D0016994

PENGUIN CLASSICS

ES'KIA MPHAHLELE

In Corner B

NORTHGATE LIBRARY

FEB -- 2011

NO LONGER PROPERTY OF
SEATTLE PUBLIC LIBRARY

PENGUIN CLASSICS

IN CORNER B

ES'KIA MPHAHLELE was born Ezekiel Mphahlele on December 17, 1919, in Marabastad, outside of Pretoria. Raised by his paternal grandmother in the rural Northern Transvaal (now the Limpopo Province) near Pietersburg (now Polokwane), in the village of Maupaneng, Mphahlele returned to Pretoria as an adolescent, only to be called "backward" by teachers and his extended family. Despite these obstacles, Mphahlele excelled and earned his teacher's certificate from Adams College, Natal, in 1940. He taught English and Afrikaans at Orlando High School in Soweto and, while teaching, published his first collection of short stories, *Man Must Live* (1947). In 1952, he was banned from teaching for campaigning against the Bantu Education proposals. Forced out of the profession, Mphahlele began working for *Drum*, a groundbreaking South African magazine; but soon became frustrated by the oppressive intellectual environment in South Africa and entered a brief exile in Basutoland—today's Kingdom of Lesotho—in 1954. He later went to Nigeria, then France, then Kenya, then Zambia, and finally to the United States, where he stayed until 1977. While abroad, he became well-known for his anti-Apartheid activism and literature, publishing his autobiography and South African classic *Down Second Avenue* (1959). He would go on to write one more autobiography, *Afrika My Music* (1984), and three novels, *The Wanderers* (1971), *Chirundu* (1980), and *Father Come Home* (1984), in addition to his short stories and nonfiction. In 1978, he returned to his native South Africa and changed his name to Es'kia, a reflection of his ongoing struggle with exile and identity. In 1986, the French government bestowed on him its Ordre des Palmes Académiques, recognizing his contribution to French language and culture. In 1998, South African president Nelson Mandela awarded him the Order of the Southern Cross. He died on October 27, 2008.

PETER N. THUYNSMA succeeded Es'kia Mphahlele as professor of African Literature at the University of the Witwatersrand,

Johannesburg. A native of South Africa and leading scholar on Mphahlele, he received his PhD in English from the University of Denver, where he studied under Mphahlele. He has written extensively on African literature and directed and founded groups such as the Council for Black Education and Research and the Institute for Human Rights Education. He currently heads the Department of Institutional Advancement at the University of Pretoria.

ES'KIA MPHAHLELE

In Corner B

Introduction by
PETER N. THUYNSMA

PENGUIN BOOKS

PENGUIN BOOKS
Published by the Penguin Group
Penguin Group (USA) Inc., 375 Hudson Street, New York, New York 10014, U.S.A.
Penguin Group (Canada), 90 Eglinton Avenue East, Suite 700, Toronto,
Ontario, Canada M4P 2Y3 (a division of Pearson Penguin Canada Inc.)
Penguin Books Ltd, 80 Strand, London WC2R 0RL, England
Penguin Ireland, 25 St Stephen's Green, Dublin 2, Ireland (a division of Penguin Books Ltd)
Penguin Group (Australia), 250 Camberwell Road, Camberwell,
Victoria 3124, Australia (a division of Pearson Australia Group Pty Ltd)
Penguin Books India Pvt Ltd, 11 Community Centre, Panchsheel Park, New Delhi – 110 017, India
Penguin Group (NZ), 67 Apollo Drive, Rosedale, North Shore 0632,
New Zealand (a division of Pearson New Zealand Ltd)
Penguin Books (South Africa) (Pty) Ltd, 24 Sturdee Avenue,
Rosebank, Johannesburg 2196, South Africa

Penguin Books Ltd, Registered Offices: 80 Strand, London WC2R 0RL, England

First published in Kenya by East African Publishing House 1967
An edition with additional selections published in South Africa
by Penguin Books (South Africa) (Pty) Ltd 2006
This edition with an introduction by Peter N. Thuynsma
published in Penguin Books (USA) 2011

1 3 5 7 9 10 8 6 4 2

Copyright © Es'kia Mphahlele, 2006
Introduction copyright © Peter N. Thuynsma, 2011
All rights reserved

Page xxvii constitutes an extension of this copyright page.

PUBLISHER'S NOTE
This is a work of fiction. Names, characters, places, and incidents either are the product
of the author's imagination or are used fictitiously, and any resemblance to actual persons,
living or dead, business establishments, events, or locales is entirely coincidental.

LIBRARY OF CONGRESS CATALOGING IN PUBLICATION DATA
Mphahlele, Es'kia, 1919–2008.
In corner B / Es'kia Mphahlele ; introduction by Peter N. Thuynsma.
p. cm. —(Penguin classics)
Includes bibliographical references.
ISBN 978-0-14-310602-9
1. Blacks—South Africa—Fiction.   2. Interpersonal relations—South Africa—Fiction.   I. Title.
PR9369.3.M67I5 2011
823'.914—dc22   2010043074

Printed in the United States of America

Except in the United States of America, this book is sold subject to the condition that it shall not, by
way of trade or otherwise, be lent, resold, hired out, or otherwise circulated without the publisher's
prior consent in any form of binding or cover other than that in which it is published and without a
similar condition including this condition being imposed on the subsequent purchaser.

The scanning, uploading and distribution of this book via the Internet or via any other means
without the permission of the publisher is illegal and punishable by law. Please purchase only
authorized electronic editions, and do not participate in or encourage electronic piracy
of copyrighted materials. Your support of the author's rights is appreciated.

Contents

Introduction

"Man Must Live" and "Mrs Plum" are stories that appear to bracket Mphahlele's corpus as theme and as metaphor. The former is a political imperative, and the latter's reference to the age-old wisdom of who sees what through a keyhole are, for me, the contextual fundamentals of Mphahlele's short stories. "Man Must Live" is the unmistakable driver, while the keyhole's panoramic one-way view of the human theater that is Apartheid South Africa supplies the perspective. Both are also intrinsically universal to anything discriminatory, bigoted, and prejudiced, further propelling the validity of Mphahlele's work beyond his native land.

Despite reading and teaching many of these stories more than fifteen years ago, I still enjoy the irresistible excitement that their titles trigger. Many unleash a warm appreciation for Mphahlele's craft as quickly as it wells up one's resentment for the Black-White encounter that was South African life under Apartheid. For readers who come to Mphahlele for the first time, here is a spectrum of the warp and weft of being Black under legislated prejudice. Here one will find the Black South African sensibility at its most observant, at its most prescient. Here one sees anger, hurt, resolve, confusion, and humiliation—all harnessed in compelling frames. And we can excuse those readers who may come to an anthology like this expecting simply a set of community tales laced with catchy African sayings or expecting a quaint vocabulary. Instead you will find compelling tales of the racial encounter in exquisite understatement and driven along by delightful turns of phrase.

This is also much more than an anthology of tales. Two short essays serve as short autobiographical introductions, and in "The Unfinished Story," Mphahlele wrestles with what he should write about, eventually commenting:

> There must surely be much more to be said than the mere recounting of an incident: about the loves and hates of my people; their desires; their poverty and affluence; their achievements and failures; their diligence and idleness; their cold indifference and enthusiasm; their sense of the comic; their full-throated laughter and their sense of the tragic with its attendant emotional sobs and ostentatious signs of pity.

These are indeed universal human traits and their contrasts set the scene for the frescoes of life Mphahlele captures in each story. Here they all swirl about the reader, often sucking one into their vortex. It is hard to be a detached reader—if there can ever be a detached reader. Mphahlele so characteristically has you sit on the writer's shoulder and look down, parallel with his eye line, at the life he so deftly unfolds.

The tales are microcosms of Apartheid in the Black residential areas—the townships, those reserves set aside for Black Africans. This is the platform upon which characters eke out their existence but Mphahlele also takes us into their thoughts. We feel and come to understand their motives, be it expediency ("The Suitcase") or appeasement ("Crossing Over," "Women and Their Men," "In Corner B," or "A Point of Identity").

I often can't decide if Mphahlele's brand of protest writing is complaint or lament. In all the impending and palpable agony surrounding his world of people—and make no mistake, the human figure looms large throughout his works—his subtlety and understatement give his characters a certain gracefulness in their survival. There is an indomitable spirit that hurls itself against an abrasive screen. Mphahlele is keenly studying his characters and how they interact. One so often gets the feeling that the writer surprises himself at the outcomes because their lives unfold so naturally, so organically—so authentically. Anger is bridled, bitterness is strangled, there is no pity, no romantic notions, and yet the sadness of the situations is nevertheless piercing and pricks the reader's political sensibility. One is made to understand the very texture of the inhumanity Apartheid wrought.

Then there is the inimitable irony so inevitable in the human condition under duress. In a possible signature story, "Man Must Live," Zungu is a bold, outwardly brash railway station police officer who enjoys herding crowds of passengers as much as he loves advising them on which train to take. But he harbors a deep shyness, which one woman passenger manages to pierce, setting in motion the character's catastrophic collapse. Mphahlele rolls Zungu about to explore his every side and probe the psyche of bravado. First published as the title story of his first anthology in 1947, the title and its tale encapsulate Mphahlele's key perspective: the need for humanity to triumph against all odds. In something of a companion piece, "The Master of Doornvlei" presents another boisterous boss-man character, exuding arrogance and control over his own farmworker people to ingratiate himself to the White farm owner. Until, of course, their bulls clash!

In "The Living and the Dead" we have another seminal narrative. Here a title and story line seem to anticipate Mphahlele's preoccupation with his future subject matter. The intricate tale surrounds a manservant, Jackson, who goes missing, juxtaposed with his White master's personal dilemma of agitating to control the flow of Black people in White neighborhoods. His man Friday's absence squeezes out how dependent he is on this person whose kind he wants to keep at bay. Then circumstances put him in possession of the letter that drew his Jackson away and his own humanity propels him into the heart of Jackson's family—anathema for a White-man agitator.

The scamp-opportunist character desperate to eke out his existence is also on display in "The Suitcase," where he is most memorable. On a bus ride, a man claims an abandoned suitcase as his own and tumbles headlong into the law. On the surface it is a story of petty thievery, but only slightly below the surface lies the desperation of a have-not in a world that alienates him. A similar structure marries backstory to main in "Grieg on a Stolen Piano"—here, too, expediency dwarfs principle.

"In Corner B," the title story, shows Mphahlele the observer at his best. Here he focuses on a widow and the activities surrounding her husband's funeral; some reverend and sublime, others dripping with human mischief and manipulation. All this theater against a backstory of the widow clutching a letter from her dead husband's mistress—compounded by the circumstances of his death and the dreaded irony of how she came by the letter. It all swivels around lines like:

How can boys just stick a knife into someone's man like that? Talita mused. Leap out of the dark and start beating up a man and then drive a knife into him. What do the parents of such boys think of them? What does it matter now? I'm sitting in this room weeping till my heart wants to burst . . .

This raw fact sits precariously against:

. . . But death humbles the most unconventional, the hardest rebel. The dead person cannot simply be packed off to the nearest cemetery. You are a person because of other human beings, you are told. The aunt from a distant province will never forgive you if she arrives and finds the deceased buried before she has seen his lifeless face for the last time. Between the death and the funeral, while the body lies in the mortuary . . . there is a wake each night. Day and night relatives and friends and *their* friends come and go, saying words of consolation to the bereaved. . . . Petty intrigues and dramatic scenes among the

> relatives . . . are innumerable. Without them, a funeral doesn't
> look like one.

These few days in the life of a bereaved household form a characteristic microcosm of Black life tainted as it is by the political circumstances of poverty and the struggle for simple dignity. Their lives are entwined in every political thread; in fact, their very existence (and death) is a political statement of sorts.

Overt protest voices and actions become trite. To take the anger, the brutal reality of a situation under siege, the protest writer needs to experiment to make it fresh. All too many Apartheid voices played victim, cast aside objectivity, and often became contemptuously autobiographical. Mphahlele experimented with structure, with time, and with under-statement. In "He and the Cat," a client is nearly consumed by his own dilemma, yet it is his presence in a lawyer's waiting room, his curiosity and perception, that eclipses the personal. Instead, it is the small human theater in the waiting room, the receptionist, and a portrait on the wall that dominate. The core story is neatly relegated without diluting the narrator's anxiety and fears—yet we are never told what business he has with the lawyer!

Tempted as one is to comment on every story on this anthology, however incompletely and no doubt deficiently, three deserve special mention: "A Point of Identity," "Mrs Plum," and "Crossing Over." All three are my personal preferences, and among them, "Mrs Plum" has attracted the most critical attention and acclaim.

"A Point of Identity" is a particularly telling story. Much less a *microcosm* (and here one is now self-conscious of redeploying those threadbare critical clichés we used so liberally as critics in the Apartheid era), this story is a reenactment of the deepest hurt racial discrimination could deliver—tear away a person's identity and you compromise his or her very self-worth. Here a character of mixed racial background (Mozambican

Portuguese father and African mother) prefers to take a Black African wife and live where he is happiest, among Africans in their township rather than among "Coloureds" in theirs. He immerses himself in conversations about being different yet the same as them.

The tale becomes an intricate exposé of prejudices, whose main character simply wants to savor the best of the Black and Coloured lifestyles. The former gives life's very essence while denying almost every other human dignity. The latter, the world of Coloured people, provides certain privileges—albeit a modicum more. Without having to make a choice our character, Karel Almeida, pays comfortable lip service to wanting to live among his Black neighbors, drink with them, laugh with them ("Karel's whole physical being seemed to be made of laughter"), play cards with them, and chat with our more intellectual narrator, "T" (unmistakably Mphahlele). When the government suddenly enforces its segregation legislation and compels Blacks to live among Blacks and Coloureds among their own, identities must be owned! At that point, Karel's expediency ("man must live") dictates it is better that he remain Coloured. Curiously, T's wife comments—quite characteristic of Rebecca Mphahlele's sobering, earthy utterances:

> Why does the man keep talking about this like someone who cannot hold hot roasted pumpkin pips in his mouth? . . . Isn't it that he thinks we blacks are nice to live with as long as he doesn't carry passes as we do and get the same wages as we do?

To carry a pass was to be known more as a number than a name, to live in an urban ghetto; a pass was necessary to seek work and possibly enter another area. Each month a person's employer had to sign the passbook indicating the person was still employed so that at any given time, the police knew whether he or she was entitled to be in White man's territory. If not, it meant spot fines and invariably jail time or hard labor on White-owned farms, with little or no opportunity to inform one's family. Tragically, those who died were often buried secretly in the bush.[1] It is this exigency that seems to keep Karel from formally embracing the identity he wants most.

When Karel dies, it is the wrangling with his own identity that resonates, rather than the clichés surrounding politically charged ghetto survival. When T learns of what Karel actually chose as his racial label, we are left gasping at the consequences while we marvel at how resigned Karel's wife is to her Apartheid fate.

And it is the consequences, not merely the circumstances, of a discriminatory theater that drive Mphahlele's stories. In a relatively obscure story, "Crossing Over," the writer consciously tackles the intricacies of working his narrative in both time and structural dimensions. Here an old woman and her family are forcibly relocated away from ancestral land and away from where her husband is buried. His inner conversations quite masterfully preclude her present but do not eclipse it. This is a technique that is most significant in Mphahlele's first autobiography (or autobiographical essay, as I prefer to see it), *Down Second Avenue.* Here it is as if Mphahlele bails out of his narrative in a series of interludes, to take stock of his life at crucial junctures. In "Crossing Over," the writer's most credible voice is that of an anguished but not embittered soul with a single purpose. It is a sensitive, almost delicate, but indeed a robust determination that propels her. In a story whose narrative is utterly disciplined yet organic, we have Ma-Selepe communing with her dead husband, who died a year after her two migrant-laborer sons were killed in a train crash en route home—all a test of her humanity. The tale runs on idiom rather than on vocabulary as it explores the *now*, the agonizing *now! How* will this picture of physical frailty resolve her agony and her anxiety, the reader continually asks, and the answer, well . . .

"Mrs Plum" is the work Mphahlele claims as his most successful. This may well be because it is a sustained narrative approaching the length of a novella, but with the techniques of an excellent short story. Mphahlele is as concerned with *how* the story is told as much as he is with its message. The narrative comes close to being an almost stream-of-consciousness, dynamic observation with personal commentary. Its central character, Karabo, is on the surface a simpleminded domestic helper who is set against her patronizing employer, Mrs. Plum. Karabo is made to eat unfamiliar food with foreign utensils at the family table, and she is treated well and paid regularly, but Mrs. Plum makes no attempt to understand her servant. Karabo grows through her initial bewilderment into an *insightful* narrator—her learning process is also ours. Her intelligence emerges from the events she witnesses and the talk among the neighborhood domestic helpers we get to overhear. Despite Mrs. Plum's liberal gestures, the racial code does not permit either one to regard the other as an individual.

The story then admits all the concomitant ingredients to complicate life in the racial arena: Mrs. Plum's daughter falls in love with a Black physician, a man Karabo fancies, too. Mrs. Plum's affection for her lap dogs, Monty and Malan, borders on the immoral; she hoses down a police raiding patrol, refuses to pay the fine, and is jailed. Against these blustering events there is Karabo, who, despite her surface simplicity, is sincere, cheerful, and consistent. She demonstrates a firm grasp of her situation and, above all, knows her limitations. Mrs. Plum, in turn, reflects the White liberal's dilemma and her position is untenable and unenviable. The way she treats her dogs reflects the view that so often pets are treated better than servants.

Ultimately, this story reflects how seriously Mphahlele regards his responsibility as a writer; no matter how narrow or trained his vision may be, he means to explore the dynamics of the South African worldview. His compulsion to tell a story is irrepressible!

Less successful inclusions in this collection are the stories written in his exile and about the non–South African encounters.

Exile presented new challenges for Mphahlele. As adults catapulted from home, he and Rebecca had to adapt to their new circumstances. As a writer, he had to observe new customs and mores, new sensibilities. But what to do with these foreign things?

"Nigerian Talking Points," "A Ballad of Oyo," and "The Barber of Bariga" find their way into the anthology as, I imagine, a contrast to the confident narration of the stories about home. Here the intellectual intellectualizes as he tries to make sense of the African diaspora in which he landed. Ever the observer, Mphahlele eavesdrops on the Nigerian perspective. In "A Ballad of Oyo," for example, we savor the very texture of life in a marketplace—life, death, competition—a cacophony of laughter, haggling, and gossip. It is a bold examination of one woman's resilience.

He sniffs at their humor, their mannerisms, and their foibles and comes away, I think, not ready to soak up Africa or exile. Originally published in 1967, these stories draw from the earliest days of his exile and his uneasiness is palpable. He comes to grips with exile much more confidently in later works, but never accepts it. What melds these three pieces to the tapestry of the other stories is the human condition that is so irresistible, so compelling.

The voice of exile was difficult to cultivate. It demanded the same critical confidence that told of life on home soil; this would take time, and the restlessness that accompanies exile doesn't afford that privilege. In many ways exile is a cauldron of irritability, dissatisfaction, and homesickness; the exile yearns for the familiar. As he writes in "My Experience as a Writer," for Mphahlele the writer, exile was a time when he:

> . . . could not feel the country, grasp it, couldn't pick up distinctive smells of places.

And he goes on to say:

> As long as I refused, consciously and unconsciously by turns, to dissolve into the American landscape and milieu, so long was

I going to continue to avoid using the American experience as novelistic or poetic material. Africa would continue to be my literary beat.

Returning to South Africa, even before Apartheid's demise, was simply inevitable.

PETER N. THUYNSMA

NOTES

1. Dissatisfaction with the Pass system is best evidenced by the 1952 Defiance Campaign and the Sharpeville Massacre of March 21, 1960. The Pass booklet was colloquially known as a *dompass*—Afrikaans for "stupid pass."

Bibliography

Books

Man Must Live and Other Stories. Cape Town: African Bookman, 1947.

Down Second Avenue (autobiography). London: Faber & Faber, 1959; Berlin: Seven Seas, 1962; New York: Doubleday, 1971. Translated into ten European languages plus Japanese and Hebrew.

The African Image (essays, literary-cultural, political). London: Faber & Faber, 1962; New York: Praeger, 1964; revised edition, Faber & Faber, 1974; Praeger, 1974. Banned in South Africa in 1966 under the Publications Control Board Act.

"A Guide to Creative Writing" (pamphlet). Nairobi: East African Literature Bureau, 1966.

In Corner B and Other Stories. Nairobi: East African Publishing House, 1967.

Voices in the Whirlwind and Other Essays. London: Macmillan, 1971; New York: Hill & Wang, 1972; London: Fontana/Collins, 1973.

The Wanderers (novel). New York: Macmillan, 1971; London: Macmillan, 1971; London: Fontana/Collins, 1973; Cape Town: David Philip, 1984.

Chirundu (novel). Johannesburg: Ravan Press, 1980; London: Thomas Nelson, 1980; New York: Lawrence Hill, 1981.

Let's Write a Novel: A Guide. Cape Town: Maskew Miller, 1981.

The Unbroken Song: Selected Writings: Poems and Short Stories. Johannesburg: Ravan Press, 1981.

Afrika My Music (second autobiography). Johannesburg: Ravan Press, 1984.

Father Come Home (novel). Johannesburg: Ravan Press, 1984.

Let's Talk Writing: Prose: A Guide for Writers. Johannesburg: Skotaville, 1987.

Renewal Time (short stories). New York: Readers International, 1988.

Es'kia: A Collection of Essays, and Public Speeches Spanning 30 Years. Kwela Books in association with Stainbank & Associates, 2002.

Es'kia Continued: A Sequel to "Es'kia"—Published in 2002: A Collection of Essays, and Public Speeches Spanning 30 Years. Stainbank & Associates, 2005.

Books Edited

Modern African Stories. London: Faber & Faber, 1964.

African Writing Today. Harmondsworth, England: Penguin, 1967, 1969.

Thought, Ideology and African Literature (short stories published in journals and not appearing in anthologies). Denver: University of Denver, 1970.

Short Stories, Poems, and Essays Anthologized by Mphahlele and Other Editors

(SS = short story; P = poem; E = essay/article)

"The Suitcase" (SS). In *New World Writing*, under pen name Bruno Esekie, 56–61. New York: New American Library, 7th Mentor Selection, 1955.

"The Living and the Dead" (SS). In *Following the Sun*. Berlin: Seven Seas Books, 1960.

BIBLIOGRAPHY xix

"African City People" (E). In *East Africa Journal*. Nairobi: East African Publishing House, June 1964.

"Grieg on a Stolen Piano" (SS). In *Pan African Stories*, edited by Neville Denny, 142–53. London: Thomas Nelson & Sons, 1965.

"He and the Cat" (SS). In *South African Writing Today*, edited by Nadine Gordimer and Lionel Abrahams, 73–77. Harmondsworth and Baltimore: Penguin, 1967.

"On the Long Road: From an African Autobiography" (E). In *African Writing Today*, edited by Ezekiel Mphahlele, 253–63. Harmondsworth and Baltimore: Penguin, 1967.

"Remarks on Negritude" (E). In *African Writing Today*, edited by Ezekiel Mphahlele, 247–53. Harmondsworth and Baltimore: Penguin, 1967.

"A Ballad of Oyo" (SS). In *Africa in Prose*, edited by O. R. Dathorne and Willfried Feuser, 289–98. Harmondsworth and Baltimore: Penguin, 1969.

"Mrs Plum" (SS). In *Modern African Stories*, edited by Charles R. Larson, 155–92. London: Collins Fontana Books, 1971.

"The Master of Doornvlei" (SS), "A Point of Identity" (SS), and "A Ballad of Oyo" (SS). In *Contemporary African History*, edited by Edris Makward and Leslie Lacy. New York: Random House, 1972.

"Death" (P). In *Poems in Context*, edited by Lee A. Jacobus and William T. Moynihan, 431–34. New York: Harcourt Brace Jovanovich, 1974.

"Mrs Plum" (SS). In *Cannon Shot and Glass Beads*, edited by George Lamming, 221–51. London: Picador Pan Books, 1974.

"Crossing Over" (SS). In *To Kill a Man's Pride and Other Stories*, edited by Norman Hodge. Johannesburg: Ravan Press, 1997.

"Down the Quiet Street" (SS). In *Telling Tales*, edited by Nadine Gordimer. London: Bloomsbury, 2004.

Selected Essays (Excluding Several Reviews),
Poems, and Stories in Anthologies, Single-Author
Volumes, and Journals

The following are only a selected few from several articles:

"A Winter Story," *Fighting Talk* (Johannesburg) (Spring 1956).

"Across Downstream," *Drum* (Johannesburg) (April 1956).

"Lesane" (a series of complete stories on the same character), *Drum* (December 1956 and January, March, and April 1957).

"The African Intellectual in Africa." In *Transition*, edited by Prudence Smith. London: Maz Reinhardt, 1958.

"Accra Conference Diary." In *An African Treasury*, edited by Langston Hughes. New York: Crown, 1960.

"Out of Africa." *Encounter* (London) (April 1960).

"Black and White," on South African literature. *New Statesman* (London) (September 10, 1960).

"The Cult of Negritude." *Encounter* (March 1961).

"For a Cultural Boycott." *Fighting Talk* (Johannesburg) (July 1962).

"Writers of Africa." *Fighting Talk* (September 1962).

"Ghana: On the Cultural Front." *Fighting Talk* (October 1962).

"African Culture Trends." In *African Independence*, edited by Peter Judd. New York: Dell, 1963.

"Exile in Nigeria" (P). In *Poems from Black Africa*, edited by Langston Hughes. Bloomington: University of Indiana Press, 1963.

Introduction to *Modern African Stories*. London: Faber & Faber, 1964.

"The Language of African Literature." *Harvard Educational Review* 34, no. 2 (Spring 1964).

"Cultural Identity: Israel and Africa." *Jewish Quarterly* (London) (1965).

"Cultural Activity in Africa." *Manas* (California) (August 25, 1965).

"Cultural Tensions in a Mixed Society." In *Racial and Communal Tensions—African Contemporary Monographs No. 3*. East African Publishing House: Nairobi, 1966.

"The Language of African Literature," revised version of the 1964 work. In *Africa: A Handbook to the Continent*, edited by Colin Legum. New York: Praeger, 1966.

"African Literature for Beginners." *Africa Today* 14, no. 1 (Denver) (1967).

Introduction, "The Long Road," and "Remarks on Negritude." In *African Writing Today*. Harmondsworth, England: Penguin, 1967, 1969.

"Langston Hughes," an essay on his poetry. In *Introduction to African Literature*, edited by Ulli Beier. Evanston, IL: Northwestern University Press, 1967.

"My Heart Said Speak Bold," a tribute to Todd Matshikiza, writer and musician, on the occasion of his death. *Topic 33*. United Information Agency: Washington, D.C., 1968.

"Rediscovery of African Culture." *Africa and the World* (London) (November 1968).

Introduction to *Emergency*, a novel by Richard Rive. New York: Collier, 1969.

"The Short Story: South Africa," from the International Symposium on the Short Story. *Kenyon Review* 126, no. 4 (1969).

"Uganda Intellectuals and the State." *Times of Zambia* (Lusaka, Zambia) (February 6, 1969).

"African Literature: A Dialogue of Two Selves." *Horizon* 11, no. 10 (Ndola, Zambia) (October 1969).

"Death," "Somewhere," and "Homeward Bound" (P). In *New African Literature and the Arts I*, edited by Joseph Okpaku. New York: Thomas Y. Crowell, in association with The Third Press, 1970.

Introduction to *Down Second Avenue*, American edition. New York: Doubleday, 1971.

Introduction to *Night of My Blood*, a book of poems by Kofi Awoonor. New York: Doubleday, 1971.

Introduction to *No Sweetness Here*, short stories by Ama Ata Aidoo. New York: Doubleday, 1971.

"The Voice of Prophecy in African Poetry." *Umoja* (Las Cruces, NM) (1973).

"The Tyranny of Place," a lecture in a symposium at the University of Missouri, Kansas City. *New Letters* (Autumn 1973).

"Why I Teach My Discipline." *Denver Quarterly* 8, no. 1 (Winter 1973).

"Notes from the Black American World" (I). *Okike* 4 (Amherst, MA) (December 1973).

"Mphahlele's Reply to Addison Gayle, Jr," a reply to Gayle's review of *Voices in the Whirlwind and Other Essays* (*Black World*, July 1973). *Black World* 23, no. 3 (January 1974).

"Notes from the Black American World" (II), on Gwendolyn Brooks. *Okike* 4 (June 1974).

"Notes from the Black American World" (III), a discussion of Askia Muhammad Toure's poetry in relation to the element of mysticism and prophecy in contemporary African American poetry. *Okike* 8 (1975).

"A Poem: For All the Victims of Racist Tyranny in Southern Africa" (P); "Death III: Variations on a Theme by John Keats, or E.M. scores 55, December 17, 1974." In *South African Voices* (African and Afro-American Studies and Research Center, in association with the Harry Ransom Center, the University of Texas at Austin, 1975).

"The Function of Literature at the Present Time: The Ethnic Imperative," a lecture in a symposium at the University of Denver. *Denver Quarterly* 9, no. 4 (Winter 1975). Abridged in *Transition* 45, Vol. 9 (ii) (Accra, Ghana), edited by Wole Soyinka.

"Death II" (P). *The Gar 18* 4 (Austin, TX) (March–April 1975).

Review of E. R. Braithwaite's *Honorary White*; account of a visit to South Africa. *New York Times Book Review* (July 13, 1975).

"The African Critic Today—Toward a Definition." In *Reading Black: Essays in the Criticism of African, Caribbean, and Black American Literature*, contributions to a symposium, edited by Houston A. Baker, Jr. (1976).

"Notes from the Black American World: Images of Africa in Afro-American Literature" (IV). *Okike* 10 (1976).

"Higher Education in South Africa," in *The International Encyclopaedia of Higher Education*. Boston: Northeastern University, 1977.

"Tribute to Leopold Sedar Senghor," a prose poem. *Presence Africaine* (1977).

"The Voice of Prophecy," an essay on African poetry. *English in Africa* (Grahamstown, South Africa) (1979).

Oganda's Journey, a verse play. *Staffrider* (Johannesburg) (July/August 1979).

"The Wisdom of Africa: Notes on the Oral Tradition." *Staffrider* (November/December 1979).

"Education: Towards a Humanistic Ideology." In *Report on the Conference on Educational Priorities in a Developing State*. Pretoria: De Jager, 1980.

"Education and the Search for Self." *Teachers' Journal* (Durban) (September 1980).

"Africa in Exile." *Daedalus: Journal of the American Academy of Arts and Sciences* (Spring 1982).

Black Africa: A Generation after Independence 111, no. 2. Proceedings of the American Academy of Arts and Sciences (Spring 1982).

"To You My People" (P). *The Classic* 3, no. 1 (Johannesburg) (1984).

Monthly column on a variety of themes. *Tribute* (Johannesburg) (starting May 1987).

"Alternative Institutions of Education for Africans in South Africa: An Exploration of Rationale, Goals and Directions." *Harvard Educational Review* 60, no. 1 (1990).

"Delmas on My Mind" (P). *Tribute* (December 1990). *Education as Community Development: Reordering of Values, Focus and Emphasis*. Johannesburg: Witwatersrand University Press, 1991.

"Somewhere" (P), in *From the Republic of Conscience: International Anthology of Poetry*, edited by Kerry Flattley and Chris Wallace-Crabbe. Flemington, Victoria, Australia: Aird Books, 1992; Fredonia, NY: White Pine Press, in association with Amnesty International, 1992.

"Silences" (P). *Tribute* (August 1992).

In Corner B

Acknowledgements

To the editors and publishers in which stories first appeared:

Drum, Fighting Talk, Africa South, the original *The Classic* and its revived counterpart of 1983 (for 'Women and Their Men').

'Crossing Over' was first included in the second edition of *To Kill a Man's Pride and Other Short Stories from South Africa,* Marcus Ramogale (ed.) (Johannesburg: Raven Press, 1996).

My Experience as a Writer

I was fifteen when I began high school at St Peter's Secondary School, Rosettenville, one of Johannesburg's southern suburbs. This was January 1935.

There was a sense in which boarding school protected one from the vulgarity, the squalor, the muck and smell of slum life such as Marabastad was – a Pretoria location (I still feel 'location' gives ghetto life a more distinctive character than the fancy name 'township' does today). At any rate during term time. The reading bug had already bitten me, so I spent hours of free time reading in the school library: Dickens, R L Stevenson, Walter Scott, Edgar Rice Burroughs (I was once thrown out of class for reading a Tarzan book during a free period), Conan Doyle, Baroness Orczy, Pearl Buck, Quiller-Couch, Buchan and so on: from Tarzan and the mystery thrillers to the sublime.

Back in Marabastad I had rummaged through a lot of junk literature donated by some suburban families and dumped on the floor of a storeroom attached to a community hall that bore the sign MUNICIPAL LIBRARY. After ploughing through boys' and girls' adventure stories (all about white kids!), through ghost stories, after throwing aside astrology books, I had one day stumbled upon Cervantes's *Don Quixote*.

In the early years of the war I was at Adams (Teachers') College, my next boarding school; I read more of the same stuff, adding to the list titles like *Gone with the Wind*. I was also an avid reader of *The Outspan* which during the war ran thrilling hunters' stories, mystery and real-crime stories about John Dillinger, Pretty Boy Floyd, Baby Face Nelson, G-Man Purvis and so on. As I was an irrepressible moviegoer who had evolved from the silent days to the talkies, I read everything

I could lay my hands on about the art and techniques of the cinema.

A story well told: this became in time an obsession with me. I retold a folk tale for a school contest at Adams and took away the first prize of ten shillings.

During my first job at Ezenzeleni Blind Institute in Roodepoort (near Johannesburg), a trade school that overlooked a valley and stood serenely on one of the many ridges around, I started to write verse, a compulsive lyricising of my immediate external nature. The impression had been left in our minds at school that poetry must be about trees, birds, the elements. We had never been taught poetry as well as we know how today. We had a compulsion to memorise in my schooldays, and it was a joy to recite and listen to the grandeur of Shakespeare on campus and during school debates. These debates were more an exercise in rhetoric than in the method of argument. The spoken word or phrase or line was the thing, damn the dialectic. So I was writing verse out of a book as it were. There was no one an apprentice could go to for advice on techniques, or merely to show a manuscript. It was a shot in the dark.

In the years that I worked at Ezenzeleni I lived in a location on the western edge of Roodepoort town. It was no less slummy than our Marabastad. Just another heap of rusted tinshacks. The same dusty potholed streets, the same communal taps, streets flowing with dirty water and littered with children's stools; the same mongrels that accentuated the would-be stillness of my nights with their howling as I sat up late studying privately for the Matric Certificate (I had only the Junior Certificate and the two-year teachers' diploma). Sailing along the night air was also the incessant hum of location life. It was a hum that seemed to suppress the bellowing, screams and shrieks and street singing that would finally burst into an orgy with a reckless fury and abandon come Saturday night. Like the people of Marabastad, my Roodepoort people were hurting, even in the process of creating their own fun, their little nook of pleasure.

The war was raging in Europe and North Africa, Maraba-stad was being bulldozed, Jan Smuts was sending troops to snuff viciously the municipal workers' strike that had burst into rioting in an African hostel adjacent to Marabastad. But Roodepoort West location was still standing in its rusted stubbornness, stretching out its lease of life till the Nationalists would blast it away during the sixties.

On those Roodepoort nights, when I had had my fill of geometrical theorems and algebraic equations and graphs and Shakespeare and Milton and the Boston Tea Party and Bismarck and the Black Hole of Calcutta, when the stench of night soil choked the night air from the waggons passing by, I would try to relax, seek refuge in the workshop of mind. I would listen to the stories milling around in the workshop, looking for words to give them form. Before I knew what I was doing I had embarked on the great adventure of storytelling. I had in earlier years fallen in love with the printed word; now it was an obsession, aching for articulation by no other person than the present narrator. The story had found me. I had never read modern short stories before and, as I recall, I turned out pages and pages of freewheeling narrative episodes.

I'm one of hundreds of writers who first came to English as a working language, a learning language, a political medium of communication in a multilingual society, rather than as a native tongue. Thus studying English, either in a formal or non-formal situation, has enhanced my writing ability. While my general reading was for pleasure, it was also for learning the language. My books are full of markings that trace the paths of a mind obsessed with idiom, the well-chosen word or phrase, the exquisite narrative and descriptive line. So private study, which took me through the University of South Africa for the BA, BA Honours and the MA, and the teaching of English in high school after Roodepoort, afforded me ample opportunity to re-educate myself in the English language via its literature.

I was reading the Scottish and English ballad for Matric when

I became enthralled by its storytelling manner. Its brooding mood accentuated by the refrain and the supernatural element, its economy of language, its dramatic 'leap' to clinch the violent happening – all these features reinforced in me an intuition about the mechanism and spirit of the short story. And my life in Marabastad, Roodepoort and later in Orlando provided that atmosphere that breeds violence, death, deprivation.

It was by mere accident that I came across an educational pamphlet brought out by Julian Rollnick's African Bookman Publications, Cape Town. I nervously put my writing together in a packet and mailed it to Mr Rollnick. He promptly sent me back the verse and said he wanted to publish five of the ten stories – a pick from a bunch I had been accumulating for six years. *Man Must Live and Other Stories* (1946) was Rollnick's first try in fiction publishing.

In the early fifties I was going through a number of literary experiences that were drastically to change my social attitudes and my writing style. I was introduced to Nadine Gordimer who immediately took an interest in my writing. She agreed to look at my stories. The discussions that followed and my initiation into Nadine's own craftsmanship in the genre gave me new insights into what I was engaged in.

I began to read the Russians: Gogol, Chekhov, Tolstoy, Gorky. Their mastery of the short story, especially that of the first three, blew my mind. By accident I discovered the African-Americans. Fanny Klenerman, the grande dame of Vanguard Booksellers in Johannesburg, had titles by Richard Wright, James Baldwin, Langston Hughes. Wright's volume of short stories, *Uncle Tom's Children*, contained the kind of violence and brutal truths about white racism that struck a common chord in me, even as they tore me up inside. I also discovered Ernest Hemingway and William Faulkner, Carl van Vechten's *Nigger Heaven*. I discovered English translations of Flaubert, Boccaccio, Rabelais. Hemingway and Wright taught me economy of language and the impressionistic concreteness of image, Faulkner taught me resonance, the Russians the totality of craftsmanship.

On the advice of Nadine, who was impressed with the story 'The Suitcase', I sent it to *New World Writing*, an international anthology published in New York. The story appeared in this collection in 1955. The late Langston Hughes read it in New York and wrote me a flattering word of appreciation, sending me at the same time his first book of poetry, *The Weary Blues*, and a book of short stories, *The Ways of White Folks*: the beginning of a long friendship. Later in the decade when I was investigating South African fiction, I was to be most favourably impressed by William Plomer's work. Over the years as I corresponded with William he wrote me commentaries on every book I published in England until the last one before his death. Yet another friendship I have valued immensely has been that of Martin Jarrett-Kerr, member of the Community of the Resurrection and critic. He also has monitored my writings all along. Martin, before his return to England, had been one of the few European patrons who came regularly to our theatre and music performances in Johannesburg.

Drum magazine was launched in 1951 and had by 1955 established itself as a vibrant monthly for black writing and the black urban proletariat. Names like Can Themba, Bloke Modisane, Casey Motsisi, Todd Matshikiza, Richard Rive, Peter Clarke, Arthur Maimane, Henry Nxumalo became *Drum's* regular literary furniture. I had myself published my first story in *Drum* in 1953. I became its fiction editor in January 1955, staying on till I left for Nigeria in September 1957. *New Age* and *Fighting Talk*, the two leftist papers of the decade, and Ronald Segal's *Africa South* also featured Alex la Guma, Alfred Hutchinson, Rive and myself. Although we were not at school in the fifties, although we had diverse interests and intellectual pursuits, even as journalists, we shared this much in common: we had found a voice. And because urban blacks in South Africa have so much in common with urban African-

Americans, almost to a man the writers of the fifties had more than just a dip into American culture: journalism, imaginative literature, jazz, innovative prose styles. There was in our styles a racy, concrete, nervously impressionistic idiom, often incorporating the grand Shakespearean image. Nxumalo, who had come to *Drum* already an experienced journalist, did not fit into this stylistic pattern.

For my part I was, as a result of all these influences, learning to be much less sentimental in my view of character, much less didactic in tone, more concrete and incisive in dramatisation and idiom. I was also trying out the same discipline in my creative writing as my UNISA mentor, Professor Edward Davis (now deceased), was putting me through my English assignments. A notorious taskmaster, but a man I admired for his sparkling intellect and critical acumen.

Exile. In 1957 I moved from one vibrant literary scene, where new things were happening, into another: West Africa. I had the privilege of working on *Black Orpheus* with writers like the Nigerians Wole Soyinka, Chinua Achebe, Christopher Okigbo, J P Clark; the Ghanaians Kofi Awoonor, Efua Sutherland, Ama Ata Aidoo, the Gambian Lenrie Peters. There was abundant theatre activity and the artists were most prolific. Independent commercial publishing was thriving, books found their way to the stalls of the open-air market square where food and miscellaneous goods were sold.

When I worked in Paris (1961–3) and was organising writers' and artists' centres, literary and educational conferences in Europe and Africa, I rubbed shoulders with Léopold Sédar Senghor, Sembene Ousmane, Bernard Dadié, Birago Diop, Aimé Césaire, and other French-speaking blacks from Africa, the French West Indies and the islands of Oceania, Madagascar.

After *Down Second Avenue* (1959) and *The African Image* (1962) I was again writing short stories. This genre had been for us in South Africa a condensed form of prose that required a few broad but incisive strokes or flashes to get the 'message' across. The writers who were creating out of a rural sensibility had been writing novels and lyric poetry that depicted the intrusion of Western-Christian values and customs into a non-aggressive pastoral humanism. The works of Thomas Mofolo, Azariele Sekese, Sol Plaatje, John Langalibalele Dube, H I E Dhlomo, B W Vilakazi, A C Jordan fell in this tradition. The more intensely urban were using the short story and reportage as a way of coming to terms with their anger, as a response to the immediate pressures of deprivation and racism.

This was no longer my milieu in West Africa and France. In Kenya and Zambia I would experience only the residual effects of a colonial presence that was receding. I was having to write out of new discontents or remembered hurts which I knew would still be the lot of those I had left behind. The element of immediacy had gone. I was among people whose discontents had reference to other historical roots, although they merged with mine at the point of Europe's colonial entry. But the discontents I found called for other responses than those demanded by racial confrontation and contemplation. My novel, *The Wanderers* (1972), was an attempt to reflect the fragmented passage of a South African black through a continent fragmented by a colonial history but trying vaguely to grope for a sense of unity on the grounds of that very shared history.

When I was waiting for something to be born in fiction I took to poetry, but more important to literary criticism. *Voices in the Whirlwind* (1972) and the revised edition of *The African Image* (1974), plus other essays that appeared in journals, are examples of these waiting intervals.

In all the nine years I was in America, I could not feel the country, grasp it, couldn't pick up distinctive smells of places. So I gave up trying to spin something out of an American-inspired imagination; except, again, to express myself on African-American life, thought and literature. As long as I refused, consciously and unconsciously by turns, to dissolve into the American landscape and milieu, so long was I going to continue to avoid using the American experience as novelistic or poetic material. Africa would continue to be my literary beat. And although *Chirundu* is about a Zambian episode, I try to capture some of the essence of Africa in general, of the African agony. It seemed to me that a 'decision' to forget the South African experience, or to allow it to recede into the background, would amount to a rejection of Africa as a whole, to lose faith in it. Such has been the measure of my pan-African sensibility, my awareness of Africa's history, my exposure to its anger and frustrations, its joys, its wisdom and humanism. West Africa kindled this awareness.

A return to South Africa would have to be the resolution of my identity as an African teacher and writer. The one has often accused and justified the other by turns, and similarly they have wept over and gloried in the other.

For the last decade I have been debating in my mind the function of literature in the present-day world and the individual writer's role in relation to this function. The writer expresses himself out of a sense of compulsion and according as his sensibility conducts him. Ideally he wants to communicate thought and feeling both as a cultural compulsion and as an act of language.

At the level of function where we contemplate the uses of literature for the individual reader and evaluate his responses, and for the writer himself, there are no violent disagreements. There is a kind of consensus about what actually happens between writer and reader. But on what literature actually does and should do to and for society, for community, there is a wide range of claims. We hear words like 'commitment', 'revolution', 'art for society', 'art for my sake', 'bourgeois art', 'elitist art', 'words must act like bullets' and so on.

The claims for literature's social role have often been expressed in moralistic, apocalyptic and transcendental terms. In some realm of our responses to it, it is supposed to be a civilising agent, supposed to spark in us revolutionary zeal and even trigger the bullet for us. As it is an art process, and all creative forms of expression called Art are supposed, in the tradition of German idealism, to be a meeting point between Mind and Nature and to reconcile them, it is taken on trust that literature belongs in that lofty realm. How does Art do this? God will take care of that.

I should hope that my writing increases the reader as much as it increases me. The larger public and institutions can do what they like with it, short of debasing it, twisting it to endorse their own immoral positions. If my work turns out not to please and increase future generations, I shall not be alive to care. I'm content with approval of what I'm doing *now*, my own gratification from what I have created, the conscious effort I make to achieve directness, clarity and richness of expression – when this has been realised: these will suffice for *now*. I am conscious of being an African writer speaking to Africans. T S Eliot's notion of a world intelligence as an audience is too ephemeral for me to cherish.

It would be a comforting thought to share fully the trans-cendental view of art, even only privately. But I'm preoccupied with grassroots responses to literature and am often too cynical to allow my mind to dwell on those possibilities that only live in the intellect.

And yet I feel outraged enough to curse those who censor literature (other than self-serving pornography) in South Africa and elsewhere. I care enough about the banning of books per se, mine or other writers', to want to howl up and down the streets and incite the reading public to wage a crusade against acts of censorship. South Africans are generally apathetic about the literature they are forbidden to read or circulate or possess: part of a more serious malaise that blunts sensitivity so that the violation of human freedoms is spoken of as 'routine checks' and accepted as such.

In the collective sense in which we speak of literary products, books, censorship today would be the only reason for caring now about what will be available and acceptable in the future. Because rather than censor our own thoughts as writers, we should consider creating undaunted, believing that if the future generations are going to be the true judges, cause for indictment should be anything but self-censorship. Intellectual dishonesty is already an act of self-condemnation.

I used to worry that because of our separate racial lives blacks and whites do not know enough about each other fully to portray character across colour and racial lines. I'm too cynical now to care any longer: blacks never asked for Apartheid.

Finally, it is an exaggerated claim for literature that it can spark a revolution. There are surely more immediate irks that incite a revolution – all those irks that arise from a sense of deprivation and loss. People expect to be incited by the language of everyday usage, not the heightened form of expression and metaphor of the kind that makes imaginative literature. By the time a writer has done composing a play, a poem, a story as a vehicle of political agitation, the revolution is under way. Literature may record, replay, inspire an ongoing process. As an act of language that renews, revitalises, it is a vehicle of thought and feeling that should increase by reliving experiences. Literature is forever stirring us up. This is its own kind of revolution.

(1978)

The Unfinished Story

I want to write; I must write; I should write; I am going to write. This is what I said to myself one moonless night under an inky black sky.

I was standing on my stoep, looking out into the darkness before me. Below my house in that darkness were masses of houses where I knew life was throbbing fast. Away in the distance a cluster of city lights twinkled softly. Now and then a wave of singing came to my ears from down there. That would be the congregation of the Bantu Church of Zion, I thought – or some section of it, that denomination having so many dissentient groups. I knew they would be dancing in circles, waving their crosses in the air, their white cassocks swooping round. They take their worship so seriously, these people, and it being a Saturday night I knew they would go on into the late hours of the morning.

Write what? you ask me. That's partly my difficulty. What shall I write? Why should I write?

So much has been written on the Bantu, but I have always felt something seriously wanting in such literature. I told myself there must surely be much more to be said than the mere recounting of incident: about the loves and hates of my people; their desires; their poverty and affluence; their achievements and failures; their diligence and idleness; their cold indifference and enthusiasm; their sense of the comic; their full-throated laughter and their sense of the tragic with its attendant emotional sobs and ostentatious signs of pity.

The singing continued. Its sound came floating wave on wave through the darkness. How could I begin? What medium of writing could I use? The essay? No. My feelings would perhaps overstep the limits of that form. Drama? Verse? No. The short story or the novel? Worth trying, I thought.

Now, what could I say to the world? Well, many things. For example, I could tell of the two men I saw on the station platform recently. One was drunk and his friend was trying to pull him away from the edge of the platform just when an express was approaching. With a final effort the sober man flung his unsteady friend away, but lost his own balance and toppled on to the line, disappearing under the train. A piercing scream seemed to jolt the drunken man to his senses and when he regained his feet he gazed with horrified stupidity at the remains of his friend strewn over the line.

But I should have to develop this theme. It seemed so scanty by itself. The stream of my thoughts ran dry. The incident seemed so silly, so commonplace.

Then I thought of another: of the woman who always had her shoes on, day and night. Everyone in our street confessed he had never seen her bare feet. She had an unusual gait which always reminded me of a duck or seal. Stories went round about the reasons for her keeping her shoes on even while she crossed a river where there was no bridge or while she slept. One day the woman got into such a frenzy against a man in a bus that for lack of a weapon nearby she took off her right shoe and flung it at the man. All eyes were suddenly riveted on her bare foot. When she observed this she dropped on the floor, covering her foot with her skirts. A whisper went round among the passengers that she had no toes on her right foot.

On another day a rash and boisterous young man burst into her kitchen, explaining hurriedly at the same time that his continuous knocking at the door had not been answered, and so ... He never finished the sentence having had to flee out of range because a dish in which she had been bathing her feet came hurtling at him. When he later related the incident he said he had seen one bare foot outside the dish. He swore it was the left foot, and it had no toes.

What of it, I thought, will this make pleasant reading for others? Besides … well, it just will not do. And so my mind goes on recalling characters I have met on station platforms, on the trains, in concert halls and other places.

Twelve o'clock midnight! The song goes on down there, half pagan and half sacred. I feel helpless. I cannot begin. I know my wings are either so heavily laden that I cannot take off or have carried me too far from communicable thoughts. Now, however much my ideas cry for an outlet, I feel hollow and flat. The last straw is the realisation of my need for money. I take a deep breath and look up at the Milky Way as if it could rain down pounds, shillings and pence.

It's useless – this effort to write. How many books lie idle and dusty on the shelves of the world's libraries? And in the bookshops? Yet I keep telling myself, I must write, if only because one day I shall find something to say, and will need to have had some practice in the way to say it.

(1949)

Man Must Live

First stop Mayfair, Langlaagte, Ikona Westbury, Newclare, Randfontein train! Randfontein train: *ikona* Westbury, Newclare, first stop Mayfair, Langlaagte, Maraisburg, Roodepoort; all stations Randfontein! *U ya pi? Nkosi yam?* (Where are you going to – My Lord!)

Khalima Zungu's voice echoed through the station platform and in the subways. Masses of people rushed into the train. Khalima Zungu was a railway policeman. He was proud of it too. So he enjoyed reciting the names of stations and sidings off pat without giving them much thought.

He had a good thundering voice too, and was pleased it was of great use here. In fact, many people said he could make an outstandingly good baritone singer. Now this did not impress him much; he did not know much about singers and singing anyhow. But what did impress him was that it was also from *women*, this remark, and if *women* said it, it must be a compliment! Not that he was conceited, but Zungu clearly had a wholesome respect for anything that a woman said. Sometimes, of course, he had to admit, more than he liked to, that it was a weakness rather than a virtue.

Khalima Zungu also overheard such remarks as: 'Isn't he fine in that uniform; look at his broad shoulders and his big strong hands!' 'God does give some people good, big and tall bodies!' Zungu did not understand where God came in, but women had said them; so why wonder? He had good reason to be proud of himself and his work.

He could control masses of people, such as this. He paced up and down along the train to see his charges into the train. Now he had to say a harsh word or two, shout at another at the other end, then he had to drag a small boy out of the crowd to save him from harm.

They were so much like cattle, some of them, he thought; not unlike those cattle he looked after when a boy in Zululand, where he had once saved a girl who was overtaken by the stampeding herd. Most of them, he admitted, were simply anxious to get home after a day's hard work to enjoy the luxury of homely relaxation.

But why, even this argument held good, should a man sometimes go into a wrong train and then ask from inside if the train was going to Orlando or Pimville or some other place? Many of this species, he reflected, were often carried away by wrong trains, or the trains carried wrong passengers, whichever way you liked to put it.

Zungu also knew that he had to put up with people who left the right train and followed another crowd dashing to a train at the opposite platform, and perhaps fell back with them like waves beating blindly against a rocky shore and splashing back. So much like sheep, some of them were, my Lord!

But he could not help feeling he was equal to the situations, although the more he thought of them the more contemptuous he felt for these two-legged sheep. Sometimes Zungu felt sympathetic towards them for their ignorance, but when people behaved like this when the Railway Administration had Khalima Zungu to assist them (which he tried to do) then surely, he thought, he was entitled to despise their lack of intelligence.

This afternoon, particularly, as he paced to and fro amidst the thick crowds of people waiting for their trains, Zungu was highly pleased with himself. He had just told a woman who had enquired from him that the Cape Town train would leave at 10.10 in the night from platform number two. He wondered if he had put enough music in that 'ten ten' and if he had swung his left arm gracefully enough to look at his watch before supplying the valuable information. But he convinced himself he must have given them the desired touches.

The woman had thanked him with a not unpleasant voice that left a smile lingering on her mouth. My Lord – what would such people do without obliging Khalima Zungu! He decided this afternoon that he liked this work, what with all the nice remarks and how nice of you smiles.

Khalima Zungu always reminded himself he had worked himself up; not without initiative too. He had run away from his little village in the heart of Zululand at the age of fifteen, where he attended a small school.

Before passing Standard VI he had openly told his guardian (he was an orphan) that he did not want to attend school any more. His reasons were that he was grown up, he could read and write, and if so much of life could be learned out of books, as his teacher had often impressed upon his mind, then practical problems of life could surely teach him a hundred times better than books.

Khalima Zungu had worked in Natal for his train fare to Johannesburg. He obtained a job as a storeman in a wholesale clothes factory, where he loaded and off-loaded bundles and bales of material as they came in and out. After five years in factory work he landed in the building trade as one of the hands in bricklaying. He remembered how he was made foreman over the non-European workers. Zungu also remembered how much he enjoyed moving from one suburb to another.

That was the way to learn about life and living. You had to know how to catch three or four bricks thrown to you at a time; you had to turn a spade dexterously this way and that in mixing cement and sand; you had to throw earth almost in a lump into a lorry with precision. When Zungu was raised to the rank of foreman, he felt, more than ever before, that he hated book-learning.

When the sixth year elapsed Zungu decided he needed a change. Soon he found himself under a road-building contractor. He knew he had to start from the beginning again, but that was as it should be. He told himself he was no novice in handling a pick or shovel. They went over miles and miles

of highway, from town to city, from city to town, from town
to dorp.

The eighth year found Zungu still splashing sparks out of
rock with a pick, flattening out concrete and tar on roads. He
still loved the sound of the pick as it went 'zip' into the earth.
It seemed to give a more majestic sound when it went in to the
accompaniment of his 'jeep'. He loved the sound of the pick as
it struck rock with a 'twing'.

Zungu was compact and muscular. He had stamina at
which even his fellow workers and employer marvelled. It
always took a long time before he sweated and when a bead
of sweat rolled down his temple he knew his muscles were
proving their worth.

At this point the primitive man in him seemed to be stirred.
He cried for more outlet, and then looked the brute as he
whacked the pick against hard ground and drove the shovel
through earth and stones. It was no wonder that he was placed
foreman in his third year on the road.

Zungu knew that most of the workers under him disliked
him. They murmured complaints among themselves that he
was 'driving them like oxen'. Some even went so far as to say
that he was only strong in appearance but weak and cowardly
within. They said he showed this in the way he cringed before
his employer and the European workers to seek their favour.

'It's strange, you know,' he overheard one saying to a group
of listeners during the rest hour, 'why is it that our people
respect and fear the word of a white man and do not show
either for their fellow men?' 'Why should a person be one man
towards his employer and be a totally different man towards
those who rub shoulders with him?' another asked.

He always remembered this as the one outstanding occasion
when he ever became very furious but mastered his anger.
He remembered how he had sneered at them inwardly after
listening. But why had he not embarrassed them by suddenly
appearing on the scene and smashing the jaws of the gossipers
so that they had a more important thing to complain about? He

could not answer this question. Instead he had only sneered at them inwardly and told himself that he, Khalima Zungu, had helped construct highways for the comfort of mankind and would not defile his noble hands on the jaws of a couple of weak good for nothing boys like these. Even more important than this, he told himself, was the fact that man must live.

Yes, man must live. Zungu had nursed this philosophy of life since he left the village in Zululand. Let men accuse, deride and ridicule you in your actions; let them complain that you don't respect or fear them; let them say you don't earn your living honestly; but they too, sooner or later, will come down to the hard, cold and indisputable fact that man must live.

That night Zungu was relaxing after the tiring heat of the rush hours in the afternoon. Even then he was not admitting that he was tired – that is, to the degree measured according to his own standard when he used to work on the road. He was only enjoying the night breeze in the quiet of the station. Zungu's thoughts were careering smoothly in his mind. He could not have been more satisfied and happier than now. He was doing well, he told himself, in the fourth year of his service under the Railway Administration. He had learned much during the past years.

Khalima Zungu had dealt with rock and sand and iron before; he had to deal with life now. If you could have a strong hold of a pick and crush stone to powder, there was no reason why you should not be able to shout at people to get into a train to Pimville instead of to Germiston if they wanted to go to Pimville.

It was even comparatively easy here, he thought; you could handle a man by the scruff of the neck and bring him down to implicit obedience, but to work at a tall building or have a pick chafe blisters out of your hand was not so easy.

He had seen people of vastly varying characteristics, many of whom had conjured up some crude impressions in his mind.

Only today, for instance, he had seen a man and a woman,

evidently his wife, who was much larger than her partner. The way she talked and looked at him made Zungu guess that he was a henpeck – the kind he had sometimes seen thrown over a fence by a woman, or locked out of the house if he had failed to carry out her instructions to her satisfaction.

Then there was the man with a hump on his back. What burdens time and space sometimes picked on one to carry, just because a man did not know he *must* live. Probably, for all Zungu knew, this might just have been one of that odd and queer section of the human race that seem to have been created expressly to amuse the rest; the type that give beggars all they have and then resort to begging themselves, with only one monument of good service – a hump!

My Lord – what afflictions the White people have brought upon us! Now, how could a man in the days of our forefathers be bald-headed in the twenties or thirties if he was sound in the brain? Surely that bald-headed man he had seen was hardly out of the thirties. How on earth could he even be impudent enough to talk to him, Khalima Zungu, a member of the Railway Police Force, as though he was facing an equal? Perhaps, he remembered thinking, the man was trying to feel inwardly big to conceal the ridiculous shortness of stature and the shame of premature baldness. Such fools should be suffered to preserve one's own dignity. Anyway, he had no time for the class to which this one apparently belonged, that read so much, and know so little how to live.

Many more Zungu had seen: the long-faced stringy woman who seemed to be engaged in an eternal war with herself; the little boy who scurried away under his mother's shawl at the sight of him (even children recognised his greatness!); the round fat man with folds in the nape of his neck, who threaded his way through the clustering crowds of people as if he was a toy that had been wound and set going in a beeline in spite of all in its way. Money-minded people usually walked this way, Zungu thought. Of course they wanted to live, he admitted, like him. But such people usually died in pursuit of life, long before they started to live. Or he might even have been the sort that was brought up softly and that frittered away their time in wielding rackets at balls or jerking their bodies in funny movements in dance to weird noises. Just soft people who were not any the better for their knowledge of a world of things.

Yet if they must live, let them: all these particles of a world that scattered with the onset of night and would reassemble tomorrow and tomorrow, each day forming an organised bundle of unlike disorganised parts – a world on Park Station.

Khalima Zungu gradually realised something must be found to help fulfil his purpose to live. Until now he had not thought seriously about marriage. He had once or twice fallen in love, but he was naturally girl-shy, although he respected a woman's word. So these incidents were of a passing nature. And he always excused his girl-shyness by telling himself woman was not yet necessary in his life project. He could live quite gaily without partnership with the female of the species. He did not necessarily deny the importance of the physical side of such partnership. In fact, if he must live, he thought, this could not be overlooked. And after all, he was just as much entitled to his ancestors' heritage as the next man was to his own.

But Zungu now thought and wished someone might meet him halfway, some woman he could win without having to exert so much effort to overcome his shyness. He knew he was standing very little chance of luck, but he hoped. Those women who had come into his life before did not satisfy the requirements of his standard of an ideal wife, the wife of his dreams and imagination ...

It was a very cold mid-July night on which Khalima Zungu paced on Platform Number Two. His hands were deep in his coat pockets, his ears buried under the lapels. One could hardly see his face under the peak of his cap, drawn well down. He looked up at the big railway clock, not feeling disposed to let his hand venture out in the act of taking out his watch. It was five minutes to twelve.

The last train to Randfontein must be pulling in now. Zungu was thinking it was late when he saw it sliding in effortlessly, if somewhat cautiously. There was only one person entering and two or three getting down; so the train did not stop long. It had scarcely disappeared when a lady came towards him, panting. She stopped abruptly and gave a sigh of despair when she looked at the hind part of the train disappearing.

Zungu approached the woman, feeling somewhat sympathetic. 'I hope you are not from far, because if so, you have no luck; that is the last train. No other till 3.15 in the morning.'

She heaved another sigh of despair. 'I am from Inanda, and can't go back now; no use, I'll just have to sit here until 3.15.'

'You are not allowed to sit here at this time,' Zungu said primly. He was dealing with a lady, but rules were rules.

'But I know nobody near here; where shall I go to?'

'I wish I knew; that's what I would like to ask you,' he replied, not without a sarcastic tone. He looked at her appealing face, then at her whole figure with a searching hard stare in his eyes. 'Em – an expensive coat, likely the rich type of woman who felt so independent that she could move about at this time of night ... 'Em – not unattractive though ...

Zungu thought for a moment of what he could do. It was not really his job, but he was human. An idea struck him. It would be outside the rules, but it could be risked. You could always explain things if questioned afterwards. Besides, if the woman continued staring at him in this can't you do something manner, there was no saying how long she might do so, and neither he nor she could afford to look at each other indefinitely in such cold weather.

He told her what he could do, and she accepted the offer. They went up the stairs to his little waiting room, where a fire was blazing happily and enticingly. She sat down with eagerness and decided that she was going to like it here, and that the little fears she had begun to have when he had suggested this scheme to her were vain.

They soon found themselves sailing on the glassy sea of easy conversation. She was a Mosotho, but could speak Zulu fluently. Khalima Zungu soon learned her name – Mrs Sophia Masite; that she was a widow, had two sons and a daughter; that they all lived with her in Randfontein. They talked about many other things.

Ten minutes past three found the two walking down the steps to the train. After the train had left Zungu went back to his fire. The crackling sound of the fire, the sound of the flames dancing happily and greedily licking the roof of the grate, the radiating gentle warmth, all these, were in tune with his inner emotions. They told him life was like the magic carpet he had read of in school. It carried you over mountain peaks, over green valleys and beautiful streams; through fearfully dark gorges and over rugged ugly boulders; over sharp unfriendly briars, through jungles and dark mysterious kingdoms, where you felt you were being swallowed up into the pit of death; and again you could emerge into the smiling world, swim in the fragrant smell of flowers, taste of the sweet, the bitter and the bitter-sweet fruit; always and for ever borne by the magic carpet – whither no one knew. Yet, whatever the end, man must live.

Zungu also felt that the hollowness, emptiness and the vague sense of defeatism that sometimes overwhelmed him were not there. The smiling face of that woman, all genuine thankfulness and obvious admiration written on it, and her gentle and communicative voice filled him with the sense of the beauty of life. And he knew the magic carpet had brought him to this stage.

A week later Zungu received a card from Mrs Masite, inviting him to a party on the occasion of her daughter's twentieth birthday. He was clearly excited and determined not to miss it.

That party was the turning point of Khalima Zungu's life, now forty years of age. It was during the party that Zungu decided to master his shyness. It was a very easy task, when he came to think of it afterwards – this business of winning women.

Zungu and Mrs Masite were married three weeks later. She was a rich woman, as Zungu had judged on the night when she was a damsel in distress. They soon decided that he should not work any more. Even if he exhausted his savings, she told him, it was no matter; he could draw on hers, which made his look like the contents of a child's money box.

It did not take long before he started to draw on his wife's money. Things went on smoothly at first between him and his wife and stepchildren. Zungu had no cause for discontent. It was a world of plenty and man must live, live abundantly.

But as time wore on and he was taking life for granted, the children began to show him that he, being no more than a stepfather, was not entitled to their respect. Zungu tried to keep his feelings to himself. The climax came when one night his stepdaughter told him unreservedly in the presence of her mother that he was 'backward', 'uncivilised' and 'conceited', and that, if he wanted to know the truth, her mother had married him out of pity because he had nothing to speak for him in trying to earn his living. So he must behave himself.

Zungu knew he had developed the habit of drinking excessively. He knew his nerves were giving way, and easy life had begun to dull his wits. But he could not take it. Such insults as his daughter had hurled at him must not be allowed to go on. In fact, they showed ill-breeding.

He looked knives at his stepdaughter, then at her mother. She was unmoved. Was she sitting there indifferently and passively without a word of reproach to her daughter? There was an expression of contempt and derision on that face of hers. Her eyes dared him to talk. Zungu was about to say something after working up his fury to a high pitch, but to his disappointment he found he had nothing to say. Suddenly a sense of defeat and hollowness came upon him. He was tired. His brain was stagnant, his muscles limp, his spirit flat.

Of course, he, Khalima Zungu, formerly of the Railway Police Force, should have seen the motive behind this woman's subtle intrigues in dragging him into marriage. He now saw it as clearly as crystal that she had married him as a convenience. She had always remained in the background when her children insulted him. Most probably she was pulling the wire and conducting this machinery. He had been to her a humble, harmless and ideal companion. She now realised his value had ended where his drinking habit began. Zungu had genuine love for his wife; of this he was sure.

In his magical world of riches and splendour Zungu had been used as a tool of vengeance by his wife. Much against his will, however much contempt he had for the so-called intelligentsia class, he had received them into the house and behaved as a gentleman would – as far as little knowledge gave him scope. Then there were the ordinary class, to which Zungu belonged. He had to refuse them admission because his wife said they had 'tried to stand in her way when she aspired for wealth and learning, out of sheer jealousy'.

On a warm breezy night Khalima Zungu walked from the beer hall, drunk as a fiddler. He could barely support himself on his legs, but he managed to struggle up to the door of his house. He knocked, but nobody answered. Again he knocked, and again, but the door was not opened. He then tried the knob. It was locked. Zungu kicked and heaved his shoulders against the door until sweat ran down his face. Then he remembered he had a duplicate key which the locksmith had made for him to use on such nights as this when he was locked out.

He entered and called roaringly, but the house was empty. Even in his state of mind Zungu could not but notice a difference. His mind struggled to diagnose the situation. Then he decided that there was no furniture, no picture; in fact, nothing but the bare skeleton of the house. He went to the bedroom. Here he found only his case of clothes on the floor. Besides this sad tale the house could tell no more. Zungu fell on the floor and remained there, a hopeless heap.

At about midnight he woke up. He wondered where he was and why he was there and not on his bed. The light was still on. Then he remembered that the scenery was not new to him. As quickly as lightning Zungu sprang to his feet. He rushed out in a speed not unlike that of a scalded cat to the outside storehouse. There was a drum of petrol, left as he thought because it was of no use to that pack of foxes.

My Lord – he, Khalima Zungu, formerly of the Railway Police Force, would teach them a lesson. Take out all the yolk and white of an egg and mock him with the empty shell! He would reduce this shell to cinders if it meant cremating himself alive in it.

Zungu carried the drum into the house and poured the contents over the floor and splashed some over the walls. He set the house on fire. He stood quite still as the flames reached out for one another madly and hungrily. Then he remembered, strangely enough, what he had been told at school about hell. The spectacle itself was hell incarnated, and here he was, fitting well into it as though he was the only evil-doer (if he was) worth burning in hell. But my Lord – he must live!

With this thought he dashed to where he thought the door must be, but hit against a naked wall. He turned this way and that, choking with fumes and burning. Presently he found an exit and staggered on to the veranda. Zungu felt nauseated and saw himself falling into someone's arms …

When Zungu came to he found himself in hospital. His mind was still hazy and misty. There were some people around his bed, whom he recognised as neighbours. One told him how he had found him, wrapped him up in some sacking and rolled him over the ground. He had known that if anybody was in that house it would most likely be Zungu himself only, because he had seen his wife and children packing away early in the day.

He was not seriously burnt, but the shock had been severe.
Zungu recovered. When he left the hospital, the problem of
where to sleep confronted him. The man who had saved him
offered him temporary food and a sleeping place because
he had a large family. Soon he realised he would have to be
a nomad, a tramp, sleeping where he could, eating what he
could get.

At the foot of a hill stands a corrugated iron shanty. Zungu
put it up for himself. His experience in building stood him
in good stead, although he admitted, not without a pang
of the sense of Time's ironic twists, this experience was not
accounting for itself at the right moment.

He can be seen going to and fro with a load on his back,
staggering on in a stooping gait. That upright muscular stature
has weathered in the test of time; that confident light stride
has slowed down to heavy, uncertain and clumsy movement,
giving him the appearance of a dog wounded after a hunt. Yet
he is only in the forties.

That world of love and plenty was a dream world, when
he thinks of it, whose glories have vanished with the dawn
of reality. Today Zungu feels as if Time takes a slow pace
purposely to lengthen his life, of which now remain a few
rags, too worn out to be patched. He still drinks and murmurs
to himself.

Zungu's eyes are expressionless, whether he be happy or
not. That twinkle is gone. But there is something in that stolid
blankness in those eyes; something of stubbornness. When he
looks at you, you cannot help but read the stubborn words:
what do you expect me to be – a magician or a superman, or a
soft learned genteel animal? My Lord – I *must* live, man!

The Suitcase

One of these days he was going to take a desperate chance, Timi thought. He would not miss it if it presented itself. Many men had got rich by sheer naked chance. Couldn't it just be that he was destined to meet such a chance?

He sat on a pavement on a hot afternoon. It was New Year's Eve. And in such oppressive heat Timi had been sitting for over an hour. An insect got into his nostril and made him sneeze several times. Through the tears that filled his eyes the traffic seemed to dance about before him.

The grim reality of his situation returned to him with all its cold and aching pain after the short interlude with the insect. Today he had been led on something like a goosechase. He had been to three places where the chance of getting work was promising. He had failed. At one firm he had been told, 'We've already got a boy, Jim.' At the second firm a tiny typist told him, 'You're too big, John. The boss wants a small boy – about eighteen, you know.' Then she had gone on with her typing, clouding her white face with cigarette smoke. At the third place of call a short pudgy white man put down his price in a squeaking voice: 'Two pounds ten a week.' Three pounds ten a week, Timi had said. 'Take it or leave it, my boy,' the proprietor had said as his final word, and snorted to close the matter. Timi chuckled softly to himself at the thought of the pudgy man with fat white cheeks and small blinking eyes.

He was watching the movements of a wasp tormenting a worm. The wasp circled over the worm and then came down on the clumsy and apparently defenceless worm. It seemed to stand on its head as it stung the worm. The worm wriggled violently, seeming to want to fly away from the earth. Then suddenly the worm stretched out as though paralysed. The winged insect had got its prey. Timi felt pity for the poor worm. An unequal fight, an unfair fight, he thought. Must it always be thus, he asked – the well-armed and agile creatures sting the defenceless to death? The wasp was now dragging the worm; to its home, evidently.

He remembered he had nothing to take home. But the thought comforted him that his wife was so understanding. A patient and understanding wife. Yes, she would say, as she had often said, 'Tomorrow's sun must rise, Timi. It rises for everyone. It may have its fortunes.' Or, 'I will make a little fire, Timi. Our sages say even where there is no pot to boil there should be a fire.'

Now she was ill. She was about to have a baby; a third baby. And with nothing to take home for the last two months, his savings running out, he felt something must be done. Not anything that would get him into jail. No, not that. It wouldn't do for him to go to jail with his wife and children almost starving like that. No, he told himself emphatically.

A white man staggered past him, evidently drunk. He stopped a short way past Timi and turned to look at him. He walked back to Timi and held out a bottle of brandy before him, scarcely keeping firm on his legs.

'Here, John, drink this stuff. Happy New Year!' Timi shook his head.

'C'mon be – be a s-sport, hic! No p-police to catch you, s-s-see?'

Timi shook his head again and waved him away.

'Huh, here's a bugger don't want to have a happy New Year, eh. Go t-to hell then.'

The white man swung round, brandishing his bottle as he tripped away.

If only that were money, Timi thought bitterly.

He remembered it was time to go home and boarded a bus to Sophiatown. In the bus he found an atmosphere of revelry. The New Year spirit, he thought; an air of reckless abandon. Happy New Year! one shouted at intervals.

Timi was looking at a man playing a guitar just opposite him, across the aisle. A girl was dancing to the rhythm of the music. The guitarist strummed on, clearly carried away in the flight of his own music. He coaxed, caressed and stroked his instrument. His long fingers played effortlessly over the strings. He glowered at the girl in front of him with a hanging lower lip as she twisted her body seductively this way and that, like a young supple plant that the wind plays about with. Her breasts pushed out under a light sleeveless blouse. At the same time the guitarist bent his ear to the instrument as if to hear better its magic notes, or to whisper to it the secret of his joy.

Two young women came to sit next to Timi. One of them was pale, and seemed sick. The other deposited a suitcase between her leg and Timi's. His attention was taken from the music by the presence of these two women. They seemed to have much unspoken between them.

At the next stop they rose to alight. Timi's one eye was fixed on the suitcase as he watched them go towards the door. When the bus moved a man who was sitting behind Timi exclaimed, 'Those young women have left their case.'

'No, it is mine,' said Timi hastily.

'No. I saw them come in with it.'

This is a chance ...

'I tell you it's mine.'

'You can't tell me that.'

Now there mustn't be any argument, or else ...

'Did you not see me come in with a case?'

I mustn't lose my temper, or else ...

'Tell the truth, my man, it bites no one.'

'What more do you want me to say?'

The people are looking at me now. By the gods, what can I do?

'It's his lucky day,' shouted someone from the back, 'let him be!'

'And if it is not his, how is this a lucky day?' asked someone else.

'Ha, ha, ha!' a woman laughed. 'You take my thing, I take yours, he takes somebody else's. So we all have a lucky day, eh? Ha, ha, ha.' She rocked with voluble laughter, seeming to surrender herself to it.

'Oh, leave him alone,' an old voice came from another quarter, 'only one man saw the girls come in with a suitcase, and only one man says it is his. One against one. Let him keep what he has, the case. Let the other man keep what he has, the belief that it belongs to the girls.' There was a roar of laughter. The argument melted in the air of a happy New Year, of revelry and song.

Timi felt a great relief. He had won.

The bus came to a stop and he alighted. He did not even hear someone behind him in the bus cry, 'That suitcase will yet tell whom it belongs to, God is my witness!' Why can't people mind their own affairs? He thought of all those people looking at him.

Once out of the bus he was seized by a fit of curiosity, anxiety and expectancy. He must get home quickly and see what is in the case.

It was a chance, a desperate chance, and he had taken it. That mattered to him most as he paced up the street.

Timi did not see he was about to walk into a crowd of people. They were being searched by the police, two white constables. He was jolted into attention by the shining of a badge. Quickly he slipped into an open backyard belonging to a Chinese. Providence was with him, he thought, as he ran to stand behind the great iron door, his heart almost choking him.

He must have waited there for fifteen minutes, during which he could see all that was happening out there in the street. The hum and buzz so common to Good Street rose to a crescendo; so savage, so cold-blooded, so menacing. Suddenly he got a strange and frightening feeling that he had excited all this noise, that he was the centre around which these angry noises whirled and circled, that he had raised a hue and cry.

For one desperate second he felt tempted to leave the case where he squatted. It would be so simple for him, he thought. Yes, just leave the case there and have his hands, no, more than that, his soul, freed of the burden. After all, it was not his.

Not his. This thought reminded him that he had done all this because it was not his. The incident in the bus was occasioned by the stark naked fact that the case was not his. He felt he must get home soon because it was not his. He was squatting here like an outlaw, because the case was not his. Why not leave it here then, after all these efforts to possess it and keep it? There must surely be valuables in it, Timi mused. It was so heavy. There must be. It couldn't be otherwise. Else why had Providence been so kind to him so far? Surely the spirits of his ancestors had pity on him: with a sick wife and hungry children. Then the wild, primitive determination rose in him; the blind determination to go through with a task once begun, whether a disaster can be avoided in time or not, whether it is to preserve worthless or valuable articles. No, he was not going to part with the case.

The pick-up van came and collected the detained men and women. The police car started up the street. Timi came out and walked on the pavement, not daring to look behind, lest he lose his nerve and blunder. He knew he was not made for this sort of thing. Pitso was coming up the pavement in the opposite direction. Lord, why should it be Pitso at this time? Pitso, the gasbag, the notorious talker whose appearance always broke up a party. They met.

'Greetings! You seem to be in a hurry, Timi?' Pitso called out in his usual noisy and jovial fashion. 'Are you arriving or going?'

'Arriving.' Timi did not want to encourage him.

'Ha, since when have you been calling yourself A J B?'

'Who says I'm A J B?'

'There, my friend.' Pitso pointed at the large initials on the case, and looked at his friend with laughing eyes.

'Oh, it's my cousin's.' Timi wished he could wipe the broad

stupid grin off the mouth of this nonentity. He remembered later how impotent and helpless he had felt. For Pitso and his grin were inseparable, like Pitso and his mouth. Just now he wished he wouldn't look so uneasy. 'I'm sorry, Pitso, my wife isn't well, and I must hurry.' He passed on. Pitso looked at his friend, his broad mouth still smiling blankly.

The Chevrolet came to a stop just alongside the pavement. Then it moved on, coasting idly and carelessly.

'Hey!' Timi looked to his left. Something seemed to snap inside him and release a lump shooting up to his throat. 'Stop, jong!' The driver waved to him.

There they were, two white constables and an African in plain clothes in the back seat. Immediately he realised it would be foolish to run. Besides, the case should be his. He stopped. The driver went up to him and wrenched the suitcase from Timi's hand. At the same time he caught him by the shoulder and led him to the car, opening the back door for Timi. The car shot away to the police station.

His knees felt weak when he recognised the black man next to him. It was the man who had sat behind him on the bus and argued that the case was not Timi's. By the spirits, did the man have such a strong sense of justice as to call God to be witness? Even on New Year's Eve? Or was he a detective? No, he could have arrested him on the bus. The man hardly looked at Timi. He just looked in front of him in a self-righteous posture, as it struck Timi.

Timi got annoyed; frantically annoyed. It was a challenge. He would face it. Things might turn round somewhere. He felt he needed all the luck fate could afford to give him.

At the police station the two constables took the case into a small room. After a few minutes they came out, with what Timi thought was a strange communication of feelings between them as they looked at each other.

'Kom, kom, jong!' one of them said, although quite gently. They put the case in front of him.

'Whose case is this?'

'Mine.'

'Do you have your things in here?'

'My wife's things.'

'What are they?'

'I think she has some of her dresses in it.'

'Why do you say *think*?'

'Well, you see, she just packed them in a hurry, and asked me to take them to her aunt; but I didn't see her pack them.'

'Hm. You can recognise your wife's clothing?'

'Some of it.' Why make it so easy for him? And why was there such cold amusement in the white man's eyes?

The constable opened the suitcase and started to unpack the articles one by one.

'Is this your wife's?' It was a torn garment.

'Yes.'

'And this? And this?' Timi answered yes to both. Why did they pack such torn clothing? The constable lifted each one up before Timi. Timi's thoughts were racing and milling round in his head. What trick was fate about to play him? He sensed there was something wrong. Had he been a dupe?

The constable, after taking all the rags out, pointed to an object inside. *'And is this also your wife's?''* He glared at Timi with aggressive eyes.

Timi stretched his neck to see.

It was a ghastly sight. A dead baby that could not have been born more than twelve hours before. A naked, white, curly-haired image of death. Timi gasped and felt sick and faint. They had to support him to the counter to make a statement. He told the truth. He knew he had gambled with chance; the chance that was to cost him eighteen months' hard labour.

Down the Quiet Street

Nadia Street was reputed to be the quietest street in Newclare. Not that it is any different from other streets. It has its own dirty water, its own flies; its own horse manure; its own pot-bellied children with traces of urine down the legs. The hawker's trolley still slogs along in Nadia Street, and the cloppity-clop from the hoofs of the overfed mare is still part of the street.

Its rows of houses are no different, either. The roofs slant forward as if they were waiting for the next gale to rock them out of their complacency and complete the work it has already started. Braziers still line the rocky pavement, their columns of smoke curling up and settling on everything around. And stray chickens can be seen pecking at the children's stools with mute relish. Nadia Street has its lean barking mongrels and its share of police raids.

Yet the street still clung to the reputation of being the quietest. Things always went on in the *next* street.

Then something happened. When it did, some of the residents shook their heads dolefully and looked at one another as if they sensed a hundred years' plague round the corner.

Old Lebona down the street laughed and laughed until people feared that his chronic bronchitis was going to strangle him. 'Look at it down the street or up the street,' he said, 'it's the same. People will always do the unexpected. Is it any wonder God's curse remains on the black men?' Then he laughed again.

'You'll see,' said Keledi, rubbing her breast with her forearm to ease the itching caused by the milk. She always said that, to arouse her listeners' curiosity. But she hardly ever showed them what they would see.

Manyeu, the widow, said to her audience: 'It reminds me of what happened once at Winburg, the Boer town down in the Free State.' She looked wistfully ahead of her. The other women looked at her and the new belly that pushed out from under the clean floral apron.

'I remember clearly because I was pregnant, expecting – who was it now? Yes, I was expecting Lusi, my fourth. The one you sent to the butcher yesterday, Kotu.'

Some people said that it happened when Constable Tefo first came to patrol Nadia Street on Sunday afternoons. But others said the 'Russians' – that clan of violent Basotho men – were threatening war. Of course, after it had happened Nadia Street went back to what its residents insisted on calling a quiet life.

If Constable Tefo ever thought that he could remain untouched by Nadia Street gossip, he was jolly well mistaken. The fact that he found it necessary to make up his mind about it indicated that he feared the possibility of being entangled in the people's private lives.

He was tall and rather good-looking. There was nothing officious about him, nothing police-looking except for the uniform. He was in many ways one of the rarest of the collection from the glass cage at Headquarters. His bosses suspected him. He looked to them too human to be a good protector of the law. Yes, that's all he was to the people, that's what his bosses had hired him for.

The news spread that Tefo was in love. 'I've seen the woman come here at the end of every month. He always kisses her. The other day I thought he was kissing her too long.' That was Manyeu's verdict.

It did not seem to occur to anyone that the woman who was seen kissing Tefo might be his wife. Perhaps it was just as well, because it so happened that he did not have a wife. At forty he was still unmarried.

Manyeu was struck almost silly when Constable Tefo entered her house to buy 'maheu' (sour mealie-meal drink).

'You'll see,' said Keledi, who rubbed her breast up and down to relieve the burning itch of the milk.

Still Tefo remained at his post, almost like a mountain: at once defiant, reassuring and menacing. He would not allow himself to be ruffled by the subtle suggestions he heard, the meaningful twitch of the face he saw, the burning gaze he felt behind him as he moved about on his beat.

One day Keledi passed him with a can of beer, holding it behind her apron. She chatted with him for a while and they both laughed. It was like that often; mice playing hide and seek in the mane of the lion.

'How's business?' Tefo asked Sung Li's wife one Sunday on the stoep of their shop.

'Velly bad.'

'Why?'

'Times is bad.'

'Hm.'

'Velly beezee, you?'

'Yes, no rest, till we get over there, at Croesus Cemetery.'

She laughed, thinking it very funny that a policeman should think of death. She told him so.

'How's China?'

'I'm not flom China, he, he, he. I'm born here, he, he, he. Funnee!' And she showed rusty rotten teeth when she laughed, the top front teeth overtaking the receding lower row, not cooperating in the least to present a good-looking jaw.

Tefo laughed loud to think that he had always thought of the Sung Lis as people from China, which conjured up weird pictures of maneating people from what he had been told in his childhood.

When he laughed, Constable Tefo's stomach moved up and down while he held his belt in front and his shoulders fluttered about like the wings of a bird that is not meant to fly long distances.

When her husband within called her, Madam Sung Li turned to go. Tefo looked at her shuffling her small feet, slippers almost screaming with the pain of being dragged like that. From behind, the edge of the dress clung alternately to the woollen black stockings she had on. The bundle of hair at the back of her head looked as if all the woman's fibre were knotted up in it, and if it were undone, Madam Sung Li might fall to pieces. Her body bent forward like a tree in the wind. Tefo observed to himself that there was no wind.

One Sunday afternoon Tefo entered Sung Li's shop to buy a bottle of lemonade. The heat was intense. The roofs of the houses seemed to strain under the merciless pounding of the sun. All available windows and doors were ajar and, owing to the general lack of verandas and the total absence of trees, the residents puffed and sighed and groaned and stripped some of their garments.

Madam Sung Li leaned over the counter, her elbows planted on the top surface, her arms folded. She might have been the statue of some Oriental god in that position but for a lazy afternoon fly that tried to settle on her face. She had to throw her head about to keep the pestilent insect away.

Constable Tefo breathed hard after every gulp as he stood looking out through the shop window, facing Nadia Street.

One thing he had got used to was the countless funeral processions that trailed on week after week. They had to pass Newclare on the way to the cemetery. Short ones, long ones, hired double-deckers, cars, lorries; poor insignificant ones, rich, snobbish ones. All black and inevitable. The processions usually took the street next to Nadia. But so many people were dying that some units were beginning to spill over into Nadia.

Tefo went out to the stoep to have a little diversion; anything to get his mind off the heat. He was looking at one short procession as it turned into Nadia when a thought crossed his mind, like the shadow of a cloud that passes under the sun.

Seleke's cousin came staggering on to the stoep. His dress

looked as if he had once crossed many rivers and drained at least one. He was always referred to as Seleke's cousin, and nobody ever cared to know his name.

Seleke lived in the next street. She was the tough sort with a lashing tongue. But even she could not whip her cousin out of his perennial stupor.

Keledi's comment was: 'You'll see, one day she'll hunt mice for food. The cats won't like it.' And she rubbed her breast. But Seleke's cousin absorbed it all without the twinge of a hair.

'Ho, chief!' Seleke's cousin hailed the constable, wobbling about like a puppet on the stage. 'Watching the coffins, eh? Too many people dying, eh? Yes, too many. Poor devils.'

Tefo nodded. A lorry drove up the street and pulled up on the side, almost opposite the Chinaman's shop.

'Dead men don't shout,' said Seleke's cousin.

'You're drunk. Why don't you go home and sleep?'

'Me drunk? Yes, yes, I'm drunk. But don't you talk to me like these pig-headed people around here. Their pink tongues wag too much. Why don't they leave me alone? There's no one in this bloody location who can read English like I do.'

'I'm sure there isn't.' Tefo smiled tolerantly.

'I like you, chief. You're going to be a great man one of these days. Now you're looking at these people going to bury their dead. One of these days those coffins will tell their story. I don't know why they can't leave me alone. Why can't they let me be, the lousy lot?'

A small funeral party turned into Nadia Street on a horse-drawn trolley cart. There were three women and four men on the cart, excluding the driver. A man who looked like their religious leader sang lustily, his voice quivering above the others.

The leader had on a frayed, fading, purple surplice and an off-white cassock. He looked rather too young for such a mighty responsibility as trying to direct departed souls to heaven, Tefo thought. The constable also thought how many young men were being fired with religious feelings these days ... The trolley stopped in front of a house almost opposite Sung Li's. Tefo looked on. The group alighted and the four men lifted the coffin down.

Tefo noticed that the leader was trembling. By some miracle his hymn book stayed in the trembling hand. He wiped his forehead so many times that the constable thought the leader had a fever and could not lift the coffin further. They obviously wanted to enter the yard just behind them. He went to the spot and offered to help.

The leader's eyes were wide and they reflected a crowd of emotions. Tefo could not understand. And then he made a surprising gesture to stop Tefo from touching the coffin. In a second he nodded his head several times, muttering something that made Tefo understand that his help would be appreciated. Whereupon the constable picked up the handle on his side, and the quartet took the corpse into the house. Soon Tefo was back on the Chinaman's stoep.

It must have been about fifteen minutes later when he heard voices bursting out in song as the party came out of the house with the coffin. Again, Tefo noticed, the leader was sweating and trembling. The coffin was put on the ground outside the gate. The others of the party continued to sing lustily, the men's voices beating down the courageous sopranos.

Tefo sensed that they wanted to hoist it on to the lorry. Something told him he should not go and help. One of these religious sects with queer rules, he thought.

At the gate the leader of the funeral party bent forward and, with a jerky movement, he caught hold of the handle and tilted the coffin, shouting to the other men at the same time to hold the handles on their side. Tefo turned sharply to look.

A strange sound came from the box. To break the downward tilt the other men had jerked the coffin up. But a cracking sound came from the bottom; a sound of cracking wood. They were going to hoist the coffin higher, when it happened.

A miniature avalanche of bottles came down to the ground.

A man jumped into the lorry, reversed it a little and drove off. The trolley cart ground its way down Nadia Street. Tefo's eyes swallowed the whole scene. He descended from the stoep as if in a trance and walked slowly to the spot. It was a scene of liquor bottles tumbling and tinkling and bumping into one another, some breaking, and others rolling down the street in a playful manner; like children who have been let out of the classroom at playtime. There was hissing and shouting among the funeral party.

'You frightened goat!'

'Messing up the whole business!'

'I knew this would happen!'

'You'll pay for this!'

'You should have stayed home, you clumsy pumpkin!'

'We're ruined this time!'

They had all disappeared by the time it had registered on Tefo's mind that an arrest must be made. More than that: a wild mob of people was scrambling for the bottles; in a moment they also had disappeared, with the bottles, the corpus delicti! A number of people gathered around the policeman.

The lousy crowd, he thought, glad that a policeman had failed to arrest! They nudged one another and others indulged in mock pity. Manyeu came forward. 'I want the box for fire, sir constable.' He indicated impatiently with the hand that she might have it. It did not escape Keledi's attention and she said to her neighbour, rubbing her breast that was full of milk: 'You'll see. Wait.'

'Ho, chief! Trouble here?' Seleke's cousin elbowed his way to the centre of the crowd. He had been told what had happened.

'Funerals, funerals, funerals is my backside! Too bad I'm late for the party! Hard luck to you, chief. Now listen, I trust these corpses like the lice on my shirt. But you're going to be a great man one day. Trust my word for that. I bet the lice on my body.'

Later that afternoon Constable Tefo sat in Manyeu's room,

drinking maheu. Keledi, rubbing her breast, was sitting on the floor with two other women. Manyeu sat on a low bench, her new belly pushing out under her floral apron like a promising melon.

Somewhat detached from the women's continuous babble, Tefo was thinking about funerals and corpses and bottles of liquor. He wondered about funeral processions in general. He remembered what Seleke's cousin had said the other day on the Chinaman's stoep. Was it an unwitting remark? Just then another procession passed down the street. Tefo stood up abruptly and went to stand at the door. If only the gods could tell him what was in that brown glossy coffin, he thought. He went back to his bench, a figure of despair.

Keledi's prophetic 'You'll see' took on a serious meaning when Tefo one day married Manyeu after her sixth had arrived. Nadia Street gasped. But then it recovered quickly from the surprise, considering the reputation it had of being the quietest street in Newclare.

It added to Keledi's social stature to be able to say after the event: 'You see!' while she vigorously rubbed her breasts that itched from the milk.

The Master of Doornvlei

The early summer rain was pouring fiercely.

In the mud and grass church house a bird flitted from one rafter to another, trapped. All was silent in the church except for a cough now and again that punctuated the preacher's sermon. Now and then, to relieve the gravity of the devotional moment, a few members of the congregation allowed themselves to be ensnared by the circling movements of the bird.

But only a few of them. Most of the people had their eyes fixed on the elderly preacher, as if they were following the motion of every line on each lip as he gave his sermon. In any case, he did not have a booming voice, like his deacon's (a point on which the old man was often plagued by a feeling of inferiority). So his listeners always watched his lips. One or two older women at the back screwed up their faces to see him better.

A nine-year-old boy was particularly charmed by the lost bird, and his eyes roved with it. Then he felt pity for it and wished he could catch it and let it out through the window which it missed several times. But the preacher went on, and his listeners soared on the wings of his sermon to regions where there was no labour or sweat or care.

Suddenly the boy saw the bird make straight for a closed window and hit against the glass and flutter to the floor. It tried to fly but could not. He went to pick it up. He hugged it and stroked it. He looked about but the people's faces looked ahead, like stolid clay figures. Why are they so cold and quiet when a bird is in pain? he asked himself.

It lay quiet in his hand and he could feel the slight beat of the heart in the little feathered form.

'And so, brothers and sisters,' the preacher concluded, 'the Holy Word bids us love one another, and do to others as we would that they do to us. Amen.' He asked his flock to kneel for prayer.

At this time Mfukeri, the foreman of Doornvlei Farm on which the makeshift church was built, came in. He looked around and spotted his target – a puny wisp of a boy with scraggy legs, the boy with the bird in his hand.

When he took the boy out the people continued to kneel, unperturbed, except for the raising of a head here and there, perhaps just to make sure who the victim was this time. As the two went out the boy's rather big waistcoat that dangled loosely from his shoulders flapped about.

It was common for Mfukeri to butt in at a prayer session to fetch a man or woman or child for a job that needed urgent attention. The congregants were labour tenants, who in return for their work earned the few square yards of earth on which they lived, and a ration of mealie-meal, sugar and an occasional piece of meat.

When they complained about such disturbances to the farmer, Sarel Britz, he said: 'I'm just to my labourers. I favour nobody above the rest. Farm work is farm work; I often have to give up my church service myself.'

The boy tried to protect the bird. He could not keep it on his person, so he put it under a tin in the fowl-run before he went about the work Mfukeri had directed him to do. The rain continued to pour.

The following day the boy took ill with pneumonia. He had got soaked in the rain. On such days the little mud and grass houses of the labourers looked wretched, as if they might cave in any time under some unseen load. The nearest hospital was fifty miles away, and if the workers wanted to see the district surgeon, they would have to travel twenty-five miles there and back. The district surgeon could only be seen once a week.

The boy ran a high temperature. When he was able to

speak he asked his mother to go and see how his bird fared in the fowl-run. She came back to tell him that the bird had been found under a tin, dead. That same night the boy died.

When the news went round, the workers seemed to run berserk.

'It has happened before ...'

'My child – not even ten yet ...!'

'Come, let's go to Sarel Britz ...!'

'No, wait, he'll be angry with us, very angry ...'

'We can also get angry ...'

'Yes, but the White man is very powerful ...'

'And truly so – where do we get work if he drives us off the farm?'

'He wants our hands and our sweat – he cannot do that ...'

'He beats us, and now he wants to kill us ...'

'Send him back to Rhodesia – this Mfukeri ...!'

'Yes, we don't do such things on this farm ...'

'By the spirits, we don't work tomorrow until we see this thing out ...!'

'Give us our trek-passes ...! Save our children ...!'

'Ho friends! I am not going with you. I have children to look after ...!'

'Come, friends, let's talk first before we march to the master of Doornvlei.'

Tau Rathebe, who could read and write, rallied the workers to an open spot not far from the main gate. Grim and rugged farm workers; shaggy; none with extra flesh on him; young and old, with tough sinewy limbs. Those who were too scared to join the march kept in the bushes nearby to watch. Women remained behind.

The men were angry and impatient. 'We want Mfukeri away from Doornvlei, or we go, trek-pass or none!' was the general cry, echoed and re-echoed.

And they marched, as they had never done before, to the master's house.

Britz and Mfukeri were standing on the front veranda, waiting. It was to be expected: the foreman had already gone to warn Britz. Apart from what knowledge he had about Tau Rathebe, it was plain from the early morning that the workers were not prepared to work.

'What is it, men?'

'The people want Mfukeri sent away,' said Tau. 'He has been using his sjambok on some workers, and now old Petrus Sechele's son is dead, because Mfukeri took him out in the rain. I've warned him about this before.'

'I'll think about it. You're asking me to do a difficult thing; you must give me time to think.'

'How long?' asked Tau.

Sarel Britz felt annoyed at the implied ultimatum and Tau's insolent manner; but he restrained himself.

'Till noon today. Just now I want you to go to your work. I'm just, and to show it, Mfukeri is not going to the fields until I've decided.'

They dispersed, each to his work, discontented and surly. When Mfukeri left Sarel Britz in conference with his mother, the usually smooth and slippery texture on the foreman's face, peculiar to Rhodesian Africans, looked flabby.

'I've told him not to use the sjambok, but he insists on doing it, just because I forbid it,' said Britz when he had gone.

'Reason?' Marta Britz asked.

'Just to make me feel I depend on him.'

'He never behaved like this when your father was alive. Once he was told he must do a thing or mustn't he obeyed.'

There was a pause during which mother and son almost heard each other's thoughts.

'You know, Mamma, when I was at university – on the experimental farm – I knew many Black and Coloured folk. Thinking back on the time, now, makes me feel Pa was wrong.'

'Wrong about what?'

'About Kaffirs being children.'

'But they are, my son. Your father himself said so.'

'No, one has to be on the alert with them. One can't afford to take things for granted.'

'How are they grown up?'

Sarel went and stood right in front of her. 'Yes, Ma, they're fully grown up; some of them are cleverer and wiser than a lot of us Whites. Their damned patience makes them all the more dangerous. Maybe Mfukeri's still somewhat of a child. But certainly not the others. Take today, for instance. A coming together like this has never been heard of on a White man's farm. And they've left everything in the hands of their leader. No disorder. They're serpent's eggs, and I'm going to crush them.'

He paused.

'I didn't tell you that Mfukeri has been keeping an eye on this Tau Rathebe. We've found out he was deported from Johannesburg. Somehow slipped into this farm. And now he's been having secret meetings with three or four of our Kaffirs at a time, to teach them what to do – like today.'

'So! Hemel!'

'So you see, Ma, Papa was wrong. I'm going to keep a sharp eye on the black swine. But first thing, I'm ready now to drive Rathebe away; out with him tomorrow.'

At noon the master of Doornvlei made his double decision known: that Tau Rathebe was to leave the farm the following morning, and that Mfukeri had been warned and would be given another chance – the last.

This caused a stir among the labourers, but Tau Rathebe asked them to keep calm.

They wanted to leave with him.

'No. The police will take you as soon as you leave here. You can't go from one farm to another without a trek-pass,' he reminded them.

He left Doornvlei ...

Sarel Britz felt confused. He kept repeating to himself what he had said to his mother earlier. These are no children, no children ... they are men ... I'm dealing with the minds of men ... My father was wrong ... All my boyhood he led me to believe that black people were children ... O Hemel, they aren't ...!

He had begun to see the weakness of his father's theory during his university years, but it was the incident with Rathebe that had stamped that weakness on his mind. Harvest time came and Doornvlei became a little world of intense life and work. The maize triangle of South Africa was buzzing with talk of a surplus crop and the threat of low prices.

'A big crop again, Mfukeri, what do you say?' said Britz.

'Yes, baas,' he grinned consent, 'little bit better than last year.'

'You know you're a good worker and foreman, Mfukeri. Without you I don't know how I'd run this farm.'

'Yes, baas. If baas is happy I'm happy.'

'Since Rathebe left there's peace here, not so?'

'Yes, baas, he makes too much trouble. Long time I tell baas he always meet the men by the valley. They talk a long time there. Sometime one man tell me they want more money and food. I'm happy for you, baas. The old baas he say I must help you all the time because I work for him fifteen years. I want him to rest in peace in his grave.'

Britz nodded several times.

The Rhodesian foreman worked as hard as ever to retain the master's praise. He did not spare himself; and the other workers had to keep up with his almost inhuman pace.

'Hey you!' Mfukeri shouted often. 'You there, you're not working fast enough.' He drove them on, and some worked in panic, breaking off mealie cobs and throwing them with the dexterity of a juggler into sacks hanging from the shoulder. Mfukeri did not beat the workers any more. On this Sarel Britz had put his foot down. 'Beat your workers and you lose them,' his father had often said. But every servant felt the foreman's presence and became jittery. And the army of black sweating labourers spread out among the mealie stalks after the systematic fashion of a battle strategy.

Sometimes they sang their songs of grief and hope while reaping in the autumn sun. Sometimes they were too tired even to sing of grief; then they just went on sweating and thinking; then there was a Sunday afternoon to look forward to, when they would go to the village for a drink and song and dance and lovemaking.

Sarel Britz became sterner and more exacting. And his moods and attitude were always reflected in his trusty Mfukeri. Britz kept reminding his tenants that he was just; he favoured no one above the others; he repeated it often to Mfukeri and to his mother. He leant more and more on his foreman, who realised it and made the most of it.

Back at university the students had had endless talks about the Blacks. Britz had discussed with them his father's theory about allowing the Black man a few rungs to climb up at a time; because he was still a child. Most of his colleagues had laughed at this. Gradually he accepted their line of thinking: the White man must be vigilant.

Often when he did his accounts and books, Sarel Britz would stop in the middle of his work, thinking and wondering what he would do if he lost much of his labour, like the other farmers. What if the towns continued to attract the Black labourer by offering him jobs once preserved for the White man. Would the Black workers continue to flow into the towns, or would the law come to the farmer's rescue by stopping the influx?

Sarel Britz lived in this fear. At the same time, he thought, it would break him if he paid his workers more than forty shillings a month in order to keep them. A mighty heap of troubles rose before his eyes and he could almost hear the shouts and yells of labour tenants from all the farms rising against their masters ...

The threat became more and more real to Britz. But Mfukeri consoled him. Britz had lately been inviting him to the house quite often for a chat about doings on the farm. If only that Kaffir didn't know so much about the farm so that he, Britz, had to depend on him more than he cared to … 'Come to the house tonight, Mfukeri, and let's talk,' he said, one afternoon in late autumn.

'All right, baas.'

Mfukeri went to see his master. He wondered what the master had to say. He found him reclining comfortably on his chair. Mfukeri could not dare to take a chair before he was told to sit down – in the same chair he always sat on.

'Thank you, baas.'

After a moment of silence, 'What do you think of me, Mfukeri?'

'Why do you ask me, baas?' – after looking about.

'Don't be afraid to say your mind.'

'You're all right, baas.'

'Sure?'

'Yes, baas.' They smoked silently.

'You still like this farm?'

'Very much, baas.'

'I'm glad. You're a good foreman – the only man I trust here.'

Mfukeri understood Britz. He wanted to assure his master that he would never desert him, that he was capable of keeping the tenants together. Hadn't he spied cleverly on Tau Rathebe and avoided an upheaval?

The foreman felt triumphant. He had never in his life dreamt he would work his way into a White man's trust. He had always felt so inferior before a White man that he despised himself. The more he despised himself the sterner and more ruthless he became towards his fellow workers. At least he could retain a certain amount of self-respect and the feeling that he was a man, now that his master looked so helpless.

As the foreman sat smoking his pipe, he thought: 'How pitiable they look when they're at a Black man's mercy … I wonder now …'

'All right, Mfukeri,' said the master. The Rhodesian rose and stood erect, like a bluegum tree, over the White man; and the

White man thought how indifferent his servant looked; just like a tree. To assert his authority once more, Britz gave a few orders.

'Attend to that compost manure first thing tomorrow morning. And also the cleaning up of the chicken hospital; see to that fanbelt in the threshing machine.'

'Yes, baas, goodnight.'

He was moving towards the door when Britz said, 'Before I forget, be careful about Donker mixing with the cows. It wasn't your fault, of course, but you'll take care, won't you?'

'Yes.' He knew his master regarded his bull Donker as inferior stock, and felt hurt.

It was a bewildered Britz the foreman left behind. The farmer thought how overwhelming his servant was when he stood before him. Something in him quaked. He was sensitive enough to catch the tone of the last 'baas' when Mfukeri left: it was such an indifferent echo of what 'baas' sounded like years before.

Mfukeri kept a bull with a squatter family on a farm adjoining Doornvlei. Labour tenants were not allowed to keep livestock on the farm on which they themselves worked, because they were paid and received food rations. Mfukeri's friend agreed to keep Donker, the bull, for him. It was a good bull, though scrub.

Two days later Sarel Britz was roused from his lunch hour sleep by noise outside. He ran out and saw workers hurrying towards a common point. In a few moments he found himself standing near Mfukeri and a group of workers. In front of the barn Britz's pedigree stallion, Kasper, was kicking out at Donker, Mfukeri's bull. Donker had the horse against the barn wall and was roaring and pawing the earth.

Kasper kicked, a quick barrage of hoofs landing square on the bull's forehead. But the stocky Donker kept coming in and slashing out with his short horns. Normally there would be ecstatic shouting from the workers. They stood in silence weaving and ducking to follow the movements of the fighters. They couldn't express their attitude towards either side, because they hated both Britz and Mfukeri; and yet the foreman was one of them.

The stallion tried to turn round, which was almost fatal; for Donker charged and unleashed more furious lightning kicks. Master and foreman watched, each feeling that he was entangled in this strife between their animals; more so than they dared to show outwardly.

Sarel Britz bit his lower lip as he watched the rage of the bull. He seemed to see scalding fury in the very slime that came from the mouth of the bull to mix with the earth.

He didn't like the slime mixing with the sand; it looked as if Donker were evoking a mystic power in the earth to keep his forehoofs from slipping.

Once the hoofs were planted in the ground the bull found an opening and gored Kasper in the stomach, ripping the skin with the upward motion of the horn.

Sarel Britz gave a shout and walked away hurriedly.

When Mfukeri saw Kasper tottering, and his beloved bull drawing back, an overwhelming feeling of victory shot through every nerve in him. What he had been suppressing all through the fight came out in a gasp and, with tears in his eyes, he shouted: 'Donker! Donker!'

There was a murmur among some of the onlookers who said what a pity it was the horse's hoofs weren't shod; otherwise the ending would have been different.

Kasper was giving his last dying kicks when Britz came back with a rifle in his hand. His face was set. The workers stood aside. Two shots from the rifle finished off the stallion.

'Here, destroy the bull!' he ordered Mfukeri, handing him the gun.

The foreman hesitated.

'I said shoot that bull!'

'Why do you want me to shoot my bull, baas?'

'If you don't want to do it, then you must leave this farm, at once!'

Mfukeri did not answer. They both knew the moment had come. He stood still and looked at Britz. Then he walked off, and coaxed his bull out of the premises.

'I gave him a choice,' Sarel said to his mother, telling her the whole story.

'You shouldn't have, Sarel. He has worked for us these fifteen years.'

Sarel knew he had been right. As he looked out of the window to the empty paddock, he was stricken with grief. And then he was glad. He had got rid of yet another threat to his authority.

But the fear remained.

The Living and the Dead

Lebona felt the letter burning in his pocket. Since he had picked it up along the railway it had nagged at him no end.

He would read it during lunch, he thought. Meantime he must continue with his work, which was to pick up rubbish that people continuously threw on the platform and on the railway tracks. Lebona used a piece of wire with a ball of tar stuck on at the end. One didn't need to bend. One only pressed the ball of tar on to a piece of paper or any other rubbish, detached it and threw it into a bag hanging from the shoulder.

A number of things crossed Lebona's mind: the man who had died the previous afternoon. Died, just like that. How could a man just die like that – like a rat or a mere dog?

The workers' rush was over. Only a few women sat on the benches on the platform. One was following his movements with her eyes. She sat there, so fat, he observed, looking at him. Just like a woman. She just sat and looked at you for no reason; probably because of an idle mind; maybe she was thinking about everything. Still he knew if he were a fly she might look at him all day. But no, not the letter. She mustn't be thinking about it. The letter in his pocket. It wasn't hers – no, it couldn't be; he had picked it up lower down the line; she could say what she liked, but it wasn't her letter.

That man: who would have thought a man could die just as if death were in one's pocket or throat all the time?

Stoffel Visser was angry; angry because he felt foolish. Everything had gone wrong. And right through his university career Stoffel Visser had been taught that things must go right to the last detail.

'Calm yourself, Stoffel.'

'Such mistakes shouldn't ever occur.'

'Don't preach, for God's sake!'

Doppie Fourie helped himself to more whisky.

'It's all Jackson's fault,' Stoffel said. 'He goes out yesterday and instead of being here in the evening to prepare supper he doesn't come. This morning he's still not here, still not here, and I can't get my bloody breakfast in time because I've got to do it myself, and you know *I must* have a good breakfast every day. Worse, my clock is out of order, buggered up, man, and the bloody Jackson's not here to wake me up. So I oversleep – that's what happens – and after last night's braaivleis, you know. It's five o'clock on a Friday morning and the bastard hasn't turned up yet. How could I be in time to give Rens the document before the Cape Town train left this morning?'

'Now I think of it, Stoffel,' said Fourie, 'I can't help thinking how serious the whole thing is. Now the Minister can't have the report to think about it before the session begins. What do we do next?'

'There'll be time enough to post it by express mail.'

Doppie Fourie looked grave.

'You don't have to look as if the sky was about to fall,' he said, rather to himself than his friend. 'Have another whisky.'

Stoffel poured one for himself and his friend. 'What a good piece of work we did, Doppie!'

'Bloody good. Did you see this?' Fourie held out a newspaper, pointing his trembling finger at a report. The item said that Africans had held a 'roaring party' in a suburban house while the white family were out. There had been feasting and music and dancing.

'See, you see now,' said Stoffel, unable to contain his emotion. 'Just what I told these fellows in the commission. Some of them are so wooden-headed they won't understand simple things like kaffirs swarming over our suburbs, living there, gambling there, breeding there, drinking there and sleeping there with girls. They won't understand, these stupid fools, until the kaffirs enter their houses and boss them about and sleep with white girls. What's to happen to white civilisation?'

'Don't make another speech, Stoffel. We've talked about this so long in the commission I'm simply choking with it.'

'Look here, Doppie Fourie, ou kêrel, you deceive yourself to think I want to hear myself talk.'

'I didn't mean that, Stoffel. But of course you have always been very clever. I envy you your brains. You always have a ready answer to a problem. Anyhow I don't promise to be an obedient listener tonight. I just want to drink.'

'C'mon, ou kêrel, you know you want to listen. If I feel pressed to speak you must listen, like it or not.'

Doppie looked up at Stoffel, this frail-looking man with an artist's face and an intellect that seldom rose to the surface. None of our rugby-playing types with their bravado, Doppie thought. Often he hated himself for feeling so inferior. And all through his friend's miniature oration Doppie's face showed a deep hurt.

'Let me tell you this, rooinek,' Stoffel said, 'you know I'd rather be touring the whole world and meeting people and cultures and perhaps be learning some art myself – I know you don't believe a thing I'm saying – instead of rotting in this hole and tolerating numskulls I'm compelled to work with on committees. Doppie, there must be hundreds of our people who'd rather be doing something else they love best. But we're all tied to some bucking bronco and we must like it while we're still here and work ourselves up into a national attitude. We haven't much time to waste looking at both sides of the question like these stupids, ou kêrel. That's why it doesn't pay any more to pretend we're being just and fair to the kaffir by controlling him. No use even trying to tell him he's going to like living in enclosures.

'Isn't it because we know what the kaffir wants that we must call a halt to his ambitious wants? The danger, as I see it, ou kêrel, isn't merely in the kaffir's increasing anger and

desperation. It also lies in our tendency as whites to believe
that what we tell him is the truth. And this might drive us to
sleep one day – a fatal day, I tell you. It's necessary to keep
talking, Doppie, so as to keep jolting the whites into a sharp
awareness. It's dangerously easy for the public to forget and
go to sleep.'

Doppie clapped his hands in applause, half-dazed, half-
mocking, half-admiring. At such times he never knew what
word could sum up Stoffel Visser. A genius? – yes, he must be.
And then Stoffel would say things he had so often heard from
others. Ag, I knew it – just like all of us – ordinarily stubborn
behind those deep-set eyes. And thinking so gave Doppie a
measure of comfort. He distrusted complex human beings
because they evaded labels. Life would be so much nicer if
one could just take a label out of the pocket and tack it on the
lapel of a man's coat. Like the one a lady pins on you to show
that you've dropped a coin into her collecting box. As a badge
of charity.

'We can't talk too much, ou kêrel. We haven't said the last
word in that report on kaffir servants in the suburbs.'

Day and night for three months Stoffel Visser had worked
hard for the commission he was secretary of – the Social Affairs
Commission of his Christian Protestant Party. The report of
the commission was to have been handed to Tollen Rens,
their representative in Parliament who, in turn, had to discuss
it with a member of the Cabinet. A rigorous remedy was
necessary, it was suggested, for what Stoffel had continually
impressed on the minds of his cronies as 'an ugly situation'.
He could have chopped his own head off for failing to keep
his appointment with Tollen Rens. And all through Jackson's
not coming to wake him up and give him the breakfast he was
used to enjoying with an unflagging appetite.

'Right, Stoffel, see you tomorrow at the office.' Doppie
Fourie was leaving. Quite drunk. He turned on his heel a bit as
he made for the door, a vacant smile playing on his lips.

Although the two men had been friends for a long time,

Doppie Fourie could never stop himself feeling humiliated after a serious talk with Stoffel. Visser always overwhelmed him, beat him down and trampled on him with his superior intellect. The more he drank in order to blunt the edge of the pain Stoffel unwittingly caused him, the deeper was the hurt Doppie felt whenever they had been talking shop. Still, if Fourie never had the strength of mind to wrench himself from Stoffel's grip, his friend did all he could to preserve their companionship, if only as an exhaust pipe for his mental energy.

Stoffel's mind slowly came back to his rooms – Jackson in particular. He liked Jackson, his cook, who had served him with the devotion of a trained animal and ministered to all his bachelor whims and eating habits for four years. As he lived in a flat, it was not necessary for Jackson to clean the house. This was the work of the cleaner hired by Stoffel's landlord.

Jackson had taken his usual Thursday off. He had gone to Shanty Town, where his mother-in-law lived with his two children, in order to fetch them and take them to the zoo. He had promised so many times to take them there. His wife worked in another suburb. She couldn't go with them to the zoo because, she said, she had the children's sewing to finish.

This was the second time that Jackson had not turned up when he was expected after taking a day off. The first time he had come the following morning, all apologies. Where could the confounded kaffir be? Stoffel wondered. But he was too busy trying to adjust his mood to the new situation to think of the different things that might have happened to Jackson.

Stoffel's mind turned around in circles without ever coming to a fixed point. It was this, that and then everything. His head was ringing with the voices he had heard so many times at recent meetings. Angry voices of residents who were gradually being incensed by speakers like him, frantic voices that demanded that the number of servants in each household be brought down because it wouldn't do for blacks to run the suburbs from their quarters in European backyards.

But there were also angry voices from other meetings: if you take the servants away, how are they going to travel daily to be at work on time, before we leave for work ourselves? Other voices: who told you there are too many natives in our yards? Then others: we want to keep as many servants as we can afford.

And the voices became angrier and angrier, roaring like a sea in the distance and coming nearer and nearer to shatter his complacency. The voices spoke different languages, different arguments, often using different premises to assert the same principles. They spoke in soft, mild tones and in urgent and hysterical moods.

The mind turned around the basic arguments in a turmoil: you shall not, we will; we can, you can't; they shall not, they shall; why must they? Why mustn't they? Some of these kaffir lovers, of course, hate the thought of having to forgo the fat feudal comfort of having cheap labour within easy reach when we remove black servants to their own locations, Stoffel mused.

And amid these voices he saw himself working and sweating to create a theory to defend ready-made attitudes, stock attitudes that various people had each in their own time planted in him: his mother, his father, his brothers, his friends, his schoolmasters, his university professors and all the others who claimed him as their own. He was fully conscious of the whole process in his mind. Things had to be done with conviction or not at all.

Then, even before he knew it, those voices became an echo of other voices coming down through the centuries: the echo of gunfire, cannon, waggon-wheels as they ground away over stone and sand; the echo of hate and vengeance. All he felt was something in his blood which groped back through the corridors of history to pick up some of the broken threads that linked his life with a terrible past. He surrendered himself to it all, to this violent desire to remain part of a brutal historic past, lest he should be crushed by the brutal necessities of the present, he should be forced to lose his identity: Almighty God, no, no! Unconsciously he was trying to pile on layers of crocodile hide over his flesh to protect himself against thoughts or feelings that might some day in the vague future threaten to hurt.

When he woke from a stupor, Stoffel Visser remembered Jackson's wife over at Greenside. He had not asked her if she knew where his servant was. He jumped up and dialled on his telephone. He called Virginia's employer and asked him. No, Virginia didn't know where her husband was. As far as she knew her husband had told her the previous Sunday that he was going to take the children to the zoo. What could have happened to her husband, she wanted to know. Why hadn't he telephoned the police? Why hadn't he phoned Virginia in the morning? Virginia's master asked him these and several other questions. He got annoyed because he couldn't answer them.

None of the suburban police stations or Marshall Square Station had Jackson's name in their charge books. They would let him know 'if anything turned up'. A young voice from one police station said perhaps Stoffel's 'kaffir' had gone to sleep with his 'maid' elsewhere and had forgotten to turn up for work. Or, he suggested, Jackson might be under a hangover in the location. 'You know what these kaffirs are.' And he laughed with a thin sickly voice. Stoffel banged the receiver down.

There was a light knock at the door of his flat. When he opened with anticipation he saw an African standing erect, hat in hand.

'Yes?'

'Yes, baas.'

'What do you want?'

'I bring you this, baas,' handing a letter to the white man, while he thought: *just like those white men who work for the railways ... it's good I sealed it ...*

'Whose is this? It's addressed here, to Jackson! Where did you find it?'

'I was clean the line, baas. Um pick up papers and rubbish on railway line at Park Stish. Um think of something as um work. Then I pick up this. I ask *my*-self, who could have dropped it? But ...'

'All right, why didn't you take it to your boss?'

'They keep letters there many months, baas, and no one comes for them.' His tone suggested that Stoffel should surely know that.

The cheek he has, finding fault with the way the white man does things.

'You lie! You opened it first to see what's inside. When you found no money you sealed it up and were afraid your boss would find out you had opened it. Not true?'

'It's not true, baas, I was going to bring it here whatever happened.'

He fixed his eyes on the letter in Stoffel's hand. 'Truth's God, baas,' Lebona said, happy to be able to lie to someone who had no way of divining the truth, thinking at the same time: *they're not even decent enough to suspect one's telling the truth!*

They always lie to you when you're white, Stoffel thought, *just for cheek.*

The more Lebona thought he was performing a just duty the more annoyed the white man was becoming.

'Where do you live?'

'Kensington, baas. Um go there now. My wife she working there.'

Yet another of them, eh? Going home in a white man's area – we'll put a stop to that yet – and look at the smugness on his mug!

'All right, go.' All the time they were standing at the door, Stoffel thought how the black man smelled of sweat, even although he was standing outside.

Lebona made to go and then remembered something. Even before the white man asked him further he went on to relate it all, taking his time, but his emotion spilling over.

'I feel very sore in my heart, baas. This poor man, he comes out of the train. There are only two lines of steps on platform, and I say to *my*-self how can people go up when others are coming down? You know, there are iron gates now, and only one go and come at a time. Now other side there's train to leave for Orlando.'

What the hell have I to do with this? What does he think this is, a complaints office?

'Now, you see, it's like this: a big crowd go up and a big crowd want to rush for their train. Um look and whistle and says to *my*-self how can people move in different ways like that? Like a river going against another!'

One of these kaffirs who think they're smart, eh.

'This man, I've been watching him go up. Then I see him pushed down by those on top of steps. They rush down and stamp on him and kick him. He rolls down until he drops back on platform. Blood comes out mouth and nose like rain and I says to *my*-self, oho he's dead, poor man!'

I wish he didn't keep me standing here listening to a story about a man I don't even care to know ...!

'The poor man died, just like that, just as if I went down the stairs now and then you hear um dead.'

I couldn't care less either ...

'As um come here by tram I think, perhaps this is his letter.'

'All right now, I'll see about that.'

Lebona walked off with a steady and cautious but firm step. Stoffel was greatly relieved.

Immediately he rang the hospital and mortuary, but there was no trace of Jackson. Should he or should he not read the letter? It might give him a clue. But, no, he wasn't a *kaffir*!

Another knock at the door.

Jackson's wife, Virginia, stood just where Lebona had stood a few minutes before.

'He's not here, Master?'

'No.' Impulsively he showed her to a chair in the kitchen. 'Where else could he have gone?'

'Don't know, Master.' Then she started to cry, softly. 'Sunday we were together, Master, at my master's place. We talked about our children and you know one is seven the other four and few months and firstborn is just like his father with eyes and nose and they have always been told about the zoo by playmates so they wanted to go there, so Jackson promised them he would take them to see the animals.'

She paused, sobbing quietly, as if she meant that to be the only way she could punctuate her speech.

'And the smaller child loves his father so and he's Jackson's favourite. You know Nkati the elder one was saying to his father the other day the day their grandmother brought them to see us – he says I wish you die, just because his father wouldn't give him more sweets, Lord he's going to be the rebel of the family and he needs a strong man's hand to keep him straight. And now if Jackson is – is – oh Lord God above.'

She sobbed freely now.

'All right. I'll try my best to find him, wherever he may be. You may go now, because it's time for me to lock up.'

'Thank you, Master.' She left.

Stoffel stepped into the street and got into his car to drive five miles to the nearest police station. For the first time in his life he left his flat to look for a black man because he meant much to him – at any rate as a servant.

Virginia's pathetic look; her roundabout unpunctuated manner of saying things; the artless and devoted Virginia; the railway worker and his I don't care whether you're listening manner; the picture of two children who might very well be fatherless as he was driving through the suburb; the picture of a dead man rolling down station steps and of Lebona pouring out his heart over a man he didn't know … These images turned round and round into a complex knot. He had got into the habit of thinking in terms of irreconcilable contradictions and opposition and categories. Black was black, white was white – that was all that mattered.

So he couldn't at the moment answer the questions that kept bobbing up from somewhere in his soul; sharp little questions coming without ceremony; sharp little questions shooting up, sometimes like meteors, sometimes like darts, sometimes climbing up like a slow winter's sun. He was determined to resist them. He found it so much easier to think out categories and to place people.

His friend at the police station promised to help him.

The letter. Why didn't he give it to Jackson's wife? After all, she had just as much right to possess it as her husband.

Later he couldn't resist the temptation to open the envelope; after all, it might hold a clue. He carefully broke open the flap. There were charming photographs, one of a man and woman, the other of two children, evidently theirs. They were Jackson's all right.

The letter inside was written to Jackson himself. Stoffel read it. It was from somewhere in Vendaland, from Jackson's father. He was very ill and did not expect to live much longer. Would Jackson come soon because the government people were telling him to get rid of some of his cattle to save the land from washing away, and will Jackson come soon so that he might attend to the matter because he, the old man, was powerless. He had only the strength to tell the government people that it was more land the people wanted and not fewer stock. He had heard the white man used certain things to stop birth in human beings, and if the white man thought he was going to do the same with his cattle and donkeys – that would be the day a donkey would give birth to a cow. But, alas, he said, he had only enough strength to swear by the gods his stock wouldn't be thinned down. Jackson must come soon. He was sending the photographs which he loved very much and would like them to be safe because he might die any moment. He was sending the letter through somebody who was travelling to the gold city.

The ending was:

May the gods bless you my son and my daughter-in-law and my lovely grandsons. I shall die in peace because I have had the heavenly joy of holding my grandsons on my knees.

It was in a very ugly scrawl without any punctuation marks. With somewhat unsteady hands Stoffel put the things back in the envelope.

Monday lunchtime Stoffel Visser motored to his flat, just to check up. He found Jackson in his room lying on his bed. His servant's face was all swollen up with clean bandages covering the whole head and cheeks. His eyes sparkled from the surrounding puffed flesh.

'Jackson!'

His servant looked up at him.

'What happened?'

'The police.'

'Where?'

'Victoria Police Station.'

'Why?'

'They call me monkey.'

'Who?'

'White man in train.'

'Tell me everything, Jackson.' Stoffel felt his servant was resisting him. He read bitterness in the stoop of Jackson's shoulders and in the whole profile as he sat up.

'You think I'm telling lie, Master? Black man always tell lie, eh?'

'No, Jackson. I can only help if you tell me everything.' Somehow the white man managed to keep his patience.

'I take children to zoo. Coming back I am reading my night-school book. One see me reading and say what's this monkey think he's doing with a book. He tell me stand up, he shouts like it's first time for him to talk to a human being. That's what baboons do when they see man. I am hot and boiling and I catch him by his collar and tie and shake him. Ever see a maroela tree that's heavy with fruit? That's how I shake him. Other white men take me to place in front, a small room. Everyone there hits me hard. At station they push me out on platform and I fall on one knee. They lift me up and take me to police station. Not in city but far away I don't know where but

I see now it must have been Victoria Station. There they charge me with drunken noise. Have you a pound? I say no and I ask them they must ring you, they say if I'm cheeky they will hell me up and then they hit and kick me again. They let me go and I walk many miles to hospital. I'm in pain.'

Jackson paused, bowing his head lower.

When he raised it again he said, 'I lose letter from my father with my beautiful pictures.'

Stoffel sensed agony in every syllable, in every gesture of the hand. He had read the same story so many times in newspapers and had never given it much thought.

He told Jackson to lie in bed and for the first time in four years he called a doctor to examine and treat his servant. He had always sent him or taken him to hospital.

For four years he had lived with a servant and had never known more about him than that he had two children living with his mother-in-law and a wife. Even then they were such distant abstractions – just names representing some persons, not human flesh and blood and heart and mind.

And anger came up in him to muffle the cry of shame, to shut out the memory of recent events that was battering on the iron bars he had built up in himself as a means of protection. There were things he would rather not think about. And the heat of his anger crowded them out. What next? He didn't know. Time, time, time, that's what he needed to clear the whole muddle beneath the fog that rose thicker and thicker with the clash of currents from the past and the present. Time, time …

And then Stoffel Visser realised he did not want to think, to feel. He wanted to do something … Jackson would want a day off to go to his father … Sack Jackson? No. Better continue treating him as a name, not as another human being. Let Jackson continue as a machine to work for him. Meantime, he must do his duty – dispatch the commission's report. That was definite, if nothing else was. He was a white man, and he must be responsible. To be white and to be responsible were one and the same thing …

He and the Cat

Take it to a lawyer. That's what my friend told me to do. Now I had never had occasion to have anything to do with lawyers. Mention of lawyers always brought to my mind pictures of courts, police: terrifying pictures. Although I was in trouble, I wondered why it should be a lawyer who would help me. However, my friend gave me the address.

And from that moment my problem loomed larger. It turned in my mind. On the night before my visit to the solicitor, my heart was full of feelings of hurt. My soul fed on fire and scalding water. I'd tell the lawyer; I'd tell him everything that had gnawed inside me for several days.

I went up the stairs of the high buildings. Whenever I met a man I imagined that he was the lawyer and all but started to pour out my trouble. On the landing I met a boy with a man's head and face and rather large ears and lips. I told him I had come to see Mr B, the lawyer. Very gently, he told me to go into the waiting room and wait my turn with the others. I was disappointed. I had wanted to see Mr B, tell him everything, and get the lawyer's cure for it. To be told to wait ...

They were sitting in the waiting room, the clients, ranged round the walls – about twenty of them, like those dolls ready to be bowled over at a merry go round fair. It didn't seem that I'd get enough time to recite the whole thing – how it all started, grew into something big and was threatening to crush me – with so many people waiting. The boy with the man's head and face and large ears came in at intervals to call the next person. I knew what I'd do: I'd go over the whole problem in my mind, so that I could even say it backwards. The lawyer must miss nothing, nothing whatever.

But in the course of it all my eyes wandered about the

room: the people, the walls, the ceiling, the furniture. A bare, unattractive room: the arms of the chairs had scratches on them that might have been made with a pin by someone who was tired of waiting. Against the only stretch of wall that was free of chairs for clients, a man of about fifty sat at a table, sealing envelopes. From a picture on the wall behind him – the only picture in the room – a cat with green eyes looked down as if supervising his work. For some reason I couldn't fathom, a small school globe stood on the table. It suggested that the man sealing the envelopes might start spinning the globe to show a class that the earth is round and turns on its axis.

Once you start to make an effort to think, a thousand and one things come into your head. You would think of the previous night's adventure, perhaps; and then your girlfriend might force herself into the front line; then you would begin on another trail. You might come back, as I did now, and look at the cat in front of you or the man at the table or the clients, one by one. For a fleeting moment the cat would seem to move. Then it would take up its former position, its whiskers aggressively proclaiming that you were a fool to have imagined it in motion.

You watched the frantic movements of a fly against the windowpane, fussing to get through at the top when the bottom was open. You looked beyond to the tall buildings of the city. The afternoon heat became so oppressive that your head was just a jumble box. You didn't even hear the boy with the man's face and large ears call 'Next one!' You seemed to float on the stagnant air in the room, and to be no more Sello or Temba in flesh, waiting in a room, but a creature in the no-time of feeling and thought.

The man at the table continued with his mechanical work. He, too, seemed to want to escape from drudgery, for he spoke to two or three clients near him. And he chuckled often, showing a benignly toothless mouth. He delighted in bringing out an aphorism or proverb after every four or five sentences. 'Our sages say that the only thing you have that's surely your own is what you've already eaten, he-he-he'; 'a city is beautiful from afar, but approach it and it disappoints you, he-he-he.'

The clients talked in groups, discussing various things. A man was found dead near Shanty Town, killed by a train, perhaps ... 'Now, look at me; I've three sons. Do you think any one of them cares to bring home a penny? They just feed and sleep and don't care where the food comes from.'

The man at the table said: 'What I always say is that as soon as you allow a child to go to a dance, you've lost her.'

'Try to catch a passing wind – hugh!' 'He cannot go far; they'll catch him.' 'Imagine it – her husband not six months in his grave, poor man, and she takes off her mourning. That's the reward a good husband gets!'

'Our sages say a herd of cattle led by a cow always falls into the ditch ... Listen to her always, as long as you know you have the last word ...'

'I once met a man ...' 'Potatoes? Everything is costly these days. Even a woman has gone up in price when you want to marry.' 'Only God knows when we are ever to go where we want to at any time.' 'Are we not here because of money? Do we not walk the streets and ride on trains and buses because of money? Is money not the thing that drives us in our wanderings?'

'Death is in the leg; we walk with it, he-he-he.'

'You have not been to Magaba, you say? Then you know nothing. Women selling fruit, everyone as red as the ground on which they stand; men and women just one with the red earth; salted meat roasting on the grid to be sold; red dust swirling above, people dashing this way and that like demons scorching in a fire – something like a dream.'

The man at the table laughed again and said, 'But horns that are put on you never stick on – so don't worry about gossip.'

'We've fallen upon evil days when a girl can beat her mother-in-law.' 'It's the first I've seen for many years. In my day a cow could give birth to a donkey if such a thing happened.' 'Oh, everybody beats everybody these days; we've lost, lost.' 'But we can't go back.'

'I'll know it's a zebra when I see the stripes.' This from the table.

'He reads too much; the white doctors say his brain is fermenting.'

'Even the eagle comes down to earth.' Another proverb.

'You and I have never had the chance to go to school, so we must send our children; they'll read and write for us.' 'Didn't you hear? They say the poor man was screaming and trying to run away before he died. He was crying and saying a mountain of sins was standing in his way.' 'Yes, his wife stood by his bed, and he said to her, he says, "Selope, take care of my son; now give me water to drink. This is the last time," he says, "I shall ever ask you to do anything for me." '

The boy with the man's face and large ears came to tell us that two white men had gone into Mr B's office. There was a moment's silence. The man at the table nodded several times. The cat glowered at him with green eyes and almost live whiskers. The fly must have found its way out. The heat was becoming a problem to reckon with.

'How many times have I come here?' said an old woman to no one in particular. 'In the meantime, my grandchildren are starving. Their good for nothing father has not sent them money since the law separated him from my daughter.' Deeper silence. A few people frowned at the old woman as the birds are said to have done when they were about to attack the owl. A few others seemed to be telling themselves that they weren't hearing what they were hearing.

'Where does the old mother come from?' It was someone next to her. Once he had started he went on with a string of questions to get her off the track.

And so the people went on patching up. During all this time I had got my facts straight in my head. Several times I had imagined myself in front of Mr B: a short man with tired eyes (I always envisioned the lawyer as small in stature). I had told him everything. Now, as I sat here in the waiting room, I already knew I'd be relieved; the burden would fall off as soon as I should have seen and talked to Mr B. I was so sure. It couldn't be otherwise.

There was little talking now. Fools! I thought. Their inner selves were smarting and curdling with past hurts (like mine); they were aching to see Mr B, to tell him their troubles. Yet here they were, pretending they had suspended their anxiety. Here they were, trying to rip this wave of heat and scatter it by so much gas talk: babbling away over things that didn't concern them, to cover the whirlpool of their own troubles. What was beneath these eddies and bubbles dancing and bursting on a heat wave – someone else's possessions, flouting of the law, unfaithfulness, the forbidden tree? And the man at the table: what right had he to pronounce those aphorisms and proverbs, old as the language of man, and bleached like a brown shirt that has become a dirty white? What right had he to chuckle like that, as though he regarded us as a shopkeeper does his customers? Next one ... the next one ... Next!

I was left alone with the man and the cat. My heart gave a hard beat when my mind switched back to what had brought me to the lawyer. Give it to a lawyer, my friend had said confidently, as though I merely had to press an electric switch. He'll help you out of the mud. A damned good solicitor. You give him the most difficult case and he'll talk you free ... Yes, I'd tell him everything; all that troubled my waking and sleeping hours. Then everything would be all right. I felt it would be so.

'The big man is very busy today, eh?' observed the man at the table.

'Yes,' I said mechanically.

My attention was drawn to the whole setting once more: a plain unpretentious room with oldish chairs; the school globe; the pile of letters and envelopes; the man; and the picture of the cat.

An envelope fell to the floor. He bent down to take it up. I watched his large hands feel about for it, fumbling. Then the hand came upon the object, but with much more weight than a piece of paper warranted.

Even before he came up straight on his chair I saw it clearly. The man at the table was blind, stone blind. As my eyes were getting used to the details, after my mind had thus been jolted into confused activity, I understood. Here was a man sealing envelopes, looking like a drawing on a flat surface. Perhaps he was flat and without depth, like a gramophone disc; too flat even to be hindered by the heat, the boredom of sitting for hours doing the same work; by too many or too few people coming. An invincible pair, he and the cat glowering at him, scorning our shames and hurts and the heart, seeming to hold the key to the immediate imperceptible and the most remote unforeseeable.

I went in to see Mr B. A small man (as I had imagined) with tired eyes but an undaunted face. I told him everything from beginning to end.

In Corner B

How can boys just stick a knife into someone's man like that? Talita mused. Leap out of the dark and start beating up a man and then drive a knife into him. What do the parents of such boys think of them? What does it matter now? I'm sitting in this room weeping till my heart wants to burst …

Talita's man was at the government mortuary, and she sat waiting, waiting and thinking in her house. A number of stab wounds had done the job, but it wasn't till he had lain in hospital for a few hours that the system caved in and he turned his back on his people as they say. This was a Thursday. But if one died in the middle of the week, the customary thing is for him to wait for a week and be buried at the first weekend after the seven days. A burial must be on a weekend to give as many people as possible an opportunity to attend it. At least a week must be allowed for the next of kin to come from the farthest part of the country.

There are a number of things city folk can afford to do precipitately: a couple may marry by special licence and listen to enquiries from their next of kin after the fact; they can be precipitate in making children and marry after the event; children will break with their parents and lose themselves in other townships; several parents do not hold coming out parties to celebrate the last day of a newborn baby's month-long confinement in the house. But death humbles the most unconventional, the hardest rebel. The dead person cannot simply be packed off to the cemetery. You are a person because of other human beings, you are told. The aunt from a distant province will never forgive you if she arrives and finds the deceased buried before she has seen his lifeless face for the last time. Between the death and the funeral, while the body lies in the mortuary (which has to be paid for) there is a wake each night. Day and night relatives and friends and *their* friends come and go, saying words of consolation to the bereaved. And all the time some next of kin must act as spokesman to relate the circumstances of death to all who arrive for the first time. Petty intrigues and dramatic scenes among the relatives as they prepare for the funeral are innumerable. Without them, a funeral doesn't look like one.

Talita slept where she sat, on a mattress spread out on the floor in a corner, thinking and saying little, and then only when asked questions like: 'What will you eat now?' or 'Has your headache stopped today?' or 'Are your bowels moving properly?' or 'The burial society wants your marriage certificate, where do you keep it?' Apart from this, she sat or lay down and thought.

Her man was tall, not very handsome, but lovable; an insurance agent who moved about in a car. Most others in the business walked from house to house and used buses and electric trains between townships. But her man's firm was prosperous and after his fifteen years' good service it put a new car at his disposal. Her man had soft gentle eyes and was not at all as vivacious as she. Talita often teased him about his shyness and what she called the weariness in his tongue because he spoke little. But she always prattled on and on, hardly ever short of topics to talk about.

'Ah, you met your match last night, mother of Luka,' her man would say teasingly.

'My what – who?'

'The woman we met at the dance and talked as if you were not there.'

'How was she my match?'

'Don't pretend to be foolish – hau, here's a woman! She talked you to a standstill and left you almost wide-mouthed when I rescued you. Anyone who can do that takes the flag.'

'Ach, get away! And anyhow if I don't talk enough my tongue will rot and grow mouldy.'

They had lived through nineteen years of married life that yielded three children and countless bright and cloudy days. It was blissful generally, in spite of the physical and mental violence around them; the privation; police raids; political strikes and attendant clashes between the police and boycotters; death; ten years of low wages during which she experienced a long spell of ill health. But like everybody else Talita and her man stuck it through. They were in an urban township and like everybody else they made their home there. In the midst of all these living conditions, at once in spite and because of them, the people of Corner B alternately clung together desperately and fell away from the centre; like birds that scatter when the tree on which they have gathered is shaken. And yet for each individual life a new day dawned and set, and each acted out his own drama which the others might never know of or might only get a glimpse of or guess at.

For Talita, there was that little drama which almost blackened things for herself and her man and children. But because they loved each other so intensely, the ugliest bend was well negotiated, and the cloud passed on, the sun shone again. This was when a love letter fell into her hands owing to one of those clumsy things that often happen when lovers become stupid enough to write to each other. Talita wondered about something, as she sat huddled in the corner of her dining-sitting room and looked at the flame of a candle nearby, now quivering, now swaying this way and that and now coming into an erect position as if it lived a separate life from the stick of wax. She wondered how or why it happened that a mistress should entrust a confidential letter to a stupid messenger who in turn sends someone else without telling him to return the letter if the man should be out; why the second messenger should give the letter to her youngest child who then opens it and calls his mother from the bedroom to read it. Accident? Just downright brazen cheek on the part of the mistress ...!

A hymn was struck and the wake began in earnest. There was singing, praying, singing, preaching in which the deceased was mentioned several times, often in vehement praise of him and his kindness. The room filled rapidly until the air was one thick choking lump of grief. Once during the evening someone fainted. 'An aunt of the deceased, the one who loved him most,' a whisper escaped from someone who seemed to know, and it was relayed from mouth to mouth right out into the yard where some people stood or sat. 'Shame! Shame!' one could hear the comment from active sympathisers. More than once during the evening a woman screamed at high pitch. 'The sister of the deceased,' a whisper escaped, and it was relayed. 'Shame! Shame!' was the murmured comment. 'Ao, God's people!' an old man exclaimed. During the prayers inside the people outside continued to speak in low tones.

'Have the police caught the boys?'

'No – what, when has a black corpse been important?'

'But they have been asking questions in Corner B today.'

'Hm.'

'When's a black corpse been important?'

'Das' right, just ask him.'

'It is Saturday today and if it was a white man lying there in the mortuary the newspapers would be screaming about a manhunt morning and evening since Thursday, the city would be upside down, God's truth.'

'Now look here you men these men don't mean to kill nobody their empty stomachs and no work to do turns their heads on evil things.'

'Ach you and your politics let one of them break into your house or ra–'

The speaker broke off short and wiped his mouth with his hand as if to remove pieces of a foul word hanging carelessly from his lip.

'Das not the point,' squeaked someone else.

Just then the notes of a moving hymn rolled out of the room

and the men left the subject hanging and joined enthusiastically in the singing, taking different parts.

Some women were serving tea and sandwiches. A middle-aged man was sitting at a table in a corner of the room. He had an exercise book in front of him, in which he entered the names of those who donated money and the amounts they gave. Such collections were meant to help meet funeral expenses. In fact they went into buying tea, coffee, bread and even groceries for meals served to guests who came from far.

'Who put him there?' asked an uncle of the deceased in an anxious tone, pointing at the money collector.

'Do I know?' an aunt said.

The question was relayed in whispers in different forms. Every one of the next of kin denied responsibility. It was soon discovered that the collector had mounted the stool on his own initiative.

'But don't you know that he has long fingers?' the same uncle flung the question in a general direction, just as if it were a loud thought.

'I'm going to tell him to stop taking money. Hei, Cousin Stoffel, take that exercise book at once, otherwise we shall never know what has happened to the money.' Cousin Stoffel was not fast, but he had a reputation for honesty.

It was generally known that the deposed young man appeared at every death house where he could easily be suspected to be related to the deceased, and invariably used his initiative to take collections and dispose of some of the revenue. But of course several of the folk who came to console Talita could be seen at other vigils and funerals by those who themselves were regular customers. The communal spirit? Largely. But also they were known to like their drinks very much. So a small fund was usually raised from the collections to buy liquor from a shebeen nearby and bring it to the wake.

Bang in the middle of a hymn a man came into the room and hissed while he made a beckoning sign to someone. Another hiss, yet another. An interested person who was meanly being left out immediately sensed conspiracy and followed those who answered the call. As they went out, they seemed to peel off a layer of the hymn and carry it out with them as they sang while moving out. In some corner of the yard or in the bedroom a group of men, and sometimes a woman or two, conducted a familiar ritual.

'God's people,' an uncle said solemnly, screwing his face at the time in an attempt to identify those who had been called. If he saw a stray one or two, he merely frowned but could do nothing about it on such a solemn occasion. The gatecrashers just stood, half-shy and half-sure of themselves, now rubbing a nose, now changing postures.

'God's people, as I was about to say, here is an ox for slaughter.' At this point he introduced a bottle of brandy. One did not simply plant a whole number of bottles on the floor: that was imprudent. 'Cousin Felang came driving it to this house of sorrow. I have been given the honour of slaughtering it, as the uncle of this clan.' With this he uncorked the bottle and served the brandy, taking care to measure with his fingers.

'This will kill the heart for a time so that it does not break from grief. Do not the English say *drown de sorry*?' He belched from deep down his stomach.

And then tongues began to wag. Anecdotes flew as freely as the drinks. And when they could not contain their mirth they laughed. 'Yes, God's people,' one observed, 'the great death is often funny.'

They did not continually take from the collections. If they felt they were still thirsty, someone went round among those he suspected felt the thirst too and collected money from them to buy more drinks for another bout.

At midnight the people dispersed. The next of kin and close friends would alternate in sleeping in Talita's house. They simply huddled against the wall in the same room and covered themselves with blankets.

Talita sat and waited at her corner like a fixture in the house. The children were staying with a relative and would come back on Sunday to see their father for the last time in his coffin. The corpse would be brought home on Saturday afternoon.

Thoughts continued to mill round in Talita's mind. A line of thought continued from where it had been cut off. One might imagine disjointed lines running around in circles. But always she wanted to keep the image of her man in front of her. Just as though it were an insult to the memory of him when the image escaped her even once.

Her man had confessed without making any scene at all. Perhaps it was due to the soft and timid manner in which Talita had asked him about the letter. She said she was sorry she had taken the letter from the child and, even when she had seen that instead of beginning 'Dear Talita' it was 'My everything', she had yielded to the temptation to read it. She was very sorry, she said, and added something to the effect that if she hadn't known, and he continued to carry on with the mistress, it wouldn't have been so bad. But the knowing it ... Her man had promised not to see his mistress again. Not that his affair had detracted in any way from the relationship between man and wife, or made the man neglect the welfare of his family. Talita remembered how loyal he had been. The matter was regarded as closed and life had proceeded unhaltingly.

A few months later, however, she had noticed things, almost imperceptible, had heard stray words outside the house, almost inaudible or insignificant, which showed that her man was seeing his mistress. Talita had gone out of her way to track 'the other woman' down. No one was going to share her man with her, full stop, she said to herself. She had found her: Marta, also a married woman. One evening Talita, when she was sure she could not be wrong in her suspicions, had followed Marta from the railway station to the latter's house in another part of Corner B. She entered shortly after the unexpecting hostess. Marta's husband was in. Talita greeted both and sat down.

'I am glad you are in, morena – sir. I have just come to ask you to chain your bitch. That is my man and mine alone.' She stood up to leave.

'Wait, my sister,' Marta's husband said. 'Marta!' he called to his wife who had walked off saying, laughingly and defyingly, 'Aha, ooh', perhaps to suppress any feeling of embarrassment, as Talita thought. She wouldn't come out.

'You know, my sister,' the man said with disturbing calm, 'you know a bitch often answers to the sniffing of a male. And I think we both have to do some fastening.' He gave Talita a piercing look, which made her drop her eyes. She left the house. So he knows too! she thought. That look he gave her told her they shared the same apprehensions. Her man had never talked about the incident, although she was sure that Marta must have told him of it. Or would she have the courage to?

Often there were moments of deep silence as Talita and her man sat together or lay side by side. But he seldom stiffened up. He would take her into his arms and love her furiously and she would respond generously and tenderly, because she loved him and the pathos in his eyes.

'You know, my man,' she ventured to say one evening in bed, 'if there is anything I can help you with, if there is anything you would like to tell me, you mustn't be afraid to tell me. There may be certain things a woman can do for her man which he never suspected she could do.'

'Oh don't worry about me. There is nothing you need do for me.' And, like someone who had at last found a refuge after a rough and dangerous journey, her man would fold her in his arms and love her.

Was this it, she wondered. But how? Did it begin during her long period of ill health – this Marta-thing? Or did it begin with a school episode? How could she tell? Her man never talked about his former boy-girl attachments, except in an oblique or vague way which yielded not a clue. Marta was pretty, no doubt. She was robust, had a firm waist and seemed

to possess in physical appearance all that could attract a man.
But if she, Talita, failed to give her man something Marta had
to offer, she could not trace it. How could she? Her man was
not the complaining type, and she often found out things that
displeased him herself and set out to put them out of his way
if she could.

In the morning, while he was asleep, she would stare into
his broad face, into his tender eyes, to see if she could read
something. But all she saw was the face she loved. Funny
that you saw your man's face every day almost and yet you
couldn't look at it while he slept without the sensation of
some guilt or something timid or tense or something held in
suspension; so that if the man stirred, your heart gave a leap as
you turned your face away. One thing she was sure of amidst
all the wild and agonising speculation: her man loved her and
their children …

'They're always doing this to me I do not matter I cannot allow
plans to be made over the body of my cousin without my being
told about it and why do they talk behind my back I don't
stand for dusty nonsense me. And someone's daughter has
the cheek to say I am nobody in the family of my cousin's and
says me, I am always going ahead of others yes I am always
running ahead of the others because I think other people are
fools what right has she to talk behind my back why does she
not tell me face to face what she thinks of me she is afraid I can
make her see her mother if once I …'

'Sh!' The senior uncle of the dead man cut in to try to keep
the peace. And he was firm. 'What do you want to turn this
house into? There is a widow in there in grief and here you are
you haven't got what the English call respection. Do you want
all the people around to laugh at us, think little of us? All of us
bury our quarrels when we come together to weep over a dear
one who has left; what *nawsons* is this?'

The cousin who felt outraged stood against the wall with

her hands hidden behind her apron like a child caught in an act of mischief. She had not been addressing herself to anyone in particular and hoped someone would pick up the challenge. And although she felt rebuked, she said, 'But uncle of the clan, these people are always whispering dirty things behind my back what should I say? And then they go and order three buses instead of four these God's people have collected money for us to hire enough buses for them I shall not be surprised if someone helped himself to some of the money –'

'Sh!' the senior uncle interrupted. 'We do not throw urine out of the chamber for everybody to see.'

Someone whispered, Mapodisa! Police! With two boys! Everyone in the yard stood still, as if to some command. An African constable came in, preceded by two dirty-looking youngsters in handcuffs.

'Stop,' he barked when they neared the door.

'Where is the widow?' the constable asked, addressing no one in particular.

Silence.

'Hela! Are these people dumb?' Silence. One of the boys blew his nose on to the ground with his free hand and wiped off the stuff from his upper lip and ran the hand down the flank of his trousers.

The constable went into the room with a firm stride, almost lifting up the boys clear off the ground in the process. Inside, he came face to face with Talita, who was sitting in her usual corner. She seemed to look through him and this unsettled him slightly. He braced himself up visibly.

'Face the mother there you fakabond!' he barked at the boys.

'I say look at the mother there, you dirty tsotsi.' He angrily lifted the drooping head of one of them.

'You know this mother?' The boys shook their heads and mumbled adolescently.

'Mother, look at these tsotsis. Have you ever seen them before? Look at them carefully, take your time.'

Talita looked at them wearily. She shook her head.

'Sure-sure?' Again she shook her head.

'I know what you do at night you fakabond.' The whole house was now full of him, the rustle of his khaki uniform and his voice and his official importance. 'You kill you steal you rape and give other people no peace. Fakabond! You saw boys attack a man the other night, did you? Dung, let me tell you! You talk dung. Pure dung! You took out your knives for the man, fakabond! You see that bucket in front of your cells? You will fill it in quick time tonight when the baas is finished with you. The big white sergeant doesn't play around with black boys like you as I do. Dung! You didn't mean to kill him, you say, just wanted to beat him up and he fought back. Dung!'

The constable had hardly said the last word when an elderly woman came out of another room, holding a stick for support.

'What is all this?' she asked. 'First you come and shake this poor child out of her peace when she has lost her man and then you use foul words at a time like this. Cannot this business wait until after the burial? Tell me who are you? Who is your father? Where were you born?'

He mumbled a few words, but the woman cut him short.

'Is this how you would like your mother or your wife to be treated, I mean your own own mother?'

'I am doing the government's work.'

'Go and tell that government of yours that he is full of dung to send you to do such things. Sies! Kgoboromente kgoboromente! You and him can go to hell where you belong. Get out!'

She took a lunge and landed her stick on him. Once, then twice, and the third time she missed because the constable dashed noisily out of the house, hauling the boys by the handcuffs. The woman pursued him with a limp, right up to the car in which was a white man in plain clothes – directly in front of the gate. The white man was obviously at pains to suppress a laugh. The constable entered with the boys in a most disorderly, undignified manner ... The vehicle started off amidst the clatter of words that continued to come from the woman's mouth.

Talita wondered: were the boys merely the arms of some monster sitting in the dark somewhere, wreaking vengeance on her man ...?

Evening came. One caucus after another was held to make sure all arrangements were intact; for this was Saturday and the corpse had arrived. The double-decker buses from the city transport garages: were they booked? You son of Kobe did you get the death certificate and permit for the cemetery? And the number plate? They want to see the dead man's pass first. Ask for it in the house ... Pass pass be damned, cannot a man go to his grave in peace without dragging his chains after him ...! Is the pastor coming tonight? Those three goats: have they been slaughtered? Right, this is how men work ... You have worked well. The caucus meetings went on ...

Word went round that the grandmother of the deceased had come. She loved Talita, so everyone who mattered testified. Heads nodded. Relatives who had not seen one another for a long time were there and family bonds were in place again. Some who were enemies tolerated each other, shooting side glances at each other. Those who loved each other tended to exaggerate and exhibit the fact.

The people came in to keep vigil for the last night. The brown coffin – nothing ostentatious enough to cause a ripple of telltale excitement – stood against a wall. A white sheet was thrown across to partition the room so that in the smaller portion the corpse lay on a mattress under a white sheet. Talita sat next to it, leaning against her man's grandmother. The days and nights of waiting had told on her face; the black head-tie that was fastened like a hood cast a shade over it. Her hair had already been reduced to look like a schoolgirl's with a pair of scissors. Singing began. The elderly ladies washed the corpse.

The tune sailed out of the room, floated in the air and was caught by those outside.

'Tomorrow after the funeral eh? Okay?'

'Yes, tomorrow after the funeral. Where?'

'At the party.'

'Oh-ja, I forgot Cy's party. I'll go home first and change, eh? But I'm scared of my Pa.'

'Let the old beard go fly a kite.'

'He's my Pa all the same.' She pushed him slightly as a reproach.

'Okay. He is, so let's not fight 'bout it. Still don't want me to come to your house?'

'You know he don't like you and he'd kill me if he saw me with you.'

'Because you work and I don't I'm sure. I'm getting a job Monday that'll fix the old beard.'

'No it's not just a job and it's not you Pa hates.'

'That's funny talk. What then?'

'Just because I'm twenty-three and I shouldn't have a boy yet.'

'Jesus! Where's the old man been living all these years? Jesus!'

'Doesn't matter, Bee. You're my boy.' She giggled.

'Just remembered my Pa asked me the other day who's that he saw me with. I say your name – Bee, I say.'

'And then?'

'And then his face becomes sour and he says Who? I say Bee. He says Where have you heard someone called Bee – *Bee* did you say? I say anybody can call his son what he likes. He says you must be mad or a tsotsi without even a decent name.'

A deep sigh and then: 'That's no funny.' He trembled slightly.

'Don't be cross Bee, you know it means nothing to me what you're called.'

'Sh – they're praying now.'

Two mouths and two tongues suck each other as he presses her against the wall of the shed that served as a fowl-run.

'Hm, they're praying,' but her words are lost in the other's mouth. He feels her all over and she wriggles against him. She allows herself to be floored ...

A hymn strikes again.

Two figures heave themselves up from the ground, panting. It has been a dark, delicious, fugitive time. They go back and join the singers, almost unnoticed.

The hymn continues. A hymn of hope, of release by death, of refuge for the weary and tormented: a surrender to death once it has been let loose among a flock of sheep. Underlying the poetry of this surrender is the one long and huge irony of endurance.

In another corner of the yard an elderly man was uncorking a bottle of whisky and pouring it into glasses. The sound of it, like water flowing down a rock crevice, was pleasing to the ear as the company squatted in front of the 'priest'. Here my children, kill the heart and as the Englishman says, *drown de sorry*. Ah, you see now ... Someone, for lack of something important or relevant to say, but out of sheer blissful expectation sighed: 'Ja madoda – yes, men, death is a strange thing. If he came to my house he would ask my woman to give him food any time and he could come any time of night and say I've come to see if you're all right and then we would talk and talk and talk. We were so close. And now he's late, just like that.' And he sobbed and sniffled.

'Ja,' the others sighed in chorus.

A woman screamed in the room and broke into sobs. The others carried her out.

'Quiet child,' a middle-aged woman coaxed. 'Quiet quiet quiet.'

Talita held out. When Sunday dawned she said in her heart God let it pass this time. The final act came and passed ...

They were walking away from the grave towards the tarmac path leading to the exit. Suddenly a woman, seemingly from nowhere, went and flung herself on the soft, red damp mound of the new grave. It was Marta. She screamed like one calling a person across a river in flood, knowing the futility of it all. 'Why did you leave me alone?' Marta yelled, her arms thrown over her head. Her legs kicked as she cried unashamedly, like a child whose toy has been wrenched out of his hand. Soon there was one long horizontal gasp as whispered words escaped the crowd, underlining the grotesqueness of the scene. Some stood stolidly, others amused, others outraged. Two men went and dragged Marta away, while she still cried, 'Come back come back why did you leave me alone?'

Talita stopped short. She badly wanted to leap clear of the hands that supported her, but she was too weak. The urge strained every nerve, every muscle of her body. The women who supported her whispered to her to ignore the female's theatrics. 'Let us go, child,' they said. 'She wants you to talk.' They propelled Talita towards the black 'family car'.

A few days later a letter arrived, addressed to Talita. She was walking about in the yard, but was not allowed to go to work or anywhere beyond her gate. The letter was in a bad but legible scrawl and read:

> Dear Missis Molamo, I am dropping this few lines for to hoping that you are living good now i want to telling you my hart is sore sore. i hold myselfe bad on the day of youre mans funeral my hart was ful of pane too much and i see myselfe already o Missis Molamo alreaddy doing mad doings i think the gods are beatting me now for holding myselfe as wyle animall forgeef forgeef i pray with all my hart child of the people.

Talita paused. These wild women who can't even write must needs try to do so in English. She felt the tide of anger and hatred mounting up, flushing her whole body, and then she wondered if she should continue to read. She planted her elbow on the table and supported her head with her hand. She felt drawn to the letter, so she obeyed the impulse to continue.

now i must tel you something you must noe quik quik thees
that i can see that when you come to my hause and then
whenn you see me kriing neer the grafe i can see you think i
am sweet chokolet of your man i can see you think in your hart
my man love that wooman no no i want to tel you that he neva
love me nevaneva he livd same haus my femily rented in Fitas
and i lovd him mad i tel you i lovd him mad i wanted him with
red eyes he was nise leetl bit nise to me but i see he sham for me
as i hav got no big ejucashin he got too much book i make nise
tea and cake for him and he like my muther and he is so nise i
want to foss him to love me but he just nise i am shoor he come
to meet me in toun even now we are 2 merryd peeple bicos
he remember me and muther looked aftar him like bruther for
me he was stil nise to me but al wooman can see whenn there
is no loveness in a man and they can see lovfulness. now he is
gonn i feel i want to rite with my al ten fingas becos i have too
muche to say aboute your sorriness and my sorriness i will help
you to kry you help me to kry and leev that man in peas with
his gods. so i stop press here my deer i beg to pen off the gods
look aftar us

                i remain your sinserity
                Missis Marta Shuping

When Talita finished reading, a great dawn was breaking upon
her, and she stood up and made tea for herself. She felt like a
foot traveller after a good refreshing bath.

A Point of Identity

It was not until a crisis broke upon Karel Almeida that I began to wonder why he, a coloured African man, should have chosen to live in a black settlement rather than among other coloured African folk. Whoever thought up the word 'Coloured' must have been one of those people who are so obsessed with the subject of 'colour' that when they belch, the reek of it hits you a mile away. Left to ourselves, we should speak of *Africans*, whether 'Coloured', 'White', 'Indian' or 'Negro'.

But I started to talk about Karel Almeida. When he came to live with us in Corner B location, seven miles out of Pretoria, it was first rumoured that he must be well to do. Then people said he *was* rich. And then people went around saying that he had won a huge bet at the race course wherever (no one cared to know where exactly) he had come from. Soon it was said that he was a coloured African. Then again they said, Ach, he's not Coloured, just one of these blacks with funny names. All these guesses arose from the fact that Karel Almeida was light in complexion, he was large in physique and he improved the appearance of his three-roomed house within two months or so of his arrival. Also Almeida laughed a lot like 'a man who had little to worry him'. But I shouldn't forget to add that he was a bachelor when he arrived, and must have been saving up and living light.

This was little less than ten years before – I mean when he came to our street and occupied a house next door to mine.

During those years Karel Almeida became 'Karel' to me and my wife and 'Uncle Karel' or 'Uncle Kale' to the children. We were very fond of each other, Karel and I. We had got to take each other for granted; so it was normal for him, when he was spending his two weeks' leave at home and my wife fell ill, to look after her and cook for her and give her medicines while I was away at school, teaching. He worked in a Jew's motor mechanic shop in the city, and lived austerely enough.

Karel's whole physical being seemed to be made of laughter. When he was going to laugh, he shook and quivered as if to 'warm up' for a take-off and then the laugh was released like a volley from deep down his large tummy, virtually bullying the listener to join in the 'feast'.

'Hm, just hear now Karel is eating laughter!' my wife would say when the sound issued from Karel's house.

'Me my mudder was African, my farder was Portugalese,' Karel often said in conversation. 'Not, mind you, de Portugalese what come an' fuck aroun' an' have a damn good time an' den dey vamoose off to Lourenço Marques. But de ole man went to LM an' he got sick.' After a pause he burst out, 'An' he die sudden, man, just like to blow a candle out, T.' He always called me 'T', which was an intimate way of referring to me as a schoolteacher.

'Where were you and your mother?'

'In Joburg, man. It's now – let me see – one, two, three, ja, three years. Died in Sibasa, man, way up nort' Transvaal. My Ma nearly died same day and followed my Pa de day he die. Fainted an' gave us hell to bring her back. She went to LM for de funeral.'

'And now, where's she?'

'Who, my mudder? She's dead – let me see – one, two, two years now. I brought her wit' me to Joburg when I was learning mechanics at de same garage what brought me here. Good Jew boss, very good. He got a son at university in Joburg. Nice boy too. Ma didn't like Joburg not dis much, so I took her back to Sibasa.'

We often teased each other with Karel, he was so full of laughter.

'I can't understand,' I said one day, 'why you cycle to work and back instead of taking a bus. Just look how the rain beats on you and the wind almost freezes you in winter.'

He laughed. 'Trouble wit' you kaffirs is you's spoiled.'

'And you Boesmans and Hotnotte are tough, you'll tell me.'

'An de Coolies, too. See how dey walk from house to house selling small t'ings. Dey's like donkeys, man. Can't catch dem de coolies, man. You and me will never catch dem. It's dey who'll always make de money while we Hotnotte an' kaffirs sleep or loaf about or stick a knife or plug a bullet into someone or jes work for what we eat an' live in an' laugh at life. Jeeslike man, dey's gone dose Coolies, dey'll beat us at makin' money all de time.'

'But Hotnotte, Boesmans and Kaffirs and coolies are all frying in the same pan, boy, and we're going to sink or swim together, you watch.'

'Okay Kaffirs, let's swim.'

'What you got, Boesman?'

'Whisky, gin and lime. But you know I'm not a Hottentot or a Bushman, I've got European blood straight from de balls no zigzag business about it.' And, as he served the drinks, his laughter rang pure and clear and solid.

'But serious now, true's God, I've always lived wit' Africans an' never felt watchimball-er-discomfortable or ashamed.' He could never say 'what you call it'. 'Damn it all man if my farder slept wit' mudder an' day made me dat's dey business. You, T, your great-great-great-grandmudder may have been white or brown woman herself. How can you be sure of anyt'ing? How can any Indian be sure he's hundred per cent India? I respec' a man what respec' me no matter his colour.'

He spoke with vehemence and compassion.

Karel took an African woman to live with him as his wife. She was a lovely woman whose background was unknown. She was hardworking and Karel treated her with great affection. She never had much to say, but she was not proud: only shy.

And then the crisis came.

If the whole thing did not begin to set members of a family against one another or individual persons against their communities, or vice versa; if it did not drive certain people to the brink of madness and to suicide; if it did not embarrass very dark-skinned people to sit in front of a white tribunal and have to claim 'mixed parentage', then we should have thought that someone had deliberately gone out of his way to have fun, or create it. The white people who governed the country had long been worried about the large numbers of coloured Africans who were fair enough to want to play white, and of Negroes who were fair enough to want to try for Coloured. They had long been worried about the prospect of one coffee-coloured race, which would shame what they called 'white civilisation' and the 'purity' of their European blood. So, maybe, after a sleepless night, someone ate his breakfast, read his morning newspapers in between bites, walked about his suburban garden, told his black 'boy' to finish cleaning his car, kissed his wife and children goodbye ('Don't expect me for supper, dear'), went to the House of Assembly and began to propel a huge legislative measure through the various formal stages to the President's desk where it would be signed as law. Whatever happened, a board was established to reclassify coloured Africans to decide whether they were to remain on the register as 'Coloured' or 'Natives'. All people who said that they were coloured had to go to the board for 'tests'.

They were ordered to produce evidence to prove their ancestry (was there a white man or woman in the family tree or not?). The onus was clearly on the subject of the inquiry to prove that he was coloured. Day after day papers were filed: birth certificates; photographs; men, women and children came and lined up before the board. A comb was put into their hair; if it fell off, they must have straight or curly hair and so one condition was fulfilled.

'How tall was your father?' a board member might ask.

'This high,' an exhibit might reply. If he indicated the height by stretching out his arm in a horizontal direction, it was likely that the exhibit was Coloured, for Negroes generally indicate height by bending the arm at the elbow so that the forearm points in a vertical direction. Another condition fulfilled or found to be an obstruction.

A family woke up one morning wondering if they had been through a dream: some of its members had been declared 'Coloured' and others 'Native'. But how was it possible that a whole family could experience the same dream? Once a 'Native', one had to carry a pass to permit him to live in an area, to enter another, to look for work in a town. It would be an indefensible criminal offence if one failed to show the pass to a policeman. Once a 'Native', one's wages had to be lowered.

'Look, man, T,' Karel said to us one cold evening after taking a seat in our kitchen. 'I must go to that board of bastards.'

He took us by surprise. He took a cup of tea from my wife and stirred it in exaggerated circular movements of his whole arm from the shoulder. He might have been paddling a canoe, with that arm that looked like a heavy club. The tea slopped over into the saucer.

'To the board? But you don't have to tell them you are a Negro African?'

Karel looked down.

'What de hell, no.' I looked at my wife and she looked at me.

'I told you my farder was Portugalese. Dat makes me Coloured, nê?'

'I know, but ...' I did not know what I wanted to say.

'Look, man, T, I – I can't go dress up in de watchimball-er-pass office dere for dis t'ing what you folks carry. Listen, T, I see youse folks get stopped by de bloody police day an' night; I see you folks when de whites at de post office want you to show your pass before dey give you a parcel or watchimball-er-registered letter; I see you folks in a line-up on Sunday mornings when police pick you up for not havin' a pass in your pocket an' dey take you to de station. Look man, T, one night you don't come home at de time your wife's waitin' to see you, eh? Now she gets frightened, she t'inks Oh my man may be locked up. She look for de pass in de house and dere it is you forgot it. She puts on her shawl an' she takes de kids next door an' she locks up de house an' she goes to de police station. Which one? Dere's too many. She t'inks I must go to de hospital? Maybe you's hurt or knocked down. But she's sure it must be some police station. No one wants to ring de different stations to fin' out. Hell man she's lost. De papers tell us all dis plenty times. Sometimes it's de last time she saw you in de morning when you goes to work. Maybe you couldn't pay your watchimball-er-admission of guilt and de police sentence you. Dere's a lorry waitin' to pick up guys like you wit' no money for admission or who t'ink you'll talk for yourself in de magistrate court. A white man takes you to his farm far way from here to work like slaves. Maybe you die dere and your wife will never see your grave, T, never-never.'

I was struck dumb. What argument could one have against this recital of things one knew only so well? Hadn't one read these accounts in the press? Hadn't one seen and known personally families who had waited for a husband, a son, a cousin, who was never going to come? Hadn't one read these accounts in the press and felt something claw inside one's insides and creep up to the throat and descend to the lower regions until one seemed untouchably hot all over.

I ventured to say feebly, 'You wouldn't be the only one, Karel. Isn't one strengthened by the fact that one is not suffering alone?'

'I ain't no coward, T. What about de wages? My wages will go down if I simply agree I'm black. Anudder coloured man may push me out of dis job.'

'But you *are* Negro, Karel. You as good as said so yourself often. You came to live with us blacks because you felt purity of blood was just lunatic nonsense, didn't you?'

'Look man, T, de word "native" doesn't simply mean one's got black blood or African blood. It's a p'litical word, man. You's a native because you carry a pass, you can't go to watchimball-er-Parliament. You can't vote, you live in dis location. One can be proud of being an African but not a *native*.'

'What does your woman say about this, Karel?'

'Oh you know she never says not'ing to dis'point me, T.'

'But do you know what she thinks?'

'Can't say, T. Sometime she seems to say Yes, sometime No, but she always say Do what you think is the right thing, Karel.'

My wife and I were sitting up one Saturday night when she said, 'Why does the man keep talking about this like someone who cannot hold hot roasted pumpkin pips in his mouth? Why not go and get the paper to show that he has Coloured paint on him instead of ringing bells everywhere to tell us he wants to go!'

'No, no, Pulane, you're not being fair. As far as we know, he talks to *us* only about it.'

'*To us only*, hugh! You should hear people talk about it in the street.'

I did not try to ascertain if she meant the whole street, but said instead, 'I think he wants to be sure first he will be doing the right thing.'

'Ach, he's just a coward, finished. Just like all Coloureds. Blacks are nice and good as long as a Coloured man is not told to become black.'

'Why should anyone want to be black?'

'Isn't it that he wants to show the white people he's Coloured? Isn't it that he thinks we blacks are nice to live with as long as he doesn't carry passes as we do and get the same wages as we do? See them. Paul Kruger told them they were like white people and were civilised. Now you go round this corner, Coloured people have better houses; you turn round that corner, Coloured people get better money; you go to the bioscope the Coloured people sit at the back and we blacks are put right in front where we can almost kiss the er-what's its name? Ach, they make me feel hot between the thighs these Coloureds!'

'Would you not want these good things they're getting?'

'Of course! What kind of question is that?'

'But you are not asking to be a Coloured woman are you?'

'Sies, me? Would you like to see me Coloured?'

'See what I mean! And you seem to want Karel to carry our burdens as a price for liking us and living with us. Who are we to say the Coloured should not want to keep the good things they have?'

'I just don't want people having it both ways, that's what. They like us as people to laugh with, not to suffer with. We are the laughing cheerful blacks, the ones full of life and entertainment, the ones they run to when they're tired of being Coloureds, Europeans, Indians. As for the Indians, they like their curry and rice and roti and money and mosques and temples too much to pretend they want us for next door neighbours, I can't blame them because they don't try to bluff anyone. Look how the Indian boys run about with Coloured girls! They want nothing more than keep their business sites and help us shout from the platform. Ach, they all make me sick these pinks.'

She stood up and took the kettle from the stove with the force it would require if it were glued on. She filled it with water and put it back on the stove, all but throwing it down.

'And you think the Indian folk who join us in protesting are merely bluffing? And the whites, the Indians and Coloureds whose homes smell of police uniform because of unending raids and who are banned and sent to prison – are they just having a good time, just putting on a performance? Well, I don't know, child of my mother-in-law, but that is a very expensive performance and not so funny.'

These had been times when I wasn't sure myself if I didn't really feel as my wife did.

After a spell of silence she got up to make tea. Meantime I went out to stand on the stoep. For some strange reason, while I looked at the blazing sky over Iscor steel works five miles away, I thought of Karel's wife. The gentle-looking nurse who never said much any time ...

Back inside the house, my wife said: 'I wonder how much longer it is going to be for us Africans to keep making allowances and to give way to the next man to turn things round in our head, to do the explaining and to think of others' comfort.'

I looked long into my cup, looking for something clever to say in reply. I could not find it. But I know it had something to do with the African revolution ...

'I got de identity card at last,' Karel said casually a few months later.

'So!'

'De white trash! Dey wanting to trap a guy all-a-time, bastards. Man, T, hulle dink altyd hulle hol'n mens toe – dey t'ink dey goin' to drive me into a dead corner, sons of white bitches.' He paused. 'Been waitin' for papers from LM. My late Ma put dem in a box and sent it to LM.' He looked tired and uninterested in his achievement. His voice and posture spelled humiliation to an embarrassing degree – or was it my own embarrassment? Perhaps. I didn't have the courage to ask him to give the details of the examination which must have dragged on for a number of days with a number of breaks.

'So you'll have to leave our location and the law's going to pull you away from your wife.'

'I been t'inking about dat, T. Dey can do all dey want dey'll never do buggerall to me and my woman, true's God. An' I don' take back my identity card. I stay Coloured and live wit' my woman.'

I thought about my wife's talk about people wanting to have it both ways.

Nor did Karel make any effort to leave Corner B. But we knew that the location's white superintendent would sooner or later be sticking a rough twig between Karel's buttocks to drive him out of the location.

Meantime, Karel's right leg had begun to give him trouble. He was complaining of sleepless nights because of it. He tried to maintain an even tempo in his life, and his laugh was still loud, clear and full. Even so, in the ear of one who knew him as well as I did, it was losing its roundness and developing sharp edges. When the autumn rains came down he complained more and more. He could not pretend any longer that he did not need to limp. He visited the General Hospital times without number. He was subjected to radio photography countless times. The doctors prescribed one thing after another – to drink, to massage.

'Ach man, T, dese white doctors are playing around wit' me now. I do everyt'in' dey tell me an' all dey do is shake dey blerry head wit' sandy brains. Dey loudmout' when dey tell us dey clever an' educated but dey know f— all. *What can I do*, man, I ask dem. Dey'll kill me wit' dat X-ray one day.'

I felt by proxy the leaping fire that must have been scorching its way through him to release the tongue of flame that spoke these words.

One night Karel's wife came to wake me up to come to him. He wanted to see me, she said. I found him on top of his blankets, his face wet with perspiration. His wife was still fully dressed, applying a hot fomentation.

'Have you ever heard of such a miracle!' his wife said. Before I could reply she said, 'Karel is talking in parables I am sure, hau. He's telling me he wants to see a witchdoctor. Hei, people, modisana!' She looked at him as she was taking out tablets from a bottle. 'Just ask him.'

'Listen man, T, I'm told some of dese watchimball-er-witchdoctor guys can do it. If de white man is beaten maybe black medicine will do it, man.'

'Now you're not going to do such a stupid thing,' his wife said. I had never heard her speak with such authority, such a bold face. Here on the question of sickness and patients, I felt, she was sure of herself. Looking at me: 'I would rather take him to another hospital far out of Pretoria, borrow money somewhere, spend all my savings to pay white doctors. Tell

him, you're his friend, tell him, maybe he'll listen to you.' She
stooped to give him his tablets. He turned and lay on his back,
with a deep round sigh.

'Listen, T, my woman here t'inks maybe I don' show t'anks
for her goodness to me, for her watchimball-er-patience, for
her good heart. Hang it man, T, I'm grateful from the bottom
of my heart, dat's jes why I want to make it possible for her to
rest a bit. She works too hard and has to sit up de whole night
a'most lookin' after me.'

'What should a woman be for if she is not there to look after
her man?'

'But – but a witchdoctor, man, Karel!' I said.

'You see him as he is,' his wife said, 'his boss has given him
a month to stay home – on full pay you hear me? If he rests
this leg for a while maybe we'll see which way we are moving.
Maybe I can get a few days off to take him out to my people in
the Free State. Just to go away from here a bit.'

'I think you should do what this good woman advises,
Karel. Forget this witchdoctor madness. Besides, soon as these
chaps start mucking around with one's body they're sure to
meddle with parts they know nothing about.'

'That is what I keep telling him, you hear.'

I was less convinced about what I was saying than I may
have sounded. There were always stories about someone or
other who had been cured by a witchdoctor or herbalist after
white doctors had failed. The performers of these wonders – as
they sounded to be – were invariably said to have come from
Vendaland in the farthest recesses of the rain-making queen's
territory of the Northern Transvaal. Some time before this a
school principal in Corner B had asked a herbalist next to his
house to give him a purgative. He had almost immediately
become ill and died on his way to hospital. The herbalist had
been arrested, but had pleaded that he had advised the teacher
to take plenty of water with and after the herb, which thing
he must have failed to do. No one had seen him take the herb
who could say whether he had followed the instructions or not.

Most of us, whether teachers or not, whether townspeople of long standing or not, believed one way or another in ancestral spirits. These same people might at the same time renounce or tolerate the Christian faith or even think their belief in ancestral spirits reinforced it. How could anyone be sure? A man like Karel trying to ride a huge wave of pain: what use was there trying to tell him not to seek help outside the hospital? What he said to me the next moment was disarming.

'Listen, T.' He paused as if he had forgotten what he was going to say. 'Listen, de doctor at de hospital says to me yesterday I'm sure you got kaffir poison. Kaffir poison, you mean what dey call native poison, I ask. He says Yes, I say You can't take out kaffir poison? An' he says No, he says, it's not for white medicine. An' again I says What do you t'ink doctor? An' he shows me he doesn't know.'

'And you think he was telling you what to do without saying so?'

'Yes, dat's not funny. You see for yourself how dese whites queue up at de African watchimball-er-herbalist's place at Selborne.'

'Those are poor whites,' his wife hastened to remark. 'Poor, poor, poor boers or whites from cheap suburbs. What do they know better than that?'

'Dey wouldn't be queuing up everyday like dat if he wasn't doing dem any good.'

'Nonsense,' was all I could say. And the cocks started to crow. Just then he dropped off into sleep. I stood up and took his wife's arm to reassure her that I was going to stay on her side.

Once again when Karel could stand up, he walked about. He seemed to have recovered his old cheerful mood again, except for thin lines under his eyes to show that pain had kicked him about and marched through him: with hobnailed boots as it were.

'I feel quite right now,' he said to me. 'Yes, a small slow pain but I t'ink it will go. I must see it goes because I'm sure de boss will not give me more days at de end of de t'irty days. Dey never do dat dese whites. Can't see myself more time in de house if I'm not getting well, and not getting paid neither.'

The note of urgency in his voice told me that he must have something on his mind. What? I wondered.

'I'm goin' to watchimball-to Selborne,' he said another day. 'I'm takin' a bus.'

Two days passed.

'Hei wena – You, our friend had a visitor this morning,' my wife reported.

'What visitor?'

'A man with a bag in his hand. The sort you see witchdoctors carry.'

So, just at the time his wife is at work, I thought.

'Are you going to tell his woman?'

I was irritated at her use of 'you' as if to disengage herself. No, I'd go and tell him a few hard things and I'd not mince words, I told her.

I did, but he only laughed and said I shouldn't be foolish. The man knew the particular ailment he had described to him. Wasn't fussy either about the fee for opening his bag. Yes man, he had thrown the bones and shells on the floor and spoke to them and they told him how things were. Someone had smeared 'some stuff' on his bicycle pedal and it had gone up his leg. Did he say the Jew boss liked him? Yes, very much. Any other black workers at the garage? Two others. Ever had a quarrel with any one of them? Now let's see. No. Was he senior to them? Yes. Some black people have clean hearts, others have black hearts. He could see the way one bone on the fringe was facing. He could hear it talk. He could see one of the garage workers going to an evil doctor to buy black magic.

'It's dere man, T, die Here weet – God knows.'

'Do you know a saying in my language that it takes a witch to track down another?' I said.

'I don't care if dis one's a witch. It's my leg gives me worryness. Man T, you can see he can't be lying. His face, his eyes are full of wisdom. He took two days to look for de trouble, *two days*. And he talks to me nice, T, takes de trouble, not like dose white watchimball-bastards at de hospital.'

I left him after his wife had entered.

The next day, instead of taking my sandwiches and tea in the staffroom, I cycled home in order to see how Karel was. My mind was full of ugly forebodings ... My wife told me that she had taken him lunch as usual but found the 'visitor' and so did not stay. Karel did not look worse than the previous day.

When I entered, the 'visitor' was not there. But Karel was lying on the bed, his leg stretched out and resting on a tiny bench. Under the bench was a rag, saturated with blood. 'What have you done, Karel!' I exclaimed.

'I feel all right, T. De leg will be all right from now. The man dug a hole in the ankle for the poison to come out. Ah!' He released a long heavy sigh. He held his hip with his still powerful hand and let it slide down his side, thigh and leg, like one pressing something out of a tube. At the same time he screwed up his face to show how much energy he was putting into the act.

'Ah, T,' came the long long sigh again, 'I can feel de watchimball-de pain moving out of the hole there. The blood is carrying it out. Oh, shit!' After a pause, he said, 'A black man like you, T, can go a long way. A black man has people around him to give him strength. I haven't.'

The facial muscles relaxed and his arm hung limp at his side. I looked at the ankle more carefully this time, as much as I could dare. The sight of the blood oozing out like that from the inside part of the ankle, and the soaking wet rag on the floor, shocked me out of my stupor and confusion. I looked around for any cloth, found it and bandaged the ankle. Without a word, I ran out to my house. I scribbled a note to my headmaster and asked my wife to go and watch over Karel while I went for a doctor a few streets up. He was out for home visiting, together with his nurse. I was frantic. Move him to hospital twelve miles away? The white hospital four miles away would not touch him. What about transport? Go to the location superintendent to ring the hospital? I gave up. I left a note for the doctor. I went back to wait.

Death came and took him away from us.

While I was helping to clear things up in the house, several days later when Karel's wife was permitted by custom to reorganise things in the house, she said to me: 'I believe Karel once told you about his identity card?'

'Yes.'

She held it in her hand. 'I don't know if I should keep it.'

My thinking machine seemed to have come to a dead stop and I couldn't utter a word.

'Ach, what use is it?' she said.

'Can I see it please?'

Below his picture appeared many other bits of information:
    NAME: KAREL BENITO ALMEIDA
    RACE: COLOURED

I gave it back. She tore it into bits.

'Did he tell you about this letter?' She handed it over to me.

It was a letter from the location's white superintendent telling Karel that he would have to leave house No. 35, Mathole Street, where he was known to live, and was forbidden from occupying any other house in Corner B as he was registered 'Coloured' and should not be in a 'Bantu location'.

She took the letter and tore it to bits.

'Soon I know I must leave this house.'

'Why? You can tell the superintendent that you are his widow. I know widows are always ejected soon as their men are under the ground. But we can help you fight it out.'

I knew this was useless heroic talk: the law of the jungle always wins in the end. But that is another story. And in any case, 'I was not married to Karel by law,' the good woman said.

Grieg on a Stolen Piano

Those were the days of terror when, at the age of fifteen, he ran away from home and made his way towards Pietersburg town. Driven by hunger and loneliness and fear he took up employment on an Afrikaner's farm at ten shillings a month plus salted mealie-meal porridge and an occasional piece of meat. There were the long scorching hours when a posse of horsemen looked for him and three other labourers while they were trying to escape. The next morning at dawn the white men caught up with them.

Those were the savage days when the whole white family came and sat on the stoep to watch for their own amusement, African labourers put under the whip. Whack! Whack! Whack! And while the leather whip was still in the air for the fourth stroke on the buttocks, he yelled, *Ma-oeeee*! As the arm came down, he flew up from the crude bench he was lying on and, in a manner that he could never explain afterwards, hooked the white foreman's arm with his two, so that for a few seconds he dangled a few feet from the ground. Amid peals of laughter from the small pavilion, the foreman shook him off as a man does a disgusting insect that creeps on his arm.

Those were the days when, in a solo flight again towards Pietersburg, terror clawed at his heart as he travelled through thick bush. He remembered the stories he had so often listened to at the communal fireplace; tales of huge snakes that chased a man on the ground or leapt from tree to tree; tales of the giant snake that came to the river at night to drink, breaking trees in its path, and before which helpless people lay flat on their stomachs wherever they might be at the time; none dared to move as the snake mercifully lifted its body above them, bent over, drank water and then, mercifully again, turned over backwards, belly facing upwards, rolling away from the people; stories that explained many mysteries, like the reason why the owl and the bat moved in the dark. Always the theme was that of man, helpless as he himself was in the bush or on a tree or in a rock cave on a hill, who was unable to ward off danger, to escape a terrible power that was everywhere around him. Something seemed to be stalking him all the time, waiting for the proper moment to pounce upon him.

But he walked on, begged and stole food and lifts on lorries, until he reached Tshwane – Pretoria.

There was the brief time in 'the kitchens', as houses of white people are called where one does domestic work, as if the white suburbs were simply a collection of kitchens. There were the brutal Sundays when he joined the Pietersburg youth, then working in the kitchens, on their wild march to the open ground just outside Bantule location for a sport of bare fisticuffs. They marched in white shorts on broad slabs of feet in tennis shoes and Vaseline-smeared legs: now crouching, now straightening up, now wielding their fists wrapped in white handkerchiefs. One handkerchief dangled out of a trouser pocket, just for show. The brutal fisticuffs; mouths flushed with blood; then the white mounted police who herded them back to the kitchens; the stampede of horses' hooves as the police chased after them, for fun ...

Those were the days when chance lifted him like a crane out of the kitchens and out of the boxing arena, and deposited him in Silverton location. This was when his aunt, having been alerted by her brother, had tracked him down.

There was regular schooling again. At twenty he began teacher training at Kilnerton Institution nearby. There were the teaching days, during which he studied privately for a junior secondary school certificate.

Those were the days when, as the first black man in the province to write an examination for this certificate, he timidly entered a government office for the first paper. The whites stared at him until he had disappeared into the room where he would write in isolation. And those were the days when a black man had to take off his hat as soon as he saw a white man approach; when the black man had to keep clear of street pavements.

Then the return home – the first time in seven years – as a hero, a teacher. The parents bubbled over with pride. Then the feast ...

It was one of those hot subtropical nights when Pretoria seems to lie in its valley, battered to insensibility by the day's heat; the night when a great friend of his was tarred and feathered by white students of the local university at Church Square; and Mr Lambeth, a British musician who had come to teach at Kilnerton, there discovered this black young man's musical talent. He had given his time free to teach him the piano. Many were the afternoons, the nights, the weekends that followed of intensive, untiring work at the instrument. What else had Mr Lambeth done wrong? He asked himself several times after the incident. The Englishman had many friends among African teachers whom he visited in their locations; he adjudicated at their music competitions.

This black young man was my uncle. He is actually a cousin of my late father's. So, according to custom, my father had referred to him as 'my brother'. As my father had no blood brothers, I was glad to avail myself of an uncle. When my father died, he charged my uncle with the responsibility of 'helping me to become a man'. It meant that I had someone nearby who would give me advice on a number of things concerned with the problem of growing up. My mother had died shortly after. Uncle has seven children, all but one of whom are earning their living independently. The last-born is still in school.

Uncle is black as a train engine; so black that his face often gives the illusion of being bluish sometimes. His gums are a deep red which blazes forth when he smiles, overwhelming the dull rusty colour of his teeth. He is tall and walks upright. His head is always close-shaven because, at sixty, he thinks he is prematurely greying, although his hair began to show grey at thirty. He keeps his head completely bald because he does not want a single grey hair to show.

His blackness has often led him into big-big trouble with the whites, as he often tells us.

'Hei! Jy!'

Uncle walks straight on, pretending not to see the bunch of them leaning against a fence. He is with a friend, a classmate.

'Hey! Jy! Die pikswart een, die bobbejaan!' – the pitch-black one, the baboon.

One of them comes towards the two and pushes his way between them, standing in front. They stop dead.

A juvenile guffaw behind sends a shiver through Uncle. He breaks through his timidity and lunges at the white boy. He pommels him. In Pietersburg boxing style he sends the body down with a knee that gets him on a strategic place in the jaw. The others are soon upon them. The Africans take to their heels …

A new white clerk is busy arranging postal orders and recording them. The queue stretches out, out of the post office building. The people are making a number of clicking noises to indicate their impatience. They crane their necks or step out of the queue in order to see what is happening at the counter.

Uncle is at the head of the queue.

'Excuse me,' he ventures, 'playtime will soon be over and my class will be waiting for me, can you serve us, please?'

The clerk raises his head.

'Look here,' he says aggressively, 'I'm not only here to serve kaffirs, I'm here to work!'

Uncle looks at him steadily. The clerk goes back to his postal orders. After about fifteen minutes he leaves them. He goes to a cupboard and all the eyes in the queue follow each movement of his. When he comes back to the counter, he looks at the man at the head of the queue, who in turn fixes his stare on him. The white man seems to recoil at the sight of Uncle's face. Then, as if to fall back on the last mode of defence, he shouts 'What are you? What are you? – just a black kaffir, a kaffir monkey, black as tar. Now any more from you and I'll bloody well refuse to serve the whole bloody lot of you. Teacher – teacher, teacher *te hel!*'

Irritation and impatience can be heard to hiss and sigh down the queue.

Uncle realises he's being driven into a corner and wonders if he can contain the situation. Something tells him it is beyond him. The supervisor of posts comes in just then, evidently called in by his junior's shout.

'Ja,' he asks, 'wat is dit?'

'Your clerk has been insulting me – calling me a Kaffir monkey.'

The clerk opens his mouth to speak, but his superior leads him round a cubicle. After a few moments, the clerk comes back, ready to serve but sulky, and mute.

Uncle says that throughout the white clerk seemed to feel insulted at the sudden confrontation of such articulate human blackness as thrust itself forward through the wire mesh of the counter.

This time, Uncle had the satisfaction of causing the removal of the white clerk after a colleague, who had been an eye witness of the incident in the post office, had obtained support from fellow teachers at Silverton to petition a higher postal authority against the clerk.

'Can you see that happening today?' he asked. 'No, man, I'd have been fired at once on a mere allegation out of the clerk's important mouth.'

Years later Uncle was promoted to the post of junior inspector of African schools (the white man being always senior). He went to live in the Western Transvaal. This is where his wife died while giving birth. He really hit the bottom of depression after this. The affection he had for his wife found a perverse expression in drink and he took to his music with a deeper and savage passion which, as he puts it, was a kind of hot fomentation to help burst the boil of grief inside him. He kept

his children with him, though. Each one had the opportunity
to go to an institution of higher education. Here he was lucky.
For although all of them were mediocre, they used what they
had profitably and efficiently. One did a degree in science;
another played the saxophone in a band; another was a teacher
and 'pop singer'; another became a librarian for an institute of
research into race relations; one daughter went in for nursing,
and a son and a daughter were still in secondary school.

There were nights of sheer terror when their father failed to
return home and they knew he must be in some drinking orgy
somewhere. Then they got to know that he was doing illicit
diamond buying. As he visited schools in his circuit, he sold or
bought small stones. But he was always skating near the edge.
Once he had the bitter experience of discovering that he had
bought a few fakes for £50 from an African agent.

Then there was the day he says he'll never forget as long
as he lives. The CID, after crossing his path several times and
picking up and losing trails, finally came to the converging
point – Uncle. They found him in a train from Johannesburg to
Kimberley. They took him to the luggage van and questioned
him. Nothing was found on him and he wouldn't talk. When
eventually they realised they might have a corpse on their
hands, they put him out on a station platform, battered,
bleeding and dazed. His suitcase was thrown in his direction.

Uncle was transferred to Johannesburg, but not without
incident. A white educational officer wanted him to carry his
typewriter – a heavy table model – to his car outside. Uncle told
him he wouldn't. He had before refused to wash the official's
car when asked to do so. As the educational authorities had
a high opinion of his work, after serving several years in the
department, they engineered a transfer for him. If you asked
him how he managed to keep his post, he will tell you, 'I made
more or less sure I don't slip up that side, and besides whites
don't like a correct black man, because they are so corrupt
themselves.'

Each time after some verbal tiff with a white man, Uncle

says, he felt his extra blackness must have been regarded as an insult by those who found themselves in the shadow it seemed to cast around him.

His arrival in Johannesburg was like surfacing. He went slow on his drinks and even became a lay preacher in the Methodist Church at Orlando. But he started to go to the races and threw himself into this kind of gambling with such passion that he resigned as preacher.

'I can't keep up the lies,' he said. 'There are people who can mix religion with gambling and the other things, but I can't. And gamble I must. As Christ never explained what a black man should do in order to earn a decent living in this country, we can only follow our instincts. And if I cannot understand the connection, it is not right for me to stand in the pulpit and pretend to know the answer.'

The 'other things' were illicit diamond dealing and trading as a travelling salesman, buying and selling soft goods, mostly stolen by some African gang or other that operated in the city. There were also workers who systematically stole articles from their employers' shops and sold them to suburban domestic servants and location customers. While he was visiting schools, he would call this man and that man round the corner or into some private room to do business.

Uncle married again. He was now living with three of his children, two of whom were still in secondary school. A cloud descended upon his life again. His wife was an unpleasant, sour woman. But Uncle woke up to it too late. She sat on the stoep like a dumpling and said little beyond smiling briefly a word of greeting and giving concise answers to questions. The children could not quarrel with her, because she said little that could offend anyone. But her antheap appearance was most irritating, because she invited no one's cooperation and gave none beyond fulfilling the routine duties of a wife. She did not seem to like mothering anyone.

Once she succeeded, perhaps in all innocence, in raining a furore in the house.

'You must find out more about the choir practice your daughter keeps going to every week,' she says to Uncle in the presence of the other children. They had stopped calling her 'Ma' because she insisted on referring to them as 'your daughter' or 'your son' when she talked to their father about them.

'It's choir practice,' Uncle said brusquely.

'Wai-i-i! I know much about choir practices, me. A man's daughter can go to them without stopping and one-two-three the next time you look at her she has a big choir practice in her stomach.'

The girl ran into her bedroom, crying.

Soon tongues were let loose upon her. But she continued to sit like an antheap, her large body seeming to spread wider and wider like an overgrown pumpkin. Her attitude seemed to suggest much Uncle would have liked to know. What *was* she hiding?

'What do you do with such a woman?' Uncle sighed when he told me about the incident.

He was prepared to go through with the 'companionship', to live with her to the end of his days. 'I promised I'd do so in church,' he remarked. 'And I was in my full senses, no one forced me into the thing.'

Another time he threatened, 'One day I'll get so angry, neph', I'll send her away to her people. And at her station I'll put her on a wheelbarrow like a sack of mealies and wheel her right into her people's house if I've to bind her with a rope.'

I knew he was never going to do it.

Uncle could only take dramatic decisions which were not going to leave him any need to exercise responsibility either to revoke them or fall back on them. He made decisions as a man makes a gamble: once made, you won or lost, and the matter rested there. It was the same with his second marriage, I think. He met the woman during a church conference, when he was by chance accommodated in her house in Randfontein together with two other delegates, according to the arrangements of the local branch. His wife had been dead twelve years. He had decided that his children were big enough not to look so helpless if a second marriage soured the home atmosphere by any chance. His personal Christian belief would not permit him to get out of a marriage contract. This was the kind of responsibility he would want to avoid. If there was a likely chance that he might have to decide to revoke a step later, he did not take it.

There was in Uncle a synthesis of the traditional and the westernised African. At various periods in his life he felt that ill luck was stalking him, because misfortune seemed to pour down on him in torrents, particularly in money matters, family relations and relations with white educational authorities. At times like these, Uncle went and bought a goat, slaughtered it and called relations to come and eat the meat and mealie-meal porridge with their bare hands, sitting on the floor. He then buried the bones in the yard. At such times his mind searched the mystery of fate, groping in some imagined world where the spirits of his ancestors and that of his dead wife must be living, for a point of contact, for a line of communion.

After the feast he felt peace settle inside him and fill his whole being until it seemed to ooze from the pores of his body as the tensions in him thawed ... Then he would face the world with renewed courage or with the reinforced secure knowledge that he was at peace with his relations, without whom he considered he would be a nonentity, a withered twig that has broken off from its tree.

Twice when I was ill, Uncle called in an African medical doctor. But when my migraine began and often seemed to hurl me into the den of a savage beast, he called in an African herbalist and witchdoctor. The man said he could divine from his bones that I had once – it didn't matter when or where – inhaled fumes that had been meant to drive me insane, prepared by an enemy. So he in turn burned a few sticks of a herb and made me inhale the smoke. It shot up my nasal cavity, hit the back of my skull, seeming to scrape or burn its path from the forehead to the nape of my neck. Each time, after repeated refusals to be seen by a witchdoctor, my resistance broke down. I felt temporary relief each time.

So he was going to keep his wife, rain or shine. When her behaviour or her sullenness depressed him, he went back to his whisky. Then he played excerpts from Grieg's piano concerto or a Chopin nocturne, or his own arrangements of Mohapeloa's 'Chuchumakhala' (the train) or 'Leba' (the dove) and others, vocalising passages the while with his deep voice. He loved to evoke from his instrument the sound of the train's siren *oi-oi-i-i* while he puffed *chu-chu, chu-chu*.

'If she knew this piano was lifted out of a shop,' he thought often, 'this dumpling would just let off steam about the fact, simply to annoy me, to make me feel I'm a failure because she knows I'm not a failure and she wants to eat me up and swallow me up raw the way she did her first husband.'

He had lately disposed of his twenty-year-old piano.

The keyboard felt the impact of these passionate moments and resounded plaintively and savagely. Self-pity, defiance, despising, endurance, all these and others, played musical chairs in his being.

'Look, neph',' Uncle said one day when he was his cheerful, exuberant self again, 'look, here's an advertisement of an African beauty contest in *Afric*.'

'Oh, there is such a rash of beauty contests these days we're all sick of them. It's the racket in every big town these days. Haven't they learned that a woman is as beautiful as your eyes make her?'

'You're just too educated, that's all. You know nothing, my boy, wait till I tell you.'

'Is it a new money-catching thing again? Don't tell me you're going to run a gambling game around the winning number.'

Uncle and beauty queens did not dovetail in my mind. What was behind that volume of blackness that frightened so many whites? I was curious to know.

'Better than that, neph'. If you want to cooperate.'

'In what?'

'Now look at the prizes: £500, £250, £150 and consolation prizes. One of these can be ours.'

'But this is a beauty contest, not a muscle show.'

'Don't be so stupid. Now, here. I know a lovely girl we can enter for this contest.'

I felt my curiosity petering out.

'I go and fetch the girl – she's a friend's daughter living in the Western Transvaal, in a village. Just the right kind of body, face, but she needs to be brought up to market standard. The contest is nine months away still, and we've time.'

'But – '

'Now listen. You put in £25, me the same. We can then keep the girl in my house – no, your aunt will curdle again – now let me think – yes, in my friend Tau's house: his wife has a beautiful heart. The money will go to feeding her and paying for her lessons at Joe's gym. Your job will be to take her out, teach her how to smile when she's introduced; how to sit – not like a brooding hen; how to stand in public – not like an Afrikaner cow. You've got to cultivate in her a sense of public attention. Leave the body work to Joe. If she wins, we give her £100 and split £400.'

Joe was one of those people who know just when to come in for profit. He set up his gym in a hired hall with the express aim of putting candidates through 'body work'.

For my part, I simply did not like the idea at all. Beauty on a platform: beauty advertised, beauty mixed up with money; that is how the thing seemed to me, a person with the simple tastes of a lawyer's clerk. To what extent Uncle had assimilated jazzy urban habits, I couldn't tell.

'Thought about it yet, neph'? We can't wait too long, you know.'

'Yes, Unc', but I just don't see the point of it. Why don't we leave beauty queens to the – er – experts?' I actually meant something much lower than experts. 'Like Joe, for instance.'

'Joe's just a spiv,' Uncle replied. 'He just loves to rub shoulders with top dogs, that's all. We are investing.'

'But I've only £30 in the post office savings; if I take out £25, I shall be almost completely out.'

'A black man never starves if he lives among his people, unless there is famine. If the worst comes to the worst, you would have to be content with simply having food, a roof over your head and clothing.'

'That's rural thinking. The extra things a man wants in the city I can't afford.'

'Two hundred pounds can give you the extras.'

I paused to think.

'No, Unc', gambling is for the rich, for those who can afford to lose, not for people like us.'

'You think I'm rich? Don't be silly, you mean to say all those hunch-backed, dried-up, yellow-coloured whites you see at the races and betting booths are rich?'

I relented after a good deal of badgering. Who knows, I thought, we may just win. What couldn't I do with £200 if it came to me!

What a girl!

Her face was well shaped all right: every organ on it was in place, although she had a dry mouth and an unpleasant complexion. She could not have been well in the Western Transvaal. Her bones stuck out at the elbows and her buttocks needed pumping a good deal.

'What is your name?' I asked her.

'Tryphina.'

I almost giggled, thinking, what names some people have!

'That name won't do, Unc',' I said to him at the house, affecting a tough showmanship. 'I can't imagine the name coming out of the mouth of the MC when he calls it out.'

'Call her "Try" or "Tryph",' he said indifferently.

'No, they sound like syllables in a kindergarten reading class. Just as bad as "Jenina" or "Judida" or "Hermina" or "Stephina".'

'Let's use her Sesotho name; she should have one I'm sure.'

'Torofina,' she said.

'No, not the school name spoken in Sesotho, I mean your real Sotho name. You see, in things like a beauty competition, people like an easy name that is smooth on the tongue (I meant *sweet to the ear*). They may even fail you for having a difficult name.'

Didn't I loathe *Afric*'s cheap slick, noisy journalism.

'Oh, Kefahliloe,' she said sweetly, which means 'something has got into my eye'. 'That is what they call me at home.'

'Nice,' I commented, meaning nothing of the sort. 'But don't you have a shorter Sesotho name?'

'No.' She was still all innocence and patience.

'Well – er – maybe you can – er – think of an English name. Just for the contest, you see, and for the newspapers and magazines. Your picture is going to appear in all the papers. We'll call you Kefahliloe – a person's name is her name, and there's nothing wrong in it. Do not hurry, you can tell us the name you've chosen later. Is it all right?'

She nodded. Things never seemed all wrong with her. Sometimes there was something pathetic about her pliability, sometimes irritating.

The next day she gave it to us, with a take it or leave it tone: Mary-Jane.

The first three months showed a slight improvement. Her weight was going up, her paleness was disappearing, the lips moistening and softening, her small eyes taking on a new liveliness and self-confidence. Joe was doing the body work efficiently. I felt then, and Uncle agreed, like one who had known it all along, that there was something latent in the girl which we were going to draw out in the next few months.

She had finished her primary schooling and done part of secondary school, so she was all right on that side.

I took her to the bioscope on certain Saturdays, especially

musicals, which appealed to her more than straight drama
or bang-bang movies. I took her to Dorkay House in Eloff
Street where African musicians go each Saturday for jazz
improvisations. There we found other boys and girls listening
eagerly, ripples of excitement visibly travelling through the
audience as now and again they whistled and clapped hands.
The girls were the type called in township slang 'rubbernecks',
the ostentatiously jazz type. We found the same type at
parties.

Mary-Jane was drinking it all in, I noticed.

I invited her to my room to listen to my collection of jazz
records. She took in small doses at a time and seemed to digest
it, and her bodily movements were taking on a city rhythm.

Uncle and I shared entertainment expenses equally. We
went for cheap but good entertainment.

After six months Uncle and I knew we were going to deliver
a presentable article of good healthy flesh, comportment and
luscious charm. Charm? Strange. Through all this I did not
notice the transformation that was taking place in this direction.
She was close on twenty-one and at the end of the next six
months I was struck by the charm that was creeping out of her,
seeming to wait for a time, far off, when it would burst into
blossom. She was filling up, but her weight was in no danger
of overshooting the mark. Her tongue was loosening up.

I was becoming aware of myself. I felt a twinge of guilt
at treating her like an article that should be ready against a
deadline. Before I could realise fully what was happening, the
storm had set in. The thing was too delicate; I would have to go
about it carefully. Particularly so because I had sensed that she
was innocent and untutored in a rustic manner about things
like love. And one didn't want the bird to take fright because
one had dived into the bush instead of carefully burrowing
in. Besides, I am a timid fellow, not unlike my uncle in other
things. Uncle had expensive photographs taken of Mary-Jane
for the press. Publicity blazed across the African newspapers,
and the air was thick with talk about *Afric*'s beauty contest at

which Miss Johannesburg would be selected. 'Who was going to be the 500-pound consignment of beauty dynamite?' the journal screamed ...

I heard a snatch of conversation in the train one morning amid the continuous din of talking voices, peals of laughter and door-slamming.

'Hey man, see dat girl's picture in *Afric*?'

'Which?'

'De one called Mary-Jen – er – Tumelo?'

'Ja-man, Jesus, she's reely top, eh!'

'God, de body, hmm, de curves, de waist, dis t'ings!' (indicating the area of the breasts).

'Ach man, dat's number one true's God jealous down.'

I warmed up towards the boys and wished they could continue.

'I've seen the three judges,' Uncle said.

'The judges? But *Afric* hasn't published the names!'

'They don't *do* such things, you backward boy.'

'How did you know them?'

'I've my contacts.'

'But we don't do such things, Uncle!' I gasped.

'What things?'

'Talking to judges about a competition in which you have vested interests.'

'Don't talk so pompously. You're talking English. Let's talk Sesotho. Now all I did is I took photographs of Mary-Jane to each one at his house, paid my respects with a bottle of whisky and asked them if they didn't think she's a beautiful girl. What's wrong with just talking?'

'What did they think?'

'What are you talking, neph'? Each one almost jumped out of his pants with excitement.'

I wanted badly to laugh, but wanted also to show him that I disapproved.

'I didn't suggest anything to them. I just said she is my niece and I was proud to see her entering the contest. They swore they hadn't seen such beauty as well photographed among all the pictures they had seen in the papers. We're near the winning post, neph', I can see the other side of September the fifteenth already – it's bright. Those judges caught my hint.'

I continued to sit with my eyes fixed on the floor, wondering whether I should feel happy or alarmed.

'By the way, neph', do you realise you have got yourself a wife, home-grown and fresh? Anything going on between you two?'

'What do you mean?' I asked without wanting an answer. His eyes told me he wasn't impressed by my affectation. He waited for me to crawl out of it.

'I haven't thought of it,' I lied. After a pause, 'Was this also on your mind when you thought of her as a beauty queen, Uncle?'

'Yes, neph'. I got to liking her very much while I visited her people during my inspection trips. I was sad to think that such a bright pretty girl would merely become another villager's wife and join the rest who are scratching the soil like chickens for what food there still remains in those desolate places. Her father and me are like twin brothers, we were at school together.'

'But the contest? Surely you could obtain a husband for her without it? And you're not sure she'll win either.'

He was silent.

'Nor are we sure she'll like me for a husband.'

'Her father knows my plans. He has told her since she came here.'

'But the contest, why that?'

Silence.

'It's too difficult to explain. All I ask you is to trust me enough to know that I'm not simply playing a game with Mary-Jane for my own amusement.'

During the next few days vanity blew me up. I abstracted the whole sequence of events from their setting and the characters who acted them out. Gradually I built up a picture of myself as someone who needs to be independent and around whom a hedge was being set up, a victim of a plot. I regarded myself as a sophisticate who couldn't willingly let others choose a sweetheart or wife for me. But in fact I sensed that the reason for my resentment was that I was actually in love with Mary-Jane but could not face the prospect of living with someone I had presumed to raise to a level of sophistication for reasons of money. I had often been moved by films in which the hero eventually married the less-privileged, artless and modest girl rather than the articulate urbanised one who goes out to get her man. Now I had the opportunity of doing the same thing, and I couldn't. In either case, I realise now, one saw a different version of male vanity at work.

Another disturbing element was my uncle's motive for doing what he did by throwing Mary-Jane into a beauty contest when he could arrive at his other objective without going to all the trouble. Although he declined to say it, I think it was his gambling urge that pushed him to it. I wondered what Mary-Jane herself thought about all this: the manner in which she was simply brought to the city and put through a machine to prepare her for a beauty competition, probably without her opinion being asked. Did she perhaps take it that this was how townspeople did things, or one of the things country people were bound to do when they came to the city. I still wonder.

Mary-Jane had to enter the competition, in spite of our vanities. She looked forward to it with zest and a certain vivacity which one would not have guessed she was capable of about nine months before. Yes, she was charming, too. How I wished I had found her like this or had arrived at it through someone else's efforts and planning!

Uncle himself infected me with his high spirits. We decided to have an Indian dinner at the Crescent, after the event.

That night came.

The lights went on full beam, washing out every bit of

shade from every corner of the hall. The Jazz Dazzlers struck up 'September in the Rain'. Masses of faces in the packed hall looked up towards the rostrum. The music stopped. The MC's voice cut through the noise in the hall and the people held their breaths, unfinished words and sentences trailing off in a sigh.

It came to me with a metallic mockery – the announcement that *Afric* had decided that this was going to be a you pick the winner show. The queen and the other two prizewinners would be chosen by popular vote. There was hilarious applause and whistling from the crowd of what must have been about two thousand people. The MC explained that as the people filed out of the hall after the contest, each person would, in the presence of supervisors at the door, drop two tickets into a box fixed at every one of the four exits. One ticket would bear the numbers of the winners of the three prizes in evening dress, and the other card numbers of the winners in beach attire. The categories were indicated on the cards. These and pencils were distributed, while the band played.

I looked at Uncle next to me. I could see he was furious. He kept saying, 'Stupid! Hoodlums! Cheats! Burn the bloody *Afric*! Nothing ever goes right in things organised by the Press. You take my word for it, neph'. Ah!'

'Anything happens in beauty competitions,' I said, for lack of a stronger remark to match my sagging mood.

'Anyway, neph',' Uncle said, his face cheering up, 'two thousand people looking with two eyes each must be better than three men looking with two eyes each, with the possibility of a squint in one of them.'

This really tickled me, in spite of myself. It gave me hope: how could one be sure that all three judges knew a lovely bust from the back of a bus or a bag of mealies? We could at least enjoy our Indian dinner and leave the rest in the hands of fate.

What use would it be to describe Mary-Jane's superb performance?

We had couples – friends – with us at dinner. Mary-Jane was most relaxed. Her ingenuous abandon and air of self-assurance went to my head. The dinner proved worth waiting for. That went to my stomach and made me feel what a glorious thing it is to have a healthy receptacle for such exquisite food.

During our twelve-mile trip by car to Orlando, I felt the warm plush body of Mary-Jane press against me slightly, and I was glad to have things in contact like that. She, in turn, seemed to respond to something of what was radiating from me.

'Are you worried about the results?' I ventured to ask, merely for the sake of saying something to relieve the drowsy, full-bellied silence in the car.

'No,' she replied warmly. 'Not a bit. But I am glad it's all over.'

We lost.

Mary-Jane wasn't in the least worried. Uncle regarded it simply as a match that was lost and couldn't be replayed. For my part, I suspected that I had often heard a faint whisper within me telling me that I should be better off if we lost. So I did not know what I ought to feel.

On a Sunday I went to Uncle's house for a casual visit. I found his wife in one of her sour moods. She greeted me with the impatience of one who waves off a fly that hovers over the face and hinders conversation. She was actually talking alone, in a querulous mood. Her right elbow was resting on her huge breast and in the cup of the left hand, the right hand stroking her cheek and nose.

I passed hastily on to the room where Uncle played and sang an excerpt from Grieg's piano concerto. He saw me as I went to seat myself, but continued to play. At the end of a passage he said, casually, 'She is gone', and continued playing. I shrugged my shoulders, thinking, 'That's beyond me.'

'She left me a note,' he said. 'Did you receive one?'

His eyes told me that he had just visited his whisky cupboard. I realised that he wasn't talking about his wife.

'Who? Are you talking about Mary-Jane?'

He nodded. 'Who do you think I mean – Vasco da Gama's daughter-in-law?' Then he shouted, 'Ja. Gone. With Joe!'

He went back to some crescendo passages of Grieg, picking them up and dropping them in turn. Then he suddenly stopped and came to sit by me.

'How's everybody in the house?' I asked.

'Still well. Except your aunt. That stupid native boy who sold me this piano comes here and finds your aunt and tells her this is a stolen piano. Just showing off, the clever fool. Setlatla sa mafelelo – fool of the first order. His mother never taught him not to confide anything in woman. Kind of lesson you suck from your mother's breast. The native! Now your aunt thinks all the house money goes out for the piano. Nothing can convince her that I'm paying £30 only, and in bits, too. So, you see, she's staging one of her boycotts.'

Uncle did not even pretend to lower his voice. Has it gone this far – no bother about what she thinks? I asked myself. No, he did care. He was too sensitive not to care. Always, when he told me about her, he spoke with a sense of hurt. Not such as a henpecked husband displays: Uncle had tremendous inner resources and plenty of diversions and could not buckle up under his wife's policy of non-collaboration, the way a henpecked man would do. This 'speaking up' was just a bit of defiance.

'She worries about a stolen piano,' Uncle continued, lying back on the divan, his eyes looking at the ceiling, his thumb playing up and down under his braces. 'She forgets she sleeps between stolen sheets; every bit of cutlery that goes into her mouth was stolen by the boys from whom I bought it; her blouses are stolen goods, her stockings.' And then, looking at me he said, 'Don't we steal from each other, lie to each other every day and know it, us and the whites?'

I said, 'Ja' and looked at my tie and shoes. But I considered this superfluous explanation.

'You know, neph',' he continued in rambling fashion. 'A few days ago I had a sickening experience involving a school I've been inspecting. A colleague of mine – let's call him JM – has been visiting the school for oral tests. At no time when his white superior calls him or asks him a question does JM fail to say 'Yes, baas', or 'No, baas', or 'I'll get it for you, baas'. Now during the lunch break, some of the staff say to him in the staffroom they feel disgraced when a black man like him says 'baas, baas' to the white man. They say they hope he'll stop it – just a nice brotherly talk, you see. Guess what JM goes and does? He goes and tells his white superior that the staff members of such and such a school don't want him to call him 'baas'! Guess what the white man does? He comes and complains to me about the bad conduct of those teachers. Now I ask you, what chance do you or I stand against idiots like these two who have so much power? We don't all have the liver to join the Congress Movement. So we keep stealing from the white man and lying to him and he does the same. This way we can still feel some pride.'

As I rose to go, I said, 'So Mary-Jane's gone off with Joe, eh?' as though her image had not been hovering over me all the time since Uncle had announced her 'flight'.

'Yes, because I've a stupid timid nephew. Are you going to wait till horns grow on your head before you marry?'

I laughed.

'Any country girl who goes off with Joe has made a real start in town living, neph'!'

As I went out, the woman in the lounge was saying: 'Kiriki, Kiriki – who do they say he is? – Kiriki with the stolen piano. Me, I cannot eat Kiriki, I want money for food. He can take that Kirikinyana and Mohapeloanyana of his, put them in the lavatory bucket.'

By saying 'He can take ...' she clearly wanted me to listen. The use of the diminutive form for the names of the musicians was meant for his ears.

'What do you do with your aunt, neph', if she does not understand Grieg and cannot like Mohapeloa?'

If you had pricked me with a pin as I was going out, I should have punctured, letting out a loud bawl of laughter which I could hardly keep back in my stomach.

Mrs Plum

My madam's name was Mrs Plum. She loved dogs and Africans and said that everyone must follow the law even if it hurt. These were three big things in Madam's life.

I came to work for Mrs Plum in Greenside, not very far from the centre of Johannesburg, after leaving two white families. The first white people I worked for as a cook and laundry woman were a man and his wife in Parktown North. They drank too much and always forgot to pay me. After five months I said to myself No. I am going to leave these drunks. So that was it. That day I was as angry as a red-hot iron when it meets water. The second house I cooked and washed for had five children who were badly brought up. This was in Belgravia. Many times they called me You Black Girl and I kept quiet. Because their mother heard them and said nothing. Also I was only new from Phokeng my home, far away near Rustenburg, I wanted to learn and know the white people before I knew how far to go with the others I would work for afterwards. The thing that drove me mad and made me pack and go was a man who came to visit them often. They said he was a cousin or something like that. He came to the kitchen many times and tried to make me laugh. He patted me on the buttocks. I told the master. The man did it again and I asked the madam that very day to give me my money and let me go.

These were the first nine months after I had left Phokeng to work in Johannesburg. There were many of us girls and young women from Phokeng, from Zeerust, from Shuping, from Koster and many other places who came to work in the cities. So the suburbs were full of blackness. Most of us had already passed Standard Six and so we learned more English where we worked. None of us likes to work for white farmers, because we know too much about them on the farms near our homes. They do not pay well and they are cruel people.

At Easter time so many of us went home for a long weekend to see our people and to eat chicken and sour milk and morogo – wild spinach. We also took home sugar and condensed milk and tea and coffee and sweets and custard powder and tinned foods.

It was a home-girl of mine, Chimane, who called me to take a job in Mrs Plum's house, just next door to where she worked. This is the third year now. I have been quite happy with Mrs Plum and her daughter Kate. By this I mean that my place as a servant in Greenside is not as bad as that of many others. Chimane too does not complain much. We are paid six pounds a month with free food and free servant's room. No one can ever say that they are well paid, so we go on complaining somehow. Whenever we meet on Thursday afternoons, which is time off for all of us black women in the suburbs, we talk and talk and talk: about our people at home and their letters; about their illnesses; about bad crops; about a sister who wanted a school uniform and books and school fees; about some of our madams and masters who are good, or stingy with money or food, or stupid or full of nonsense, or who kill themselves and each other, or who are dirty – and so many things I cannot count them all.

Thursday afternoons we go to town to look at the shops, to attend a women's club, to see our boyfriends, to go to bioscope some of us. We turn up smart, to show others the clothes we bought from the black men who sell soft goods to servants in the suburbs. We take a number of things and they come round every month for a bit of money until we finish paying. Then we dress the way of many white madams and girls. I think we look really smart. Sometimes we catch the eyes of a white woman looking at us and we laugh and laugh and laugh until we nearly drop on the ground because we feel good inside ourselves.

What did the girl next door call you? Mrs Plum asked me the first day I came to her. Jane, I replied. Was there not an African name? I said yes, Karabo. All right, Madam said. We'll call you Karabo, she said. She spoke as if she knew a name is a big thing. I knew so many whites who did not care what they called black people as long as it was all right for their tongue. This pleased me, I mean Mrs Plum's use of *Karabo*, because the only time I heard the name was when I was at home or when my friends spoke to me. Then she showed me what to do: meals, mealtimes, washing and where all the things were that I was going to use.

My daughter will be here in the evening, Madam said. She is at school. When the daughter came, she added, she would tell me some of the things she wanted me to do for her every day.

Chimane, my friend next door, had told me about the daughter Kate, how wild she seemed to be, and about Mr Plum who had killed himself with a gun in a house down the street. They had left the house and come to this one.

Madam is a tall woman. Not slender, not fat. She moves slowly and speaks slowly. Her face looks very wise, her forehead seems to tell me she has a strong liver: she is not afraid of anything. Her eyes are always swollen at the lower eyelids like a white person who has not slept for many many nights or like a large frog. Perhaps it is because she smokes too much, like wet wood that will not know whether to go up in flames or stop burning. She looks me straight in the eyes when she talks to me, and I know she does this with other people too. At first this made me fear her, now I am used to her. She is not a lazy woman, and she does many things outside, in the city and in the suburbs.

This was the first thing her daughter Kate told me when she came and we met. Don't mind mother, Kate told me. She said, She is sometimes mad with people for very small things. She will soon be all right and speak nicely to you again.

Kate, I like her very much, and she likes me too. She tells me many things a white woman does not tell a black servant. I mean things about what she likes and does not like, what her mother does or does not do, all these. At first I was unhappy and wanted to stop her, but now I do not mind.

Kate looks very much like her mother in the face. I think her shoulders will be just as round and strong-looking. She moves faster than Madam. I asked her why she was still at school when she was so big. She laughed. Then she tried to tell me that the school where she was was for big people, who had finished with lower school. She was learning big things about cooking and food. She can explain better, me I cannot. She came home on weekends.

Since I came to work for Mrs Plum Kate has been teaching me plenty of cooking. I first learned from her and Madam the word *recipes*. When Kate was at the big school, Madam taught me how to read cookery books. I went on very slowly at first, slower than an ox-waggon. Now I know more. When Kate came home, she found I had read the recipe she left me. So we just cooked straightaway. Kate thinks I am fit to cook in a hotel. Madam thinks so too. Never never! Cooking in a hotel is like feeding oxen. No one can say thank you to you. After a few months I could cook the Sunday lunch and later I could cook specials for Madam's or Kate's guests.

Madam did not only teach me cooking. She taught me how to look after guests. She praised me when I did very very well; not like the white people I had worked for before. I do not know what runs crooked in the heads of other people. Madam also had classes in the evenings for servants to teach them how to read and write. She and two other women in Greenside taught in the church hall.

As I say, Kate tells me plenty of things about Madam. She says to me she says, My mother goes to meetings many times. I ask her I say, What for? She says to me she says, For your people. I ask her I say, My people are in Phokeng far away. They have got mouths, I say. Why does she want to say something for them? Does she know what my mother and what my father want to say? They can speak when they want to. Kate raises her shoulders and drops them and says, How can I tell you Karabo? I don't say your people – your family only. I mean all the black people in this country. I say Oh! What do the black people want to say? Again she raises her shoulders and drops them, taking a deep breath.

I ask her I say, With whom is she in the meeting?

She says, With other people who think like her.

I ask her I say, Do you say there are people in the world who think the same things?

She nods her head.

I ask, What things?

So that a few of your people should one day be among those who rule this country, get more money for what they do for the white man, and – what did Kate say again? Yes, that Madam and those who think like her also wanted my people who have been to school to choose those who must speak for them in the – I think she said it looks like a Kgotla at home who rule the villages.

I say to Kate I say, Oh I see now. I say, Tell me Kate why is Madam always writing on the machine, all the time every day nearly?

She replies she says, Oh my mother is writing books.

I ask, You mean a book like those? – pointing at the books on the shelves.

Yes, Kate says.

And she told me how Madam wrote books and other things for newspapers and she wrote for the newspapers and magazines to say things for the black people who should be treated well, be paid more money, for the black people who can read and write many things to choose those who want to speak for them.

Kate also told me she said, My mother and other women who think like her put on black belts over their shoulders when they are sad and they want to show the white government they do not like the things being done by whites to blacks. My mother and the others go and stand where the people in government are going to enter or go out of a building.

I ask her I say, Does the government and the white people listen and stop their sins? She says, No. But my mother is in another group of white people.

I ask, Do the people of the government give the women tea and cakes? Kate says, Karabo! How stupid; oh!

I say to her I say, Among my people if someone comes and stands in front of my house I tell him to come in and I give him food. You white people are wonderful. But they keep standing there and the government people do not give them anything.

She replies, You mean strange. How many times have I taught you not to say *wonderful* when you mean *strange*! Well, Kate says with a short heart and looking cross and she shouts, Well they do not stand there the whole day to ask for tea and cakes stupid. Oh dear!

Always when Madam finished to read her newspapers she gave them to me to read to help me speak and write better English. When I had read she asked me to tell her some of the things in it. In this way, I did better and better and my mind was opening and opening and I was learning and learning many things about the black people inside and outside the towns which I did not know in the least. When I found words that were too difficult or I did not understand some of the things I asked Madam. She always told me You see this, you see that, eh? With a heart that can carry on a long way. Yes, Madam writes many letters to the papers. She is always sore about the way the white police beat up black people; about the way black people who work for whites are made to sit at the Zoo Lake with their hearts hanging, because the white people say our people are making noise on Sunday afternoon when they want to rest in their houses and gardens; about many ugly things that happen when some white people meet black man on the pavement or street. So Madam writes to the papers to let others know, to ask the government to be kind to us.

In the first year Mrs Plum wanted me to eat at table with her. It was very hard, one because I was not used to eating at table with a fork and knife, two because I heard of no other kitchen worker who was handled like this. I was afraid. Afraid of everybody, of Madam's guests if they found me doing this. Madam said I must not be silly. I must show that African servants can also eat at table. Number three, I could not eat some of the things I loved very much: mealie-meal porridge with sour milk or morogo, stamped mealies mixed with butter beans, sour porridge for breakfast and other things. Also, except for morning porridge, our food is nice when you eat with the hand. So nice that it does not stop in the mouth or the throat to greet anyone before it passes smoothly down.

We often had lunch together with Chimane next door and our garden boy – Ha! I must remember never to say *boy* again when I talk about a man. This makes me think of a day during the first few weeks in Mrs Plum's house. I was talking about Dick her garden man and I said 'garden boy'. And she says to me she says Stop talking about a 'boy', Karabo. Now listen here, she says, You Africans must learn to speak properly about each other. And she says White people won't talk kindly about you if you look down upon each other.

I say to her I say Madam, I learned the word from the white people I worked for, and all the kitchen maids say 'boy'.

She replies she says to me, Those are white people who know nothing, just low class whites. I say to her I say I thought white people know everything.

She said, You'll learn my girl and you must start in this house, hear? She left me there thinking, my mind mixed up.

I learned. I grew up.

If any woman or girl does not know the Black Crow Club in Bree Street, she does not know anything. I think nearly everything takes place inside and outside that house. It is just where the dirty part of the City begins, with factories and the market. After the market is the place where Indians and Coloured people live. It is also at the Black Crow that the buses turn round and back to the black townships. Noise, noise, noise all the time. There are women who sell hot sweet potatoes and fruit and monkey nuts and boiled eggs in the winter, boiled mealies and the other things in the summer, all these on the pavements. The streets are always full of potato and fruit skins and monkey nut shells. There is always a strong smell of roast pork. I think it is because of Piel's cold storage down Bree Street.

Madam said she knew the black people who work in the Black Crow. She was happy that I was spending my afternoon on Thursdays in such a club. You will learn sewing, knitting, she said, and other things that you like. Do you like to dance? I told her I said, Yes, I want to learn. She paid the two shillings fee for me each month.

We waited on the first floor, we the ones who were learning sewing; waiting for the teacher. We talked and laughed about madams and masters, and their children and their dogs and birds and whispered about our boyfriends.

Sies! My Madam you do not know – mojuta oa'nete – a real miser ...

Jo – jo – jo! You should see our new dog. A big thing like this. People! Big in a foolish way ...

What! Me, I take a master's bitch by the leg, me, and throw it away so that it keeps howling, tjwe – tjwe! Ngo – wu ngo – wu! I don't play about with them, me ...

Shame, poor thing! God sees you, true ...!

They wanted me to take their dog out for a walk every afternoon and I told them I said It is not my work in other houses the garden man does it. I just said to myself I said they can go to the chickens. Let them bite their elbow before I take out a dog, I am not so mad yet ...

Hei! It is not like the child of my white people who keeps a big white rat and you know what? He puts it on his bed when he goes to school. And let the blankets just begin to smell of urine and all the nonsense and they tell me to wash them. Hei, people ...!

Did you hear about Rebone, people? Her Madam put her out, because her master was always tapping her buttocks with his fingers. And yesterday the madam saw the master press Rebone against himself ...

Jo – jo – jo! people ...!

Dirty white man!

No, not dirty. The madam smells too old for him.

Hei! Go and wash your mouth with soap, this girl's mouth is dirty ...

Jo, Rebone, daughter of the people! We must help her to find a job before she thinks of going back home.

The teacher came. A woman with strong legs, a strong face and kind eyes. She had short hair and dressed in a simple but lovely floral frock. She stood well on her legs and hips. She had a black mark between the two top front teeth. She smiled as if we were her children. Our group began with games, and then Lilian Ngoyi took us for sewing. After this she gave a brief talk to all of us from the different classes.

I can never forget the things this woman said and how she put them to us. She told us that the time had passed for black girls and women in the suburbs to be satisfied with working, sending money to our people and going to see them once a year. We were to learn, she said, that the world would never be safe for black people until they were in the government with the power to make laws. The power should be given to the Africans who were more than the whites.

We asked her questions and she answered them with wisdom. I shall put some of them down in my own words as I remember them.

Shall we take the place of the white people in the government?

Some yes. But we shall be more than they as we are more in the country. But also the people of all colours will come together and there are good white men we can choose and there are Africans some white people will choose to be in the government.

There are good madams and masters and bad ones. Should we take the good ones for friends?

A master and a servant can never be friends. Never, so put that out of your head, will you! You are not even sure if the ones you say are good are not like that because they cannot breathe or live without the work of your hands. As long as you need their money, face them with respect. But you must know that many sad things are happening in our country and you, all of you, must always be learning, adding to what you already know, and obey us when we ask you to help us.

At other times Lilian Ngoyi told us she said, Remember your poor people at home and the way in which the whites are moving them from place to place like sheep and cattle. And at other times again she told us she said, Remember that a hand cannot wash itself, it needs another to do it.

I always thought of Madam when Lilian Ngoyi spoke. I asked myself, What would she say if she knew that I was listening to such words. Words like: a white man is looked after by his black nanny and his mother when he is a baby. When he grows up the white government looks after him, sends him to school, makes it impossible for him to suffer from the great hunger, keeps a job ready and open for him as soon as he wants to leave school. Now Lilian Ngoyi asked she said, How many white people can be born in a white hospital, grow up in white streets, be clothed in lovely cotton, lie on white cushions; how many whites can live all their lives in a fenced place away from people of other colours and then, as men and women learn quickly the correct ways of thinking, learn quickly to ask questions in their minds, big questions that will throw over all the nice things of a white man's life? How many? Very very few! For those whites who have not begun to ask, it is too late. For those who have begun and are joining us with both feet in our house, we can only say Welcome!

I was learning. I was growing up. Every time I thought of Madam, she became more and more like a dark forest which one fears to enter, and which one will never know. But there were several times when I thought, This woman is easy to understand, she is like all other white women.

What else are they teaching you at the Black Crow, Karabo?

I tell her I say, nothing Madam. I ask her I say Why does Madam ask?

You are changing.

What does Madam mean?

Well, you are changing.

But we are always changing Madam.

And she left me standing in the kitchen. This was a few days after I had told her that I did not want to read more than one white paper a day. The only magazines I wanted to read, I said to her, were those from overseas, if she had them. I told her that white papers had pictures of white people most of the time. They talked mostly about white people and their gardens, dogs, weddings and parties. I asked her if she could buy me a Sunday paper that spoke about my people. Madam bought it for me. I did not think she would do it.

There were mornings when, after hanging the white people's washing on the line Chimane and I stole a little time to stand at the fence and talk. We always stood where we could be hidden by our rooms.

Hei, Karabo, you know what. That was Chimane.

No – what? Before you start, tell me, has Timi come back to you?

Ach, I do not care. He is still angry. But boys are fools they always come back dragging themselves on their empty bellies. Hei you know what?

Yes?

The Thursday past I saw Moruti KK. I laughed until I dropped on the ground. He is standing in front of the Black Crow. I believe his big stomach was crying from hunger. Now he has a small dog in his armpit, and is standing before a woman selling boiled eggs and – hei home-girl! – tripe and intestines are boiling in a pot – oh – the smell! You could fill a hungry belly with it, the way it was good. I think Moruti KK is waiting for the woman to buy a boiled egg. I do not know what the woman was still doing. I am standing nearby. The dog keeps wriggling and pushing out its nose, looking at the boiling tripe. Moruti keeps patting it with his free hand, not so? Again the dog wants to spill out of Moruti's hand and it gives a few sounds through the nose. Hei man, home-girl! One two three the dog spills out to catch some of the good meat. It misses falling into the hot gravy in which the tripe is swimming I do not know how. Moruti KK tries to chase it. It has tumbled on to the woman's eggs and potatoes and all are in the dust. She stands up and goes after KK. She is shouting to him to pay, not so? Where am I at that time? I am nearly dead with laughter the tears are coming down so far.

I was holding myself tight on the fence so as not to fall through laughing. I held my stomach to keep back a pain in the side.

I ask her I say, Did Moruti KK come back to pay for the wasted food?

Yes, he paid.

The dog?

He caught it. That is a good African dog. A dog must look for its own food when it is not time for meals. Not those stupid spoiled angels the whites keep giving tea and biscuits.

Hmm.

Dick our garden man joined us, as he often did. When the story was repeated to him the man nearly rolled on the ground laughing.

He asks who is Reverend KK?

I say he is the owner of the Black Crow.

Oh!

We reminded each other, Chimane and I, of the round minister. He would come into the club, look at us with a smooth smile on his smooth round face. He would look at each one of us, with that smile on all the time, as if he had forgotten that it was there. Perhaps he had, because as he looked at us, almost stripping us naked with his watery shining eyes – funny – he could have been a farmer looking at his ripe corn, thinking many things.

KK often spoke without shame about what he called ripe girls – matjitjana – with good firm breasts. He said such girls were pure without any nonsense in their heads and bodies. Everybody talked a great deal about him and what they thought he must be doing in his office whenever he called in so-and-so.

The Reverend KK did not belong to any church. He baptised, married and buried people for a fee who had no church to do such things for them. They said he had been driven out of the Presbyterian Church. He had formed his own, but it did not go far. Then he later came and opened the Black Crow. He knew just how far to go with Lilian Ngoyi. She said although she used his club to teach us things that would help us in life, she could not go on if he was doing any wicked things with the girls in his office. Moruti KK feared her, and kept his place.

When I began to tell my story I thought I was going to tell you mostly about Mrs Plum's two dogs. But I have been talking about people. I think Dick is right when he says What is a dog! And there are so many dogs cats and parrots in Greenside and other places that Mrs Plum's dogs do not look special. But there was something special in the dog business in Madam's house. The way in which she loved them, maybe.

Monty is a tiny animal with long hair and small black eyes and a face nearly like that of an old woman. The other, Malan, is a bit bigger, with brown and white colours. It has small hair and looks naked by the side of the friend. They sleep in two separate baskets which stay in Madam's bedroom. They are to be washed often and brushed and sprayed and they sleep on pink linen. Monty has a pink ribbon which stays on his neck most of the time. They both carry a cover on their backs. They make me fed up when I see them in their baskets, looking fat, and as if they knew all that was going on everywhere.

It was Dick's work to look after Monty and Malan, to feed them, and to do everything for them. He did this together with garden work and cleaning of the house. He came at the beginning of this year. He just came, as if from nowhere, and Madam gave him the job as she had chased away two before him, she told me. In both those cases, she said that they could not look after Monty and Malan.

Dick had a long heart, even although he told me and Chimane that European dogs were stupid, spoiled. He said One day those white people will put ear rings and toe rings and bangles on their dogs. That would be the day he would leave Mrs Plum. For, he said, he was sure that she would want him to polish the rings and bangles with Brasso.

Although he had a long heart, Madam was still not sure of him. She often went to the dogs after a meal or after a cleaning and said to them Did Dick give you food sweethearts? And I could see that Dick was blowing up like a balloon with anger. These things called white people! he said to me. Talking to dogs!

I say to him I say, People talk to oxen at home do I not say so?

Yes, he says, but at home do you not know that a man speaks to an ox because he wants to make it pull the plough or the waggon or to stop or to stand still for a person to inspan it. No one simply goes to an ox looking at him with eyes far apart and speaks to it. Let me ask you, do you ever see a person where we come from take a cow and press it to his stomach or his cheek? Tell me!

And I say to Dick I say, We were talking about an ox, not a cow.

He laughed with his broad mouth until tears came out of his eyes. At a certain point I laughed aloud too.

One day when you have time, Dick says to me, he says, you

should look into Madam's bedroom when she has put a notice outside her door.

Dick, what are you saying? I ask.

I do not talk, me. I know deep inside me.

Dick was about our age, I and Chimane. So we always said moshiman'o when we spoke about his tricks. Because he was not too big to be a boy to us. He also said to us Hei, lona banyana kelona – Hey you girls, you! His large mouth always seemed to be making ready to laugh. I think Madam did not like this. Many times she would say What is there to make you laugh here? Or in the garden she would say This is a flower and when it wants water that is not funny! Or again, If you did more work and stopped trying to water my plants with your smile you would be more useful. Even when Dick did not mean to smile. What Madam did not get tired of saying was, If I left you to look after my dogs without anyone to look after you at the same time you would drown the poor things.

Dick smiled at Mrs Plum. Dick hurt Mrs Plum's dogs? The cows can fly. He was really – really afraid of white people, Dick. I think he tried very hard not to feel afraid. For he was always showing me and Chimane in private how Mrs Plum walked, and spoke. He took two bowls and pressed them to his chest, speaking softly to them as Madam speaks to Monty and Malan. Or he sat at Madam's table and acted the way she sits when writing. Now and again he looked back over his shoulder, pulled his face long like a horse's making as if he were looking over his glasses while telling me something to do. Then he would sit on one of the armchairs, cross his legs and act the way Madam drank her tea; he held the cup he was thinking about between his thumb and the pointing finger, only letting their nails meet. He did these things, of course, when Madam was not home. And where was I at such times? Almost flat on my stomach, laughing.

But oh how Dick trembled when Mrs Plum scolded him! He did his house-cleaning very well. Whatever mistake he made, it was mostly with the dogs; their linen, their food. One

white man came into the house one afternoon to tell Madam
that Dick had been very careless when taking the dogs out
for a walk. His own dog was waiting on Madam's stoep. He
repeated that he had been driving down our street; and Dick
had let loose Monty and Malan to cross the street. The white
man made plenty of noise about this and I think he wanted to
let Madam know how useful he had been. He kept on saying
Just one inch, *just* one inch. It was lucky I put on my brakes
quick enough ... but your boy kept on smiling – Why? Strange.
My boy would only do it twice and only twice and then ...! His
pass. The man moved his hand like one writing, to mean that
he would sign his servant's pass for him to go and never come
back. When he left, the white man said Come on Rusty, the
boy is waiting to clean you. Dogs with names, men without,
I thought.

Madam climbed on top of Dick for this, as we say.

Once one of the dogs, I don't know which – Malan or
Monty – took my stocking – brand new, you hear – and tore
it with his teeth and paws. When I told Madam about it, my
anger as high as my throat, she gave me money to buy another
pair. It happened again. This time she said she was not going to
give me money because I must also keep my stockings where
the two gentlemen would not reach them. Mrs Plum did not
want us ever to say Voetsek when we wanted the dogs to go
away. Me I said this when they came sniffing at my legs or
fingers. I hate it.

In my third year in Mrs Plum's house, many things
happened, most of them all bad for her. There was trouble with
Kate; Chimane had big trouble; my heart was twisted by two
loves; and Monty and Malan became real dogs for a few days.

Madam had a number of suppers and parties. She invited
Africans to some of them. Kate told me the reasons for some
of the parties. Like her mother's books when finished, a visitor
from across the seas and so on. I did not like the black people
who came here to drink and eat. They spoke such difficult
English like people who were full of all the books in the world.

They looked at me as if I were right down there whom they thought little of – me a black person like them.

One day I heard Kate speak to her mother. She says I don't know why you ask so many Africans to the house. A few will do at a time. She said something about the government which I could not hear well. Madam replies she says to her You know some of them do not meet white people often, so far away in their dark houses. And she says to Kate that they do not come because they want her as a friend but they just want a drink for nothing.

I simply felt that I could not be the servant of white people and of blacks at the same time. At my home or in my room I could serve them without a feeling of shame. And now, if they were only coming to drink!

But one of the black men and his sister always came to the kitchen to talk to me. I must have looked unfriendly the first time, for Kate talked to me about it afterwards as she was in the kitchen when they came. I know that at that time I was not easy at all. I was ashamed and I felt that a white person's house was not the place for me to look happy in front of other black people while the white man looked on.

Another time it was easier. The man was alone. I shall never forget that night, as long as I live. He spoke kind words and I felt my heart grow big inside me. It caused me to tremble. There were several other visits. I knew that I loved him, I could never know what he really thought of me, I mean as a woman and he as a man. But I loved him, and I still think of him with a sore heart. Slowly I came to know the pain of it. Because he was a doctor and so full of knowledge and English I could not reach him. So I knew he could not stoop down to see me as someone who wanted him to love me.

Kate turned very wild. Mrs Plum was very much worried. Suddenly it looked as if she were a new person, with new ways and new everything. I do not know what was wrong or right. She began to play the big gramophone aloud, as if the music were for the whole of Greenside. The music was wild and she twisted her waist all the time, with her mouth half open. She did the same things in her room. She left the big school and every Saturday night now she went out. When I looked at her face, there was something deep and wild there on it, and when I thought she looked young she looked old, and when I thought she looked old she was young. We were both twenty-two years of age. I think that I could see the reason why her mother was so worried, why she was suffering.

Worse was to come.

They were now openly screaming at each other. They began in the sitting room and went upstairs together, speaking fast hot biting words, some of which I did not grasp. One day Madam comes to me and says You know Kate loves an African, you know the doctor who comes to supper here often. She says he loves her too and they will leave the country and marry outside. Tell me, Karabo, what do your people think of this kind of thing between a white woman and a black man? It *cannot* be right is it?

I reply and I say to her We have never seen it happen before where I come from.

That's right, Karabo, it is just madness.

Madam left. She looked like a hunted person.

These white women, I say to myself I say these white women, why do they not love their own men and leave us to love ours!

From that minute I knew that I would never want to speak to Kate. She appeared to me as a thief, as a fox that falls upon a flock of sheep at night. I hated her. To make it worse, he would never be allowed to come to the house again.

Whenever she was home there was silence between us. I no longer wanted to know anything about what she was doing, where or how.

I lay awake for hours on my bed. Lying like that, I seemed to feel parts of my body beat and throb inside me, the way I have seen big machines doing, pounding and pounding and pushing and pulling and pouring some water into one hole which came out at another end. I stretched myself so many times so as to feel tired and sleepy.

When I did sleep, my dreams were full of painful things.

One evening I made up my mind, after putting it off many times. I told my boyfriend that I did not want him any longer. He looked hurt, and that hurt me too. He left.

The thought of the African doctor was still with me and it pained me to know that I should never see him again, unless I met him in the street on a Thursday afternoon. But he had a car. Even if I did meet him by luck, how could I make him see that I loved him? Ach, I do not believe he would even stop to think what kind of woman I am. Part of that winter was a time of longing and burning for me. I say part because there are always things to keep servants busy whose white people go to the sea for the winter.

To tell the truth, winter was the time for servants; not nannies, because they went with their madams so as to look after the children. Those like me stayed behind to look after the house and dogs. In winter so many families went away that the dogs remained the masters and madams. You could see them walk like white people in the streets. Silent but with plenty of power. And when you saw them you knew that they were full of more nonsense and fancies in the house.

There was so little work to do.

One week word was whispered round that a homeboy of ours was going to hold a party in his room on Saturday. I think we all took it for a joke. How could the man be so bold and stupid? The police were always driving about at night looking for black people; and if the whites next door heard the party noise – oho! But still, we were full of joy and wanted to go. As for Dick, he opened his big mouth and nearly fainted when he heard of it and that I was really going.

During the day on the big Saturday Kate came.

She seemed a little less wild. But I was not ready to talk to her. I was surprised to hear myself answer her when she said to me Mother says you do not like a marriage between a white girl and a black man, Karabo.

Then she was silent.

She says But I want to help him, Karabo.

I ask her I say You want to help him to do what?

To go higher and higher, to the top.

I knew I wanted to say so much that was boiling in my chest. I could not say it. I thought of Lilian Ngoyi at the Black Crow, what she said to us. But I was mixed up in my head and in my blood.

You still agree with my mother?

All I could say was I said to your mother I had never seen a black man and a white woman marrying, you hear me? What I think about it is my business.

I remembered that I wanted to iron my party dress and so I left her. My mind was full of the party again and I was glad because Kate and the doctor would not worry my peace that day. And the next day the sun would shine for all of us, Kate or no Kate, doctor or no doctor.

The house where our homeboy worked was hidden from the main road by a number of trees. But although we asked a number of questions and counted many fingers of bad luck until we had no more hands for fingers, we put on our best pay while you wear dresses and suits and clothes bought from boys who had stolen them, and went to our homeboy's party. We whispered all the way while we climbed up to the house. Someone who knew told us that the white people next door were away for the winter. Oh, so that is the thing! we said.

We poured into the garden through the back and stood in front of his room laughing quietly. He came from the big house behind us, and were we not struck dumb when he told us to go into the white people's house! Was he mad? We walked in with slow footsteps that seemed to be sniffing at the floor, not sure of anything. Soon we were standing and sitting all over on the nice warm cushions and the heaters were on. Our homeboy turned the lights low. I counted fifteen people inside. We saw how we loved one another's evening dress. The boys were smart too.

Our homeboy's girlfriend Naomi was busy in the kitchen preparing food. He took out glasses and cold drinks – fruit juice, tomato juice, ginger beers and so many other kinds of soft drink. It was just too nice. The tarts, the biscuits, the snacks, the cakes, woo, that was a party, I tell you. I think I ate more ginger cake than I had ever done in my life. Naomi had baked some of the things. Our homeboy came to me and said I do not want the police to come here and have reason to arrest us, so I am not serving hot drinks, not even beer. There is no law that we cannot have parties, is there? So we can feel free. Our use of this house is the master's business. If I had asked him he would have thought me mad.

I say to him I say, You have a strong liver to do such a thing.

He laughed.

He played pennywhistle music on gramophone records – Miriam Makeba, Dorothy Masuka and other African singers and players. We danced and the party became more and more noisy and more happy. Hai, those girls Miriam and Dorothy, they can sing, I tell you! We ate more and laughed more and told more stories. In the middle of the party, our homeboy called us to listen to what he was going to say. Then he told us how he and a friend of his in Orlando collected money to bet on a horse for the July Handicap in Durban. They did this each year but lost. Now they had won two hundred pounds. We all clapped hands and cheered. Two hundred pounds, woo!

You should go and sit at home and just eat time, I say to him. He laughs and says You have no understanding not one little bit.

To all of us he says Now my brothers and sisters enjoy yourselves. At home I should slaughter a goat for us to feast and thank our ancestors. But this is town life and we must thank them with tea and cake and all those sweet things. I know some people think I must be so bold that I could be midwife to a lion that is giving birth, but enjoy yourselves and have no fear.

Madam came back looking strong and fresh.

The very week she arrived the police had begun again to search servants' rooms. They were looking for what they called loafers and men without passes who they said were living with friends in the suburbs against the law. Our dog's meat boys became scarce because of the police. A boy who had a girlfriend in the kitchens, as we say, always told his friends that he was coming for dog's meat when he meant he was visiting his girl. This was because we gave our boyfriends part of the meat the white people bought for the dogs and us.

One night a white and a black policeman entered Mrs Plum's yard. They said they had come to search. She says no, they cannot. They say, Yes they must do it. She answers No. They forced their way to the back, to Dick's room and mine. Mrs Plum took the hose that was running in the front garden and quickly went round to the back. I cut across the floor to see what she was going to say to the men. They were talking to Dick, using dirty words. Mrs Plum did not wait, she just pointed the hose at the two policemen. This seemed to surprise them. They turned round and she pointed it into their faces. Without their seeing me I went to the tap at the corner of the house and opened it more. I could see Dick, like me, was trying to keep down his laughter. They shouted and tried to wave the water away, but she kept the hose pointing at them, now moving it up and down. They turned and ran through the back gate, swearing the while.

That fixes them, Mrs Plum said.

The next day the morning paper reported it.

They arrived in the afternoon – the two policemen – with another. They pointed out Mrs Plum and she was led to the police station. They took her away to answer for stopping the police while they were doing their work.

She came back and said she had paid bail.

At the magistrate's court, Madam was told that she had done a bad thing. She would have to pay a fine or else go to prison for fourteen days. She said she would go to jail to show that she felt she was not in the wrong.

Kate came and tried to tell her that she was doing something silly going to jail for a small thing like that. She tells Madam she says This is not even a thing to take to the high court. Pay the money. What is £5?

Madam went to jail.

She looked very sad when she came out. I thought of what Lilian Ngoyi often said to us: You must be ready to go to jail for the things you believe are true and for which you are taken by the police. What did Mrs Plum really believe about me, Chimane, Dick and all the other black people? I asked myself. I did not know. But from all those things she was writing for the papers and all those meetings she was going to where white people talked about black people and the way they are treated by the government, from what those white women with black bands over their shoulders were doing standing where a white government man was going to pass, I said to myself I said This woman, hai, I do not know she seems to think very much of us black people. But why was she so sad?

Kate came back home to stay after this. She still played the big gramophone loud-loud-loud and twisted her body at her waist until I thought she was going to break. Then I saw a young white man come often to see her. I watched them through the opening near the hinges of the door between the kitchen and the sitting room where they sat. I saw them kiss each other for a long long time. I saw him lift up Kate's dress and her white-white legs begin to tremble, and – oh I am afraid to say more, my heart was beating hard. She called him Jim. I thought it was funny because white people in the shops call black men Jim.

Kate had begun to play with Jim when I met a boy who loved me and I loved. He was much stronger than the one I sent away and I loved him more, much more. The face of the doctor came to my mind often, but it did not hurt me so any more. I stopped looking at Kate and her Jim through openings. We spoke to each other, Kate and I, almost as freely as before but not quite. She and her mother were friends again.

Hello, Karabo, I heard Chimane call me one morning as I was starching my apron. I answered. I went to the line to hang it. I saw she was standing at the fence, so I knew she had something to tell me. I went to her.

Hello!

Hello, Chimane!

O kae?

Ke teng. Wena?

At that moment a woman came out through the back door of the house where Chimane was working.

I have not seen that one before, I say, pointing with my head.

Chimane looked back. Oh, that one. Hei, daughter of the people, hei, you have not seen miracles. You know this is Madam's mother-in-law as you see her there. Did I never tell you about her?

No, never.

White people, nonsense. You know what? That poor woman is here now for two days. She has to cook for herself and I cook for the family.

On the same stove?

Yes. She comes after me when I have finished.

She has her own food to cook?

Yes, Karabo. White people have no heart no sense.

What will eat them up if they share their food?

Ask me, just ask me. God! She clapped her hands to show that only God knew, and it was His business, not ours.

Chimane asks me she says, Have you heard from home?

I tell her I say, Oh daughter of the people, more and more deaths. Something is finishing the people at home. My mother has written. She says they are all right, my father too and my sisters, except for the people who have died. Malebo, the one who lived alone in the house I showed you last year, a white house, he is gone. Then teacher Sedimo. He was very thin and looked sick all the time. He taught my sisters not me. His mother-in-law you remember I told you died last year – no, the year before. Mother says also there is a woman she does not think I remember because I last saw her when I was a small girl she passed away in Zeerust she was my mother's greatest friend when they were girls. She would have gone to her burial if it was not because she has swollen feet.

How are the feet?

She says they are still giving her trouble. I ask Chimane, How are your people at Nokaneng? They have not written?

She shook her head.

I could see from her eyes that her mind was on another thing and not her people at that moment.

Wait for me Chimane eh, forgive me, I have scones in the oven, eh! I will just take them out and come back, eh!

When I came back to her Chimane was wiping her eyes. They were wet.

Karabo, you know what?

E – e. I shook my head.

I am heavy with child.

Hau!

There was a moment of silence.

Who is it, Chimane?

Timi. He came back only to give me this.

But he loves you. What does he say have you told him?

I told him yesterday. We met in town.

I remembered I had not seen her at the Black Crow.

Are you sure, Chimane? You have missed a month?

She nodded her head.

Timi himself – he did not use the thing?

I only saw after he finished, that he had not.

Why? What does he say?

He tells me he says I should not worry I can be his wife.

Timi is a good boy, Chimane. How many of these boys
with town ways who know too much will even say Yes it is
my child?

Hai, Karabo, you are telling me other things now. Do you
not see that I have not worked long enough for my people?
If I marry now who will look after them when I am the only
child?

Hm. I hear your words. It is true. I tried to think of
something soothing to say.

Then I say You can talk it over with Timi. You can go home
and when the child is born you look after it for three months
and when you are married you come to town to work and can
put your money together to help the old people while they are
looking after the child.

What shall we be eating all the time I am at home? It is not
like those days gone past when we had land and our mother
could go to the fields until the child was ready to arrive.

The light goes out in my mind and I cannot think of the
right answer. How many times have I feared the same thing!
Luck and the mercy of the gods that is all I live by. That is all
we live by – all of us.

Listen, Karabo. I must be going to make tea for Madam. It
will soon strike half past ten.

I went back to the house. As Madam was not in yet, I threw
myself on the divan in the sitting room. Malan came sniffing at
my legs. I put my foot under its fat belly and shoved it up and
away from me so that it cried tjunk – tjunk – tjunk as it went
out. I say to it I say Go and tell your brother what I have done
to you and tell him to try it and see what I will do. Tell your
grandmother when she comes home too.

When I lifted my eyes he was standing in the kitchen door,
Dick. He says to me he says Hau! Now you have also begun to
speak to dogs!

I did not reply. I just looked at him, his mouth ever
stretched out like the mouth of a bag, and I passed to my room.

I sat on my bed and looked at my face in the mirror. Since

the morning I had been feeling as if a black cloud were hanging over me, pressing on my head and shoulders. I do not know how long I sat there. Then I smelled Madam. What was it? Where was she? After a few moments I knew what it was. My perfume and scent. I used the same cosmetics as Mrs Plum's. I should have been used to it by now. But this morning – why did I smell Mrs Plum like this? Then, without knowing why, I asked myself I said, Why have I been using the same cosmetics as Madam? I wanted to throw them all out. I stopped. And then I took all the things and threw them into the dustbin. I was going to buy other kinds on Thursday; finished!

I could not sit down. I went out and into the white people's house. I walked through and the smell of the house made me sick and seemed to fill up my throat. I went to the bathroom without knowing why. It was full of the smell of Madam. Dick was cleaning the bath. I stood at the door and looked at him cleaning the dirt out of the bath, dirt from Madam's body. Sies! I said aloud. To myself I said, Why cannot people wash the dirt of their own bodies out of the bath? Before Dick knew I was near I went out. Ach, I said again to myself, why should I think about it now when I have been doing their washing for so long and cleaned the bath many times when Dick was ill. I had held worse things from her body times without number ...

I went out and stood midway between the house and my room, looking into the next yard. The three-legged grey cat next door came to the fence and our eyes met. I do not know how long we stood like that looking at each other. I was thinking, Why don't you go and look at your grandmother like that? when it turned away and mewed hopping on three legs. Just like someone who feels pity for you.

In my room I looked into the mirror on the chest of drawers. I thought Is this Karabo this?

Thursday came, and the afternoon off. At the Black Crow I did not see Chimane. I wondered about her. In the evening I found a note under my door. It told me if Chimane was not back that evening I should know that she was at 660 Third

Avenue, Alexandra Township. I was not to tell the white
people.

I asked Dick if he could not go to Alexandra with me after I
had washed the dishes. At first he was unwilling. But I said to
him I said, Chimane will not believe that you refused to come
with me when she sees me alone. He agreed.

On the bus Dick told me much about his younger sister
whom he was helping with money to stay at school until she
finished; so that she could become a nurse and a midwife.
He was very fond of her, as far as I could find out. He said he
prayed always that he should not lose his job, as he had done
many times before, after staying a few weeks only at each job;
because of this he had to borrow monies from people to pay
his sister's school fees, to buy her clothes and books. He spoke
of her as if she were his sweetheart. She was clever at school,
pretty (she was this in the photo Dick had shown me before).
She was in Orlando Township. She looked after his old people,
although she was only thirteen years of age. He said to me he
said Today I still owe many people because I keep losing my
job. You must try to stay with Mrs Plum, I said.

I cannot say that I had all my mind on what Dick was telling
me. I was thinking of Chimane: what could she be doing? Why
that note?

We found her in bed. In that terrible township where night
and day are full of knives and bicycle chains and guns and the
barking of hungry dogs and of people in trouble. I held my
heart in my hands. She was in pain and her face, even in the
candlelight, was grey. She turned her eyes at me. A fat woman
was sitting in a chair. One arm rested on the other and held her
chin in its palm. She had hardly opened the door for us after
we had shouted our names when she was on her bench again
as if there were nothing else to do.

She snorted, as if to let us know that she was going to
speak. She said There is your friend. There she is my own-own
niece who comes from the womb of my own sister, my sister
who was make to spit out my mother's breast to give way for

me. Why does she go and do such an evil thing. Ao! you young girls of today you do not know children die so fast these days that you have to thank God for sowing a seed in your womb to grow into a child. If she had let the child be born I should have looked after it or my sister would have been so happy to hold a grandchild on her lap, but what does it help? She has allowed a worm to cut the roots, I don't know.

Then I saw that Chimane's aunt was crying. Not once did she mention her niece by her name, so sore her heart must have been. Chimane only moaned.

Her aunt continued to talk, as if she was never going to stop for breath, until her voice seemed to move behind me, not one of the things I was thinking: trying to remember signs, however small, that could tell me more about this moment in a dim little room in a cruel township without street lights, near Chimane. Then I remembered the three-legged cat, its grey-green eyes, its *miaw*. What was this shadow that seemed to walk about us but was not coming right in front of us?

I thanked the gods when Chimane came to work at the end of the week. She still looked weak, but that shadow was no longer there. I wondered Chimane had never told me about her aunt before. Even now I did not ask her.

I told her I told her white people that she was ill and had been fetched to Nokaneng by a brother. They would never try to find out. They seldom did, these people. Give them any lie and it will do. For they seldom believe you whatever you say. And how can a black person work for white people and be afraid to tell them lies. They are always asking the questions, you are always the one to give the answers.

Chimane told me all about it. She had gone to a woman who did these things. Her way was to hold a sharp needle, cover the point with the finger and guide it into the womb. She then fumbled in the womb until she found the egg and then pierced it. She gave you something to ease the bleeding. But the pain, spirits of our forefathers!

Mrs Plum and Kate were talking about dogs one evening

at dinner. Every time I brought something to table I tried to catch their words. Kate seemed to find it funny, because she laughed aloud. There was a word I could not hear well which began with *sem*–: whatever it was, it was to be for dogs. This I understand by putting a few words together. Mrs Plum said it was something that was common in the big cities of America, like New York. It was also something Mrs Plum wanted and Kate laughed at the thought. Then later I was to hear that Monty and Malan could be sure of a nice burial.

Chimane's voice came up to me in my room the next morning, across the fence. Hei child of my father, here is something to tickle your ears. You know what? What? I say. She says, These white people can do things that make the gods angry. More godless people I have not seen. The madam of our house says the people of Greenside want to buy ground where they can bury their dogs. I heard them talk about it in the sitting room when I was giving them coffee last night. Hei, people, let our forefathers come and save us!

Yes, I say, I also heard the madam of our house talk about it with her daughter. I just heard it in pieces. By my mother one day these dogs will sit at table and use knife and fork. These things are to be treated like people now, like children who are never going to grow up.

Chimane sighed and she says Hela batho, why do they not give me some of that money they will spend on the ground and on gravestones to buy stockings! I have nothing to put on, by my mother.

Over her shoulder I saw the cat with three legs. I pointed with my head. When Chimane looked back and saw it she said Hm, even *they* live like kings. The mother-in-law found it on a chair and the madam said the woman should not drive it away. And there was no other chair, so the woman went to her room.

Hela!

I was going to leave when I remembered what I wanted to tell Chimane. It was that five of us had collected £1 each to lend her so that she could pay the woman of Alexandra for having done that thing for her. When Chimane's time came to receive money we collected each month and which we took in turns, she would pay us back. We were ten women and each gave £2 at a time. So one waited ten months to receive £20. Chimane thanked us for helping her.

I went to wake up Mrs Plum as she had asked me. She was sleeping late this morning. I was going to knock at the door when I heard strange noises in the bedroom. What is the matter with Mrs Plum? I asked myself. Should I call her, in case she is ill? No, the noises were not those of a sick person. They were happy noises but like those a person makes in a dream, the voice full of sleep. I bent a little to peep through the keyhole. What is this? I kept asking myself. Mrs Plum! Malan! What is she doing this one? Her arm was round Malan's belly and pressing its back against her stomach at the navel, Mrs Plum's body in a nightdress moving in jerks like someone in fits ... her leg rising and falling ... Malan silent like a thing to be owned without any choice it can make to belong to another.

The gods save me! I heard myself saying, the words sounding like wind rushing out of my mouth. So this is what Dick said I would find out for myself!

No one could say where it all started; who talked about it first; whether the police wanted to make a reason for taking people without passes and people living with servants and working in town or not working at all. But the story rushed through Johannesburg that servants were going to poison the white people's dogs. Because they were too much work for us: that was the reason. We heard that letters were sent to the newspapers by white people asking the police to watch over the dogs to stop any wicked things.

Some said that we the servants were not really bad, we were being made to think of doing these things by evil people in town and in the locations. Others said the police should watch out lest we poison madams and masters because black people did not know right from wrong when they were angry. We were still children at heart, others said. Mrs Plum said that she had also written to the papers.

Then it was the police came down on the suburbs like locusts on a cornfield. There were lines and lines of men who were arrested hour by hour in the day. They liked this very much, the police. Everybody they took, everybody who was working was asked, Where's the poison eh? Where did you hide it? Who told you to poison the dogs eh? If you tell us we'll leave you to go free, you hear? and so many other things.

Dick kept saying It is wrong this thing they want to do to kill poor dogs. What have these things of God done to be killed for? Is it the dogs that make us carry passes? Is it dogs that make the laws that give us pain? People are just mad they do not know what they want, stupid! But when white policemen spoke to him, Dick trembled and lost his tongue and the things he thought. He just shook his head. A few moments after they had gone through his pockets he still held his arms stretched out, like the man of straw who frightens away birds in a field. Only when I hissed and gave him a sign did he drop his arms. He rushed to a corner of the garden to go on with his work.

Mrs Plum had put Monty and Malan in the sitting room, next to her. She looked very much worried. She called me. She asked me she said Karabo, you think Dick is a boy we can trust? I did not know how to answer. I did not know whom she was talking about when she said *we*. Then I said I do not know, Madam. You know! she said. I looked at her. I said I do not know what Madam thinks. She said she did not think anything, that was why she asked. I nearly laughed because she was telling a lie this time and not I.

At another time I should have been angry if she lied to me, perhaps. She and I often told each other lies, as Kate and I also did. Like when she came back from jail, after that day when she turned a hosepipe on two policemen. She said life had been good in jail. And yet I could see she was ashamed to have been there. Not like our black people who are always being put in jail and only look at it as the white man's evil game. Lilian Ngoyi often told us this, and Mrs Plum showed me how true those words are. I am sure that we have kept to each other by lying to each other.

There was something in Mrs Plum's face as she was speaking which made me fear her and pity her at the same time. I had seen her when she had come from prison; I had seen her when she was shouting at Kate and the girl left the house; now there was this thing about dog poisoning. But never had I seen her face like this before. The eyes, the nostrils, the lips, the teeth seemed to be full of hate, tired, fixed on doing something bad; and yet there was something on that face that told me she wanted me on her side.

Dick is all right Madam, I found myself saying. She took Malan and Monty in her arms and pressed them to herself, running her hands over their heads. They looked so safe, like a child in a mother's arm.

Mrs Plum said All right you may go. She said Do not tell anybody what I have asked about Dick eh?

When I told Dick about it, he seemed worried.

It is nothing, I told him.

I had been thinking before that I did not stand with those who wanted to poison the dogs, Dick said. But the police have come out, I do not care what happens to the dumb things now.

I asked him I said Would you poison them if you were told by someone to do it?

No. But I do not care, he replied.

The police came again and again. They were having a good holiday, everyone could see that. A day later Mrs Plum told Dick to go because she would not need his work any more.

Dick was almost crying when he left. Is madam so unsure of me? he asked. I never thought a white person could fear me! And he left.

Chimane shouted from the other yard. She said, Hei ngoana'rona, the boers are fire-hot eh!

Mrs Plum said she would hire a man after the trouble was over.

A letter came from my parents in Phokeng. In it they told me my uncle had passed away. He was my mother's brother. The letter also told me of other deaths. They said I would not remember some, I was sure to know the others. There were also names of sick people.

I went to Mrs Plum to ask her if I could go home. She asks she says When did he die. I answer I say It is three days, Madam. She says So that they have buried him? I reply Yes Madam. Why do you want to go home then? Because my uncle loved me very much Madam. But what are you going to do there? To take my tears and words of grief to his grave and to my old aunt, Madam. No you cannot go, Karabo. You are working for me you know? Yes, Madam. I, and not your people pay you. I must go Madam, that is how we do it among my people, Madam. She paused. She walked into the kitchen and came out again. If you want to go, Karabo, you must lose the money for the days you will be away. Lose my pay, Madam. Yes, Karabo.

The next day I went to Mrs Plum and told her I was leaving for Phokeng and was not coming back to her. Could she give me a letter to say that I worked for her. She did, with her lips shut tight. I could feel that something between us was burning like raw chillies. The letter simply said that I had worked for Mrs Plum for three years. Nothing more. The memory of Dick being sent away was still an open sore in my heart.

The night before the day I left, Chimane came to see me in my room. She had her own story to tell me. Timi, her boyfriend, had left her – for good. Why? Because I killed his baby. Had he not agreed that you should do it? No. Did he show he was worried when you told him you were heavy? He was worried, like me as you saw me, Karabo. Now he says if I kill one I shall eat all his children up when we are married. You think he means what he says? Yes, Karabo. He says his parents would have been very happy to know that the woman he was going to marry can make his seed grow.

Chimane was crying, softly.

I tried to speak to her, to tell her that if Timi left her just like that, he had not wanted to marry her in the first place. But I could not, no, I could not. All I could say was Do not cry, my sister, do not cry. I gave her my handkerchief.

Kate came back the morning I was leaving, from somewhere very far I cannot remember where. Her mother took no notice of what Kate said asking her to keep me, and I was not interested either.

One hour later I was on the Railway bus to Phokeng. During the early part of the journey I did not feel anything about the Greenside house I had worked in. I was not really myself, my thoughts dancing between Mrs Plum, my uncle, my parents and Phokeng, my home. I slept and woke up many times during the bus ride. Right through the ride I seemed to see, sometimes in sleep, sometimes between sleep and waking, a red car passing our bus, then running behind us. Each time I looked out it was not there.

Dreams came and passed. He tells me he says You have killed my seed I wanted my mother to know you are a woman in whom my seed can grow ... Before you make the police take you to jail make sure that it is for something big you should go to jail for, otherwise you will come out with a heart and mind that will bleed inside you and poison you ...

The bus stopped for a short while, which made me wake up.

The Black Crow, the club women ... Hei, listen! I lie to the madam of our house and I say I had a telegram from my mother telling me she is very very sick. I show her a telegram my sister sent me as if mother were writing. So I went home for a nice weekend ...

The laughter of the women woke me up, just in time for me to stop a line of saliva coming out over my lower lip. The bus was making plenty of dust now as it was running over part of the road they were digging up. I was sure the red car was just behind us, but it was not there when I woke.

Any one of you here who wants to be baptised or has a relative without a church who needs to be can come and see me in the office ... A round man with a fat tummy and sharp hungry eyes, a smile that goes a long, long way ...

The bus was going uphill, heavily and noisily.

I kick a white man's dog, me, or throw it there if it has not been told the black people's law ... this is Mister Monty and this is Mister Malan. Now get up you lazy boys and meet Mister Kate. Hold out your hands and say hello to him ... Karabo, bring two glasses there ... Wait a bit – What will you chew boys while Mister Kate and I have a drink? Nothing? Sure?

We were now going nicely on a straight tarred road and the trees rushed back. Mister Kate. What nonsense, I thought.

Look Karabo, madam's dogs are dead. What? Poison. I killed them. She drove me out of a job did she not? For nothing. Now I want her to feel she drove me out for something. I came back when you were in your room and took the things and poisoned them ... And you know what? She has buried them in clean pink sheets in the garden. Ao, clean clean good sheets. I am going to dig them out and take one sheet do you want the other one? Yes, give me the other one I will send it to my mother ... Hei, Karabo, see here they come. Monty and Malan. The bloody fools they do not want to stay in their hole. Go back you silly fools. Oh, you do not want to move eh? Come here, now I am going to throw you in the big pool. No, Dick! No Dick! no, no! Dick! They cannot speak do not kill things that cannot speak. Madam can speak for them she always does. No! Dick ...!

I woke up with a jump after I had screamed Dick's name, almost hitting the window. My forehead was full of sweat. The red car also shot out of my sleep and was gone. I remembered a friend of ours who told us how she and the garden man had saved two white sheets in which their white master had buried their two dogs. They went to throw the dogs in a dam.

When I told my parents my story Father says to me he says, So long as you are in good health my child, it is good. The worker dies, work does not. There is always work. I know when I was a boy a strong sound body and a good mind were the biggest things in life. Work was always there and the lazy man could never say there was no work. But today people see work as something bigger than everything else, bigger than health, because of money.

In reply I say, Those days are gone Papa. I must go back to the city after resting a little to look for work. I must look after you. Today people are too poor to be able to help you.

I knew when I left Greenside that I was going to return to Johannesburg to work. Money was little, but life was full and it was better than sitting in Phokeng and watching the sun rise and set. So I told Chimane to keep her eyes and ears open for a job.

I had been at Phokeng for one week when a red car arrived. Somebody was sitting in front with the driver, a white woman. At once I knew it to be that of Mrs Plum. The man sitting beside her was showing her the way, for he pointed towards our house in front of which I was sitting. My heart missed a few beats. Both came out of the car. The white woman said Thank you to the man after he had spoken a few words to me.

I did not know what to do and how to look at her as she spoke to me. So I looked at the piece of cloth I was sewing pictures on. There was a tired but soft smile on her face. Then I remembered that she might want to sit. I went inside to fetch a low bench for her. When I remembered it afterwards, the thought came to me that there are things I never think white people can want to do at our homes when they visit for the first time: like sitting, drinking water or entering the house. This is how I thought when the white priest came to see us. One year at Easter Kate drove me home as she was going to the north. In the same way I was at a loss what to do for a few minutes.

Then Mrs Plum says, I have come to ask you to come back to me, Karabo. Would you like to?

I say I do not know, I must think about it first.

She says, Can you think about it today? I can sleep at the town hotel and come back tomorrow morning, and if you want to you can return with me.

I wanted her to say she was sorry to have sent me away, I did not know how to make her say it because I know white people find it too much for them to say Sorry to a black person. As she was not saying it, I thought of two things to make it hard for her to get me back and maybe even lose me in the end.

I say, You must ask my father first, I do not know, should I call him?

Mrs Plum says, Yes.

I fetched both Father and Mother. They greeted her while I brought benches. Then I told them what she wanted.

Father asks Mother and Mother asks Father. Father asks me. I say if they agree, I will think about it and tell her the next day.

Father says, It goes by what you feel my child.

I tell Mrs Plum I say, If you want me to think about it I must know if you will want to put my wages up from £6 because it is too little.

She asks me, How much will you want?

Up by £4.

She looked down for a few moments.

And then I want two weeks at Easter and not just the weekend. I thought if she really wanted me she would want to pay for it. This would also show how sorry she was to lose me.

Mrs Plum says, I can give you one week. You see you already have something like a rest when I am in Durban in the winter.

I tell her I say I shall think about it.

She left.

The next day she found me packed and ready to return with her. She was very much pleased and looked kinder than I had ever known her. And me, I felt sure of myself, more than I had ever done.

Mrs Plum says to me, You will not find Monty and Malan.

Oh?

Yes, they were stolen the day after you left. The police have not found them yet. I think they are dead myself.

I thought of Dick ... my dream. Could he? And she ... did this woman come to ask me to return because she had lost two animals she loved?

Mrs Plum says to me she says, You know, I like your people, Karabo, the Africans.

And Dick and me? I wondered.

Nigerian Talking Points

Olatunji, a Nigerian, and Alex Johnson, an Englishman, are friends of mine. Olatunji, or Tunji, is a 'native of Ibadan', as Nigerians like to say. Both he and Alex are civil servants, but in different departments.

Tunji is a squat fellow with a broad round face and a large mouth. There are few things as spectacular as a Nigerian when he is amazed or incredulous. He stands with his mouth wide open; and for that time – it could be ten seconds – the functioning of every other part of his body, every other facial organ, is suspended.

He is a 'been-to' – London School of Economics and all that, and he represents the new blood of his country, is part of its hope. And as with many of his kind, a bit of Nigerian hauteur breaks through his good-natured disposition now and again. That's when he is being accommodating.

Alex has the inevitable British long nose, and his mouth and chin are always threatening to disappear into his head or somewhere. He is tall and slim. Before he was married, he used to say some nice things about Nigerian girls. Although he still says them, he is not extravagant and indiscriminate in his remarks which, he admits, came of a colonial romanticism. Now he is just humanly kind.

Although we are both expatriates, there is a sense in which Alex is still regarded by Nigerians as a representative of power which I'm not. He is also part of a way of life that has registered favourably with Nigerians. I am the side of the Nigerian's life which he takes for granted. So there is just that much difference in the weight of our words when they are assessed by Nigerians. But as we are both uncommitted in our context, it doesn't matter really.

Alex is not one of that petty class of Whites you find in rest houses – a famous institution in Nigeria – or in Kipling-haunted clubs (to borrow a phrase from Orwell), swallowing quarts and quarts of beer, talking about petty things.

'What department are you in?' opens a conversation the same way weather talk does in England. They are representatives of commercial firms and civil servants. The men of the Public Works Department will come in, looking desperately wan and shuffling along with a prehistoric gait. Then they sit and complain about their African workers; lazy ... no sense of urgency ... shamming illness ... they can never do without us Whites (belching importantly at intervals for emphasis). Or they gossip about their African superiors. One of this type can often be seen at sundown in his garden, stripped to the waist, the breasts hanging down in cliffs of rubber. Next to him may be his wife; the two will stand in an attitude of primal expectancy, scouring the horizon with their eyes as if for some elemental sign – a sign that is to determine their instinctive move for the hour or season.

No, Alex is not one of these. He is the quiet sort who has neither an exaggerated sense of mission nor that back to the womb look which characterises so many Whites who have come to work in Africa. He has been in Nigeria five years and he's due to go back to Britain. His son must go to grammar school and so the family won't come back. It's always happening. White children of grammar school age are invariably wrenched from the country and that almost always means the whole family must call it a day as far as expatriate service goes.

'Why don't your children go to Nigerian grammar schools?' I ask Alex.

'They'll eventually have to go to English universities, and so they might as well do their preparatory work in familiar conditions.'

'You're sure it has nothing to do with popular White expatriate opinion of Nigerian educational standards?'

'It has, partly. But one could get over that hurdle somehow. The main thing is simply that I'm not a Nigerian and don't intend to become one, so there is no point in my children attending school with Africans. Integration for me's out of the question.'

'But what about these multiracial private primary schools like those at Ibadan?' Tunji asks.

'No, for the same reasons.'

'It's a pity, you know, that there are no state-aided multiracial schools,' I say. 'The more there are of them, the less anxiety there will be about standards. For instance, I simply couldn't think of sending my children to a multiracial school at Ibadan. The African children are a minority and people have come to attach a snob value to the school. So I send them to a Nigerian school and feel happy about it.'

'You wait,' says Tunji. 'Now we're independent all these snob institutions will vanish.'

'But there is class snobbery among Blacks themselves, isn't there, Tunji?' I say teasingly.

'Yes, but it can't get out of hand if it's indigenous and not imposed from outside.'

'Just what I always say,' Alex leaps in. 'We're supposed to be the regular Jonahs in every colonial situation.'

'Wait-wait-wait,' says Tunji. '*You* people brought in the snob values – the acquisitive urge, professional distinctions, high-powered advertising and so many other accessories.'

'Oh, we never get anywhere in this sort of talk,' says Alex despairingly.

Another time I prod Tunji in the ribs: about Nigerian women. They work too hard; in many cases, maintaining men who generally want to have a good time.

He doesn't like my references to the males. As for the women, Tunji says: 'They are perfectly happy that way.'

Yes, they are up at dawn and take their posts at the numerous markets. They stay there all day, and in some towns a greater part of the night. The Nigerian market woman is tough and independent. Pregnant or suckling, she sticks to her post with extraordinary patience. She will defend her rights, no matter what it costs; just as if she felt if she had conceded so much to man, and here at the market stall, or street kiosk, a boundary has to be drawn. Talk of emancipation of women! Once the Nigerian woman has launched out as a trader, she becomes independent of the male species for maintenance. There is in her a mixture of relentless grit and a traditional feminine pliability.

At dawn you can see droves of these women walking down to the market with huge baskets on their heads or bundles of firewood or sheaves of leaves used for wrapping food in; you see their profiles, slender as twilight at first, and then taking solid shape as they move into daylight; you see some of them suckling babies on their hips while they walk; you sense an inborn endurance in that loop of an arm round the baby, in that upward curve of an arm holding the load on the head.

A strange kind of independence. For these women are not at all sophisticated to the point where they have any use for modern appliances and conveniences (except electric lighting where it exists), or good furniture, even where they can afford these things. The educated woman herself, with very few exceptions, has not given herself over to urbanised life and urban thinking. In contrast, the semi-literate or illiterate urban woman in South Africa thinks in terms of a systematically furnished house, even in Shanty Town; in terms of a radio, modern appliances where there is electricity; in terms of a women's club. Man and woman are much more interdependent; oppression is no doubt responsible for this. Insecurity – yes, but of a different order, easily related to the political and economic hardships.

In West Africa, one senses a feeling of insecurity among women that has very much to do with social ills that go much deeper than any that could be released by a colonial situation. One hears much too often, during a women's radio programme, a speaker give a cooking recipe and say: 'I'm sure that delicious dish will keep your man at home and he's not likely to wander away in search of company.'

Insecurity is also indicated by the large numbers of people who can be seen crowded round a magician, looking entranced. On another plane, it must be responsible for the large distribution of the monthly magazine *Psychology*, in Nigeria. This is one of those journals that thrive on the cult of success and purport to supply the answer to the individual's quest for personal release from the forces that spell failure. Perhaps it is a form of escape from some sense of failure that so many of those we may call 'the masses' flock to cinemas to see Indian pictures. These films have a grand stage and a somewhat unearthly setting; they often tell a fairy-like story of love and adventure – old style – and the audiences simply live the enchantment of all this, making audible sounds in response to the action throughout.

Tunji tells me a man would never die of hunger in the country.

'Because food is plentiful, or because of a communal sense of responsibility?' I ask.

'Because of the latter *and* because native foods are cheap and the average man eats simply.'

'But your children, Tunji,' Alex observes. 'This child labour is bad for society. Look at these children carrying heavy baskets on their heads. What chance have they got in life?'

'No parent is forced to make his child work for him – I mean it isn't the organised genocide of your Victorian industrialism.'

'If the government doesn't legislate against it, it can only mean your rulers wink at it.'

'Would you say because the British government keeps throwing out Fenner Brockway's Bill that makes race discrimination illegal, then government winks at this bad practice?' Tunji says impatiently.

'Yes. Or if it doesn't, it's indifferent. Just as bad.'

'Give us time, give us time. Sometimes I'm tempted to ask you to stay longer with us to try and help us reconstruct.'

'Irony apart, sometimes I feel wanted, and then just as often I feel someone is very glad to see me go. By the way, has there been a war here?'

'Why?'

'I think you said *reconstruct*.'

Tunji laughs.

'Tell me,' I say, 'I've always been treated most respectfully by the police here – at police stations and on the road. All too overwhelming, of course, for a South African. But I'm told they are pretty tough with illiterate-looking or simple folk. Why?'

'Yes. I think they are like police all over. Because they're generally not liked, don't they compensate by power demonstration? And what's the level of education in our Force after all?'

And so we continue to enjoy the Nigerian sun and the gloriously cool evenings in abundance; the shilling night clubs, and high-life dancing; and now and again we sit and listen to the earthy juju high-life in some smaller, misty and intimate joint, where the combo usually consists of an electric guitar, two drums, a miniature xylophone and the players sing with throaty gusto. When I fail to understand one aspect of Nigeria or another, I know Tunji is here to interpret things for me. There are those features which simply hit you between the eyes at a glance and then you feel you have entered a country too huge for you even to bother to ask: questions seem so superfluous, so irrelevant, even in their relevancy.

I'm thinking of the beggars, blind and crippled, that swarm Lagos, Ibadan and other towns and cities; mostly from the Northern Region. Often a bunch of blind women can be seen with children on their backs or a female cripple on her knees with a child in the arms of a companion – all this, no doubt, to tug at the onlookers' heartstrings. The size of the whole social malady makes you feel so insignificant.

And if you are a teacher like me, you shrink back in your protective shell and cuddle in the vanity that you are wanted, because Nigeria's desperate need for teachers is not going to be fully met for a long time. Again, if you are an exile, like me, you'll be happiest if you don't try to live on your own terms.

And the slums? – those ulcerous portions of Lagos (now being cleared) and Ibadan (far from being cleared, even on blueprint). Nothing in South Africa comes near some of these areas. Yet there is no sign of depression in Nigerian slum living: an invincible gaiety and an intensity of being – yes. In South Africa there is depression that breeds violence, mental and physical, as an expression of the same intensity of being. As it was in Gorky's world, suffering man at one stage turns his anger against himself and neighbour.

All this notwithstanding, Tunji, the symbol of the new Nigeria, feels confident. He has come into his own. He has become, to the millions still under the heel in this continent, the epitome of the fulfilment towards which Africa is striving.

'I wish our people realised this one thing,' Tunji remarks, 'that it's not enough that they are free to sign treaties, agreements and other documents. They've got to be mentally free, not tethered to a system of values simply because it's European. Talk of brainwashing – we need it badly.'

As a 'been-to', Tunji, like so many others of his status, has absorbed a good deal of Western thought. His cultural entertainment is not that of villagers or peri-urban folk. He thinks in terms of Western democracy. Only when he feels a little guilty that all these Western conveniences – material and philosophic – have muffled the echoes of his traditional past, only at such times does he become enthusiastic about the 'African personality'. But he feels consoled when he remembers his last defences will never be broken down: his national dress, his food habits, his language.

Something radiates from him when he is in this national attitude that tells you he feels he has arrived. Tricky business, this national consciousness: especially when you keep thinking that it is your duty to vindicate yourself as a black man, to show that you are worthy of the epithet *emergent*, even while you try to make yourself heard above the tin-can clatter of commercial radio and vie with your syndicated 'Maverick' for first consideration on the country's TV programmes. For although his part of the country boasts the first TV in Africa, Tunji realises all too poignantly that this is a cultural invasion of no mean implications.

(1961)

A Ballad of Oyo

Ishola (also called Mama-Jimi because her first son was Jimi) found a tramp on her counter slab at Oyo's central market, where she took her stand each day to sell vegetables and fruit. Furiously she poked the grimy bundle with a broom to tell him a few things he had better hear: there are several other places where he could sleep; she sells food off this counter, not firewood – like him; so he thought to lie on a cool slab on a hot night, eh? – why does he not sleep under a running tap? And so on. With a sense of revulsion she washed the counter.

These days, when market day began, it also meant that Ishola was going to have to listen to her elder sister's endless prattling during which she spun words and words about the younger sister's being a fool to keep a useless husband like Balogun in food and clothing. Off and on, for three months, Ishola had tried to fight against the decision to tell Balogun to go look for another wife while she went her own way. Oh, why did her sister have to blabber like this? Did her sister think that she, Ishola, liked being kicked about by her man the way Balogun did? Her sister might well go on like this, but she could not divine the burning questions that churned inside Ishola.

That is right Ishola, her sister, who sold rice next to her, would say. You are everybody's fool, are you not? Lie still like that and let him come and sit and play drums on you and go off and get drunk on palm wine, come back and beat you, scatter the children – children of his palm wine-stained blood, (spitting) like a hawk landing among chicks then you have no one to blame only your stupid head (pushing her other breast forcibly into her baby's mouth for emphasis). How long has he been giving you so much pain like this? How long are you going to try to clean a pig that goes back into the mud? You are going to eat grass very soon you will tell me and do not keep complaining to me about his ways if my advice means nothing to you.

And so goes the story of Ishola, Ishola who was called Mama-Jimi, a mother of three children. Slender, dark and smooth skin with piercing eyes that must have seen through dark nights.

Day and night the women of Oyo walk the black road, the road of tarmac to and from the market. They can be seen walking riding the dawn, walking into sunrise; figures can be seen, slender as twilight; their feet feel every inch of the tarmac, but their wares press down on the head and the neck takes the strain, while the hip and legs propel the body forward. A woman here, a woman there in the drove has her arm raised in a loop, a loop of endurance, to support the load, while the other arm holds a suckling child in a loop, a loop of love. They must walk fast, almost in a trot, so that they may not feel the pain of the weight so much.

The week before the week before Mama-Jimi started for Oyo Market, her body feeling the seed of another child grow that had not yet begun to give her sweet torment, bitter ecstasy in the stomach. The night before her husband had told her he was going to the north to see his other wives. He would come back – when? When he was full of them and they of him, Mama-Jimi knew. When he should have made sure that the small trade each was doing went well, he said.

Mama-Jimi looked at his shadow quivering on the wall in the light of the oil lamp as he stooped over her and loneliness swept over her in a flood. They loved and they remained a promontory rising above the flood. And Mama-Tunji again took her place in the order of things: one of three wives giving all of her to one she loved and taking what was given by her

man with a glad heart. Oyo will always be Oyo whatever
happens to it, the market will always be there, come rain, come
blood, come malaria.

It was the week before only the week before when the rain
caught the market women on the tarmac to market. The sky
burst and the rain caught the market women on the tarmac
to market. The sky burst and the rain came down with power.
It rumbled down the road in rivulets. Mama-Jimi felt the load
inside become heavy knotting up beneath her navel. Her feet
became heavy, the hips failed to twist. But she tried to push on.
She could see the others way ahead through the grey of the
rain. Mama-Jimi's thoughts were on the market, the market of
Oyo: she must reach it. For if she should fall, she thought, or
feel sicker, other women were there.

But the woman sagged and fell and dragged herself out of
the road. She felt the blood oozing, warm and cold. A life was
running out of her, she was sure of it. A life dead just as soon
as born and sprouting in her ...

Two women found her body on the roadside: cold, wet.

Whispers bounced and rebounced at the market that Mama-
Jimi was dead, dead, Mama-Jimi was gone, gone in the rain.

Did she know it was there?

Ehe, she did she told me so.

And her man gone to the north, a-ah? So it is said.

Are they going to call him? They must. Only yesterday
night we were together and she was glad she was going to give
her man a second child.

To die when your people are far far away from you, a-ah!

We are most of us strangers here.

It is true.

This was a week before, and the market at Oyo jingles and
buzzes and groans, but it goes on as it has done for many years
before when the first Alafin came here.

You know what the market is like every morning, not so?
Babbling tongues, angry tongues, silent tongues. Down there

a woman was suckling a baby while she sold. Near to Ishola a woman was eating gari and okaran and gravy out of a coloured enamel bowl. Someone else next to her handled her sales for her. As the heat mounted a lad was pouring water on bunches of lettuce to keep them from wilting and thus refusing to be sold. But the lad seemed to be wilting himself, because as soon as he leaned back against a pole, sleep seized him and his head tilted back helplessly like a man having a shave in a barber's chair.

The mouth opened and the lettuce lost its importance for a while. Mostly oyingbo – white people – came to buy lettuce. On and off while he slept, someone sprinkled water on his face. This seldom jolted him out of his stupor. He merely ran his hand over his face, stared at the lettuce and then poured water on it. Some fat women opposite Ishola's counter were shouting and one seldom knew whether they were angry or simply zealous. They also splashed water over the pork they were selling so as to keep away blue flies that insisted on sitting on it. All the would-be buyers who stood at the pork counter fingered the pieces: they lifted them up, turned them round, put them back, picked them up again. There was no exchange of smiles here.

Ten shillings, said the pork woman who herself seemed to have been wallowing in grease.

Four shillings, suggested the customer.

Eight shillings last.

Five (taking it and putting it back as if disgusted).

Seven las' price.

With a long-drawn sound between the teeth to signify disgust, the customer left. The pork woman looked at her fellow vendor, as if to say Stupid customers!

Oyingbo women did not buy meat at these markets. They said they were appalled by the number of hands that clutched at it. They bought imported meat in the provision stores at prices fixed seemingly to annoy expatriates. One missionary woman had been known to bring a scale for the vendor to weigh the meat in order to get her money's worth. What! she had exclaimed, you don't weigh meat in this market? Ridiculous! The meat woman had looked baffled. The next time the missionary brought her own balance. This time *they* thought something was ridiculous, and they laughed to show it. Even after weighing a piece, she found that she still had to haggle and bargain. Enthusiasm had flagged on her part and after this she came to the market only to rescue some of the lettuce and parsley from continual drenching and to buy fruit.

So did the other white women. One of them turned round in answer to a shout from a vendor, Custumah, custumah! She approached Ishola's counter where there were heaps of carrots and tomatoes. She was smiling as one is expected to do from behind a counter.

Nice car-*rot* madam.

How much?

Shilling (picking up a bunch).

Sixpence.

No madam, shilling (smiling).

Sixpence.

Ha-much madam wan' pay? (with no smile).

All right, seven pence.

Ni'pence.

Seven.

No, 'gree madam (smiling).

The customer realised that she had come to the end of the road. She yielded, but not before saying Ninepence is too much for these.

A-ah madam. If not to say madam she buy for me many times I coul' 'ave took more moni for you.

Towards sunset Ishola packed up. She had made up her mind to go to Baba Dejo, the president of the court of the local authority. She firmly believed that the old man had taken a bribe. Either her father-in-law or Balogun himself, her delinquent husband, could have offered it. This, she believed must be the reason why the court could not hold a hearing of her case against her husband. Twice Ishola had asked him to hear her case. Each time the old man said something to delay it. The old fox, she thought. This time she fixed simply on putting five pounds in front of the president. He cannot refuse so much money, Ishola thought. But go back to that animal of a husband, never – no more, he is going to kill me one of these days I do not want to die I do not want to die for nothing I want to work for my children I want to send them to school I do not want them to grow old on the market place and die counting money and finding none. Baba Dejo must take the money he must listen to my case and let the law tell Balogun to leave me alone with the children and go his way I will go mine I know his father has gone and bribed him to keep the matter out of the court and why? – because he does not want to lose his son's children and because – I do not know he is very fond of me he has always stood up for me against his son – yes he loves me but I am married to his son not to him and his love does not cure his son's self-made madness. Lijadu loves me and I want him let my heart burst into many pieces if he does not take me as his wife I want him because he has such a pure heart.

Ishola was thinking of the day Lijadu came to fetch her in his car and they went to Ijebude for that weekend of love and heartbreaks: heartbreaks because she was someone else's wife someone who did not care for her and even then had gone to Warri without telling her. Now Lijadu was ready to give Balogun the equivalent of the bride price he had paid to Ishola's parents and so release her to become his wife. Balogun and his father had refused Lijadu's money.

Just what irritates me so, Ishola thought. I could burst into a hundred parts so much it fills me with anger. So they want to stop me from leaving their useless son, useless like dry leaves falling from a tree. Just this makes me mad and I feel I want to stand in the middle of the road and shout so as everyone can hear me. That man! – live with him again? He beats me he leaves me no money he grows fat on my money he does not care for the children the children of his own own blood from his very own hanging things …

I wonder how much the old man will want? The thought flashed across Ishola's mind, like a streak of lightning that rips across the milling clouds, illuminating the sky's commotion all the more.

If your father-in-law Mushin were not my friend, says the president of the court, Dejo, when Ishola tells him the business of his visit, I should not let you come and speak to me on a matter like this. It is to be spoken in court only.

You do not want me to bring it to court sir.

I would do it if, if –

How much, sir?

Give me what you have, my daughter. He looks disdainful in the face as he says so. It does not please the young woman. He takes five pounds in paper money from her hand.

What is this I hear from your father-in-law, that you want to leave your husband? Ishola feels resentful at the thought that her case must have been chewed dead by these old men. But she presses the lid hard to keep her feelings from bubbling over. I beg that you listen, sir, she says. Balogun beats me he does not work he eats and sleeps he does not care for the children of his own own blood, sir, he drinks too much palm wine this is too much I have had a long heart to carry him so far but this is the end of everything no no this is all I can carry.

Is he a man in bed?

Not when he is drunk and that is many times sir. She was looking at the floor at this time.

Hm, that is bad that is bad my child, that is bad. What does he say when you talk to him about his ways?

Nothing, sir. He just listens he listens and just listens that is all.

A man has strange ways and strange thoughts.

There is silence.

So he drinks himself stupid. I know there are certain places in Oyo where you can hear the name of Balogun spoken as if he were something that smells very bad. So he drinks himself stupid until he is too flabby to do his work in bed, a-ah! How many children have you by the way?

Three, sir.

The youngest is how old?

Two years, sir.

If a man gets too drunk to hoe a field another man will and he shall regret, he will see. He seems to be talking to himself. But a man who comes home only as a he-goat on heat, the old man continues, and not as a helper and father is useless. I will tell him that I will tell Balogun that myself. Animals look for food for their mates and their brood, why cannot a man?

You have talked to him twice before, sir.

Oh yes oh yes I have my child I know.

Silence.

But your father-in-law Mushin loves you so much so much my child.

I love him too but I am his son's wife not his.

You speak the truth there.

Silence.

It would break his heart all the same. Look at it whichever way you like. You fill a space left in his heart by the death of his wife and often defiled by the deeds of a worthless son. Dejo's face is one deep shadow of gravity.

I do not like that boy Balogun not one little moment, he goes on, but his father will weep because he holds you like his own own daughter.

Ishola's head is full of noises and echoes of noises, for she has heard all this a few times before. She has determined her course and she shall not allow her tender sentiments to take her out of it, she mustn't, no, not now. Perhaps after, when tender feelings will be pointless. She still bears a little love for Balogun, but she wants her heart to be like a boulder so as not to give way.

Let me go and call my wife to talk with you more about

this, Old Dejo says as he leaves the room. As he does so, he stretches out his hand to place a few crumpled notes of money in Ishola's hand, whispering Your heart is kind, my child, it is enough that you showed the heart to give, so take it back.

Ishola feels a warm and cold air sweep over and through her. She trembles a little and she feels as if something were dangling in space and must fall soon.

Old Dejo's wife enters, round-bellied: the very presence of life's huge expectation.

But – such an old man! Ishola thinks ...

I can see it in her eyes Balogun I can see it in her eyes, Mushin said in his son's house one morning. Ishola is going to leave us.

She is at the market now, Papa. She loves me too much to do a foolish thing like that.

When are you going to wake up you useless boy. He gasped, as he had often done before. What kind of creature was given me for a son! What does your mother say from the other world to see you like this?

Balogun poured himself palm wine and drank and drank and drank. I can see the blade of a cutlass coming to slash at my heart, the older man said, I can feel it coming.

Go and rest father, you are tired.

And Balogun walked out into the blazing shimmering sun, stopped to buy cigarettes at a small stall on the roadside and walked on, the very picture of aimlessness.

When are you going to stop fooling like this with Balogun I ask you? Ishola's sister said rasping out as she sat behind her counter. Her baby who was sucking looked up into her face with slight but mute concern in its eyes.

She does not know she does know this woman she ... will never know she will know what I am made of ...

I would never allow a man to come stinking of drink near me in the blankets (spitting). I told you long ago to go to court and each time you allow that old Dejo with his fat wife to talk you out of it. Are you a daughter of my father?

Oh what a tiresome tongue sister has ... You wait you, you just wait ...

Just a black drunken swine that is what he is. A swine is even better because it can look for rubbish to eat. Balogun does not know what people are he would not go a long way with me no he would not he does not know people. Eat sleep and lay a pile of dung, eat sleep and lay a pile of dung while men of his age group are working: the woman who gave birth to that man ...!

Sister! Leave that poor woman to lie quiet in her grave!

I will but not that wine-bloated creature called Balogun.

Lijadu must not forget to send Mushin's money of the bride-price ...

That piece of pork? a customer asked.

Ten shillings.

Five.

Nine.

Six.

No 'gree.

Six and six.

No 'gree. Eight las' price.

Seven.

No 'gree.

And the market roar and chatter and laughter and exclamations and smells put together seemed to be a live symphony quite independent of the people milling around.

Black shit! Ishola's sister carried on ...

Ishola was out of Oyo in the evening, going towards Oshogbo with her three children. Lijadu would follow the next day and join them in a small village thirty miles out so as to make pursuit fruitless.

Lijadu joined her at noon the next day, looking pale and blue and shaken.

What is it with you Lijadu? Why are you so pale? Are you sick?

Silence.

Lijadu what is it?

He sat on the ground and said Mushin has passed away. He passed away about midnight. One of the neighbours found him lying cold in the passage. People say they heard him cry the last time: Ishola, my grandchildren!

Ishola could not move for a few moments. She seemed frozen cold cold cold.

At break of day each morning you will see the women of Oyo with their baskets on their heads. You can see them on the black tarmac going to the market, their bodies twisting at the hip the strong hip. You can see their feet feel their way on the dark tarmac as they ride the dawn, riding into daylight. Their figures are slender as twilight. You can see Ishola, too, because she came back, came back to us. She told us that when she heard of the death of her father-in-law she thought This is not good for my future life with Lijadu I will go back to that cripple.

The Barber of Bariga

'Ha ha ha! Na be fonny worl' dees. A mahn mos' always have to lawve ay-gain un ay-gain.'

Anofi turned the round head to the left with his large hand as if he were spinning a toy. The head was indeed getting out of hand as Bashiru laughed riotously. And he continued to plough through his client's hair with his clippers. Anofi came to Bashiru's house each month to 'barb' his hair, as they say.

'Who be your woman dees mont', chief?' Anofi asked with tight-jawed grimness.

'Ha ha ha! A yong yong tender t'ing, my frien'.'

'Bot you no be happy for your t'ree wive?'

'Yes, bot I wan' be more happy. You know what oyingbo say: he say De more de merry merrier merriest. Now no be vex my frien' Anofi, no be vex. I see for mirror na be so.'

The barber was annoyed indeed to see the lines of his frown on the forehead. He pushed his client's head to one side with a fury-driven thumb.

'No, no be vex me. I jos' be feah.'

'For wettin' you feah?'

'She be married.'

'Y-yes. Bot no be worry she no be ole she be fresh un quick un lawvely as anyt'ing. Yes, yes, clever to make lawve and stupid for up deer.' He indicated his head.

'Das for why I be feah, chief. Why no leave um de married wawn? Na be plenty woman wit'out man for dis Lagos.' Anofi drew breath through his teeth to make a hissing noise as a sign of disgust.

Another shove of the head with his finger.

'Take time take time, no be vex for my head, Anofi.'

'Who's she?'

'A secret.'

There was a brief pause.

'People be talkin' for dis in Bariga,' Anofi said.

'What people – wettin' dey talk?'

'You un som' woman.'

'Dey say who?'

Anofi knew Bashiru's head very well; round with an eternal pimple or blackhead on the side near the ear and an old scar in the form of a slight dent in the flesh of the skull. It was an easy head to handle for a cut. Often when Anofi propelled his clippers through the hair, he seemed to fondle the head, pushing it deftly this way and that with his thumb or forefinger. The barber seemed to own the head; as if there were a point of identity with it, as if he would be hurt if someone else gave it a haircut. As his clippers nibbled down the slopes, he seemed more conscious of his skill. And his client relaxed the more, conscious of his physical ease and the good job being done of his cut.

The barber put the finishing touches and Bashiru looked tidy. He grunted approval, like a purring oversized cat that is being stroked, when Anofi held the mirror behind for him to see the trimming effects at the back of his head.

'T'ank you,' Bashiru said, giving the barber three shillings and adjusting his agbada. 'Odabo, sah – remain in peace.'

He went out into the sun. He knew his father would be entertaining the waiting customers in his shop to some of his funny stories.

For the last ten years or so Anofi's father came to sit in the shop while the barber worked. The old man featured in his memory mostly in the posture in which he sat on the bench in the shop: one leg bent and resting almost all on the bench, and the other bent leg shooting up vertically so that he could plant his elbow on the knee and prop up the head with his open palm. The old man often struck that pose when he was sure what he said would be regarded as expert counsel or a statement that could brook no argument. He was more often sure than not, and he seldom failed to raise an argument with the clients. Each morning he came into the shop through the back door, shuffled his feet to the front door, looking cool in his buba and surveyed the street life. Then he turned round and went to take his post on the bench.

Often Anofi's old man spoke in a monotone, apparently not caring whether anyone was listening or not. Or he chewed away at his kola nut, his jaws moving like a goat's. Indeed there was something goatlike about his face, altogether; almost sneezed as weakly and coughed as fussily as a goat. When he smiled to deride an argument, he would emphasise this by stretching out his lips so as to push out bits of kola nut with the inside lining of his cheeks so they should not escape the onslaught of his scattered molars. In the process his rusty-coloured front teeth came into full view, looking like the remaining few pillars of a demolished building.

Anofi went on with his work, seldom turning round to engage in conversation with his father. When he was working his father hovered somewhere in his subconscious or somewhere on the fringe of awareness. On one of the few occasions when father and son exchanged ideas, the older man said in the middle of the morning, 'I am sure if you collected all the hair you cut off and found someone to buy it, you would get rich.' He chewed his stick for cleaning his teeth.

'Rich – how, Papa?'

'I don't know why the white man cannot use people's hair.'

'Why, Papa?'

'The white people use sheep's hair, the hair of wild animals.'

Now he moved his stick, which had split into broomlike bristles at the end, in vertical strokes. All this gave his words a sarcastic ring he may not have intended them to contain.

'Are you joking, Papa?'

'No.'

'But people's hair is so dirty.' Anofi's body twitched from a sensation of disgust.

'The white man can do many things. He can make machines to wash the hair. The white man seems to be clever.'

'Why always white man white man? Cannot the black man do these things?' Anofi said in spite of his disgust.

'What machines have we ever made?'

'But we use them very well. You, Papa, you are like the woman who came out of the office of the dentist and said to us who were waiting, "Oyingbo – the white man is wonderful, he has made things to take out a tooth without pain." And you know who had taken out her tooth? A Black woman doctor. Oho, you are like that.'

There was a moment of silence while the client was shaking off hair from his clothes, slapping the back of his neck several times. Then he straightened up. Looking at Anofi's father he took out a ballpoint pen. 'Look,' the customer said. He pressed the end of the protruding stick in so that the writing tip shot out. He pressed the clip and the tip disappeared. He repeated the operation a few times and then said: 'Na whitemahn na wonderful – o. Look wettin' he make.' He smiled and walked out, leaving Anofi in fits of laughter from which he only recovered several minutes later. Papa looked upset and, to express it, he noisily sucked air through the central gap between the top biting teeth in order to push in a morsel of kola nut.

Most times Anofi said very little, and looked exasperatingly unruffled. It seemed that he never wanted to stir up things. He seemed incapable of nervous tension, of anger or malice.

He saw much of what happened in the street through the window. Masqueraders passed by, frightening children and beating drums, sprawling all over the place and prancing as if they itched to do something desperate or exciting. 'They are looking for fun, and they will get it,' Anofi would say to himself. Wedding and funeral processions passed by and groups of women in party uniform – on all these, he seldom voiced a comment. He consciously or unconsciously refused to be emotionally involved, seeming to despise the whole show. He did not, however, despise it. He liked much of the music booming out of the loudspeaker in the opposite shop where they played gramophone records or opened the radio throughout the day.

The current high-life favourite was 'Corner Love'. The vocalist said how much he disliked 'corner love' and mistrusted it. He warned the young woman against the lad who drew her into a street corner to propose love. 'I no like corner-corner love', the singer insisted forebodingly. One customer thought the singer was wasting his time and vocal energy because 'na be no corner-lawve for dis Lagos a-ah!! He jos tok-tok for not'ing cawm ot for his head. If to say you hask 'im he woul'n't know.'

One Saturday morning a car drove down the street with a white couple in it. Anofi was moving towards his signboard EXPERT BARBAR to adjust it (the 'r' in *expert* perched on top of the 'e' and the 't' with a sign to indicate that the signwriter had forgotten it, or simply had not known it should be there). He saw the car stop at the crossroads and a cyclist drive into a wedge between the car and a wall. Just then, the car moved again. To Anofi, who had stopped short in front of his signboard, it was quite clear that the cyclist was going to be in trouble.

The bumper caught the spokes of the front wheel. The rider was unseated. The rider was suspended in air for a split second, his agbada ballooning as he made the forced landing, with a cry, 'What ees wrong!'

The driver pulled up short in the middle of the cross street on sensing the trouble, by which time Anofi was in a seizure of torrential laughter, such as he was never known to have the capacity for. He did not move away from the signboard, but clung to one of the two poles holding it up as if he were afraid he would take off.

In a short time a number of people had gathered at the place of the accident. The white man was having an argument with the cyclist who was claiming money for repairs. Always people gathered around some place where something was happening that was not daily routine: a man changing a tyre; a petrol attendant checking tyres; a motorist stopping to drink tea out of a flask and so on. Whenever there had been an accident, the crowd had many observations and opinions to air, far more of the latter than the former.

The white man soon felt overwhelmed by the presence of the chattering and murmuring crowd and anger was beginning to choke him. The cyclist was now clearly crying. Small children pointed fingers at him and giggled. He looked at his agbada in between complaining and claiming compensation.

Suddenly the white woman came out of the car. She seemed beside herself with fury. She started to drag her husband back to the car, shouting to the cyclist the while: 'Go to the police then, go to the police and have us arrested, but you're not getting a farthing out of us!' Then again, 'Why don't you go and report the matter if you're not satisfied? You came in between the car and the fence.' Dropping her voice a little, 'Let's go, Andrew, let's go. Come-come into the car. We've got to go, we haven't got time to be wasting listening to this silly talk.'

The man Andrew put the brakes on somewhere in his legs. He was tall and thin and his small head was swaying above all the others. His face was a deep pink from wanton perspiration. He was also suppressing an itching sensation in one of his now wet armpits. He felt if he scratched it now it would blunt the edge of the point he was trying to make, like suddenly coughing in the middle or at the beginning of a venomous phrase during a quarrel or a reprimand. Perhaps he did not want to feel that he had arbitrarily decided that he was in the right, if in fact the other man was. And then there was a chance that they might both be wrong or right. Moreover, the other man's crying act was embarrassing him.

'No go say I um seely,' the cyclist barked.

'I think you're just being silly,' the woman insisted.

'Joo can't abuse me like dat, a-ah. It's un insolt. I say joo can't abuse me. Um not your stewart.'

'No, you're too silly to be anybody's stewart.'

'A-Ah, she's abusing me ay-gain, a-ah! Do you hear-ah?' Then he broke into Yoruba, definitely appealing to the sensibilities of the crowd.

'Slap her!' someone shouted.

'If not to say she's a woo-man, I coul' 'ave slapped her. But what is she besides – just oyingbo.'

The woman, realising that Andrew was not obeying her command, left the crowd and walked towards Anofi, who was still standing by the signboard. He had only just recovered from his fits of laughing.

'You were looking at us as we were coming on, what did you see? Please tell them what you saw.' *Them* referred to the crowd, just as if she had begun to accept the incident as a communal concern.

They looked in the direction of the barber-shop.

Anofi shrugged his narrow shoulders, shook his head: 'I never know, I never see not'ing, I mean moch.' And he walked into his shop.

The woman gave a deep sigh and she said to Andrew again, 'Let's go, it'll do us no good talking like this.'

'Let's give the man ten shillings for his repairs.'

'Over my dead body!'

He took out the money and walked towards the cyclist with his arm outstretched.

'Andrew, come here! Don't just give away money like that!'

He was just barely able to hear the cyclist say: 'T'ank you. Na we be frien's now.' There was loud cheering from the group of people as though an armistice had been declared. He went to join his protesting wife in the car, feeling anything but heroic.

'Between that wretched lying barber and your stupid self,'

she said, 'the devil alone knows how these people mean to build a nation.'

'That's a problem for the nation-builders, darling. Besides, how can you be sure that simply because a man was looking at us, as you say the barber was doing, he must have seen what happened?'

'Oh he knows he did.' She looked in the direction of the shop door and saw that Anofi was looking at them. 'The African always wins when those of his kind are in authority.'

'It's *our* turn to learn that lesson, darling.'

And the car shot forward.

There must have been several times when Anofi himself could not say whether he had actually seen what he thought he had seen, or in his perpetual mood of detachment he told himself that he was not seeing what he was seeing. When a blind beggar came to his door, he dug his hand into his pocket, took out a coin and, as if in a dream, walked to the door and dropped it in the beggar's enamel bowl. Three blind women might stop at his door with children on their backs. They would wail their incantations to Allah with heartrending effect, so that Anofi's father's jaws pounded harder on the kola nut and, with the aid of the tongue, drew air through the side teeth to hiss his bewilderment and pride. Anofi, for his part, usually went to the door in a kind of tremor to tell the party to move away. On approaching them, he saw their grey lifeless but solicitous eyes quivering beneath the eyelids, and he saw their red teeth and the footprints of smallpox on their faces. And something deep deep down in the pit of his stomach would stir. He would give something and return quickly to his customer.

'These beggars!' a customer would sometimes say. 'Dey give too moch troble, a-ah! Dey be blind nu dey go born piccin, a-ah! Foolish nort'erner woman.'

Anofi would keep mute, some chord inside him still quivering.

About a month after the last haircut Anofi gave Bashiru, the man of property, a large man entered the shop and literally threw himself on to a bench near Anofi's father. He was quite out of breath. Anofi's old father felt very tiny near such a mountain of man and it irritated him.

'Have you ever hear soch a t'ing Anofi,' Okeke puffed out. 'I go kill him true, believe me I go slaughter dat man. He goes ay-bout wit' a dead title, dead-dead title and rascally t'ings.'

'Who's dat,' Anofi asked.

'Bashiru.'

'Wettin' he don'?'

'He t'ink becos na he be rich,' and he began ticking the items off his sausage-like fingers, 'he got plenty moni, plenty houses, plenty upstairs, plenty wives, plenty piccin, plenty farm, so he can't keep his man inside his pants for his wives only. Even he take oder people's wives too.'

'Bot wettin' he don'?'

'Look um. His grand-dad don' eat his chief's title. His dad don' try to force it out to be made chief un he don' fail. Bot his dad was clever un he don' take oder people's houses un moni. He don' t'ief t'ief everyt'ing un now his son Bashiru take de blod of t'ief from his dad un t'ief t'ief wife un moni un houses all over now he be fat un rich ...'

'Wettin' he don'?'

'Foolish mahn, I tell him what Bashiru don' don' un he still hask what he don', a-ah! Na you be no idi-awt, Anofi.' He rose to take the chair for a cut. 'Bashiru be tryin' to t'ief my wife.'

'Your wife na she be wantin' to be t'iefed?'

'You make me vex, Anofi. How can my wife want to be t'iefed? Don't tell me you don't know ay-bout it. Everybody in Bariga knows it.'

The answer startled Anofi. Bashiru had boasted about his latest exploit, but he could never have thought that Okeke's wife would be so foolish as to be seduced.

'Moni ay-gain, you see for dat? Now I know Bashiru has

been takin' my wife when I'm wo'kin' in town. Believe me I go kill dat mahn. I no sleep at night becos of wawry, I don't chop becos of wawry and Bashiru chop chop bellyful becos he no wawry.'

'Please be no too vex I beg you Okeke. No be good to kill -o. Jos' beat him das all.'

Okeke's neck stiffened, and Anofi had to wait a few seconds before he could turn the man's head to a desired angle. So he did it, that Bashiru! he thought. Okeke's voice filled him with unhappy thoughts.

For a reason he could not explain he felt he was being sucked into the affair between the three persons. He did not know what was happening to him and he did not seem to have the power to resist being sucked in.

When Okeke left, he and his father looked at each other for a spell, as if their thoughts had found a confluence and were rushing down the same mainstream, and there was nothing more to say about it.

When two days later a message came to Anofi that Bashiru had died by accident at a wedding, he sensed evil in the air. He was called to come and shave Bashiru's head to prepare him for burial, according to the rules of a religious cult to which the deceased belonged. He soon found himself in the death room. The group of people in there made way for him to pass and kneel beside the corpse. He sat down and put the head on his lap. The thought that this head, the contour lines of which he knew so well, was now like a stone, made him shiver.

When there was still a patch of hair left, Anofi's clippers struck against something hard. He ran his clippers against the obstacle once more and the sound told him it was metal. He shaved around it until it emerged: the head of a nail that told him in no doubtful terms that it was a long thick one.

With a sudden movement the barber lifted up the head on to the pillow on the floor, jumped up and said to the people in the room: 'Why you no go tell me dat dis man was killed de way of a t'ief?'

He did not wait for a reply but dashed out of the house. Outside he stood still in the street. He stood like a man who, feeling a fever coming on, seems to be tuning in to the mechanism that is the body in an attempt to feel the throb of it, perhaps to reassure himself. Then he walked on.

Dusk was creeping in, but from the elevated end of the street where Anofi was the rusted iron roofs of Bariga's houses were still clearly defined in all their recklessly uneven outlines. Shopkeepers and petty street traders were pumping their pressure lamps. Soon lights would be exploding in various places from candles, pressure lamps and other manual contraptions. People coming in from Lagos where they worked. Anofi only faintly heard the continuous roar of human noises, absorbed as he was in other things.

'Make we walk togeder,' someone said coming from a side street.

Anofi merely looked at Okeke and walked on.

'You cawmin' from Bashiru's house?'

'Yes.' He was not sure whether he wanted to talk to someone or not. 'You don' kill man, Okeke.'

'Som' people dey don' kill um.'

'You don' kill man, Okeke,' Anofi repeated, as if his mind pounded at regular intervals, heedless of any other sound.

'Som' people not me. But he don' die way na he want.'

'You don' kill a *mahn*! A *mahn*, you don' take de life of a man to buy de lawve of a woman. Na be what kind of lawve dis? Not to say you can't beat your woman for stick, you savvy? You can beat your woman un kick her if she sleep for anoder man's bed, beat her un send her to hospitule. Na she got madness for head un hotness for flesh you can kick dem ot, dis madness and hotness. Not to kill anoder man a-ah.' He looked straight ahead of him all the time, as if there were no one beside him.

His insistence irritated Okeke, but it also made him uncomfortable. But he wasn't going to be frightened out of his course. All the time they walked on without looking at each other.

'Das how dey kill t'iefman for my contry,' Okeke said gloat-
ingly but with self-confidence. 'Bashiru don' t'ief som't'ing for
som'body.'

'Un you don' send um to kill.'

'Jos savvy me, Anofi, I no wan' no palaver me son of Okeke.
I hate big mahn strong mahn who eats from hand of de poor
people wi'out no moni, fat mahn who chop chop bellyful moni
dat is oder people's own. Now he t'inks he's God almighty un
he wan' chop oder people's wives a-ah!'

'Na you hate him becos he was rich and fat not becos he
don' t'ief your woman?'

'Is for same t'ing Anofi. You no be borned yesternight. Is
samet'ing. Poor man t'ief small small becos he's afraid for big
moni, rich man t'ief big becos he's afraid for big moni, rich man
t'ief big becos he got protec-shon un he buy police*mahn*.'

'Un your wife be fool woman un cheap if she stand for de
middle of de road for him to jomp on top of her.'

'If not to say you be my frien' I coul' 'ave feel vex. Bot even
you know Bashiru is not jos any cock. He got moni and no
woman fit for say no when she see moni in front of her eyes.'

'How you t'ink you escape for police?'

'Moni for his pocket un he shot op for mout' and let his
tongue sleep.'

'Even you don' get rich now, you? Okeke dis is a big terrible
t'ing. Even I nevah know what I go say for police an dey hask
me ...'

'Only what you saw for inside, his big dead head. Make you
say not'ing pass dat at all at all at all.'

'Why?'

'Becos Bashiru he don' make lawve for you wife too, idi-
awt! Wake op! She waitin' to tell you for house. See you nex'
tomorrow.'

Okeke left him.

Many things began to make sense to him. He saw his
wife's beauty for what it was. Indeed she leapt into his field
of awareness as she had seldom ever done in her physical

form. This rediscovery of her loveliness fused with the anger in him so that the world around him seemed so small, so overcrowded.

He made a detour without meaning to, often running into dead ends. He felt numb. 'Tomorrow,' he said aloud in his language and with an air of finality, 'we must go away from this place. The whole house.'

And as Anofi walked on, radio music exploded from a nearby shop and set his nerves quivering:

> No moni, no bus,
> Even na you be clever
> pass every-wawn:
> No moni, no bus.

Women and Their Men

Townships may burn; people may plunder and loot; police may shoot and unleash bloodthirsty hounds and let fly tear gas upon crowds; vehicles may overturn and go up in flames. Petrol bombs may go off – Soweto *boom*! Pretoria *boom*! Cape Town *boom*! Port Elizabeth *boom*! Durban *boom*! Sibasa *boom*! Middelburg *boom*! Kimberley *boom*!

People may be detained, strung up on a rafter in a cell, skulls may be bashed in, noses broken, necks twisted out of joint. All these and many more may throw a nation into unspeakable tremors. But still people will love and hate each other. People will still marry and divorce; they'll betray one another, slander one another. Man will still beat up wife; woman will maul another's face in a fit of jealousy. Children will defy parents, parents will renounce and disown children. Gangs will still shoot it out. Corpses will still be paraded to cemeteries on weekends … We shall weep and laugh. The preacher of Zion will still bellow his incantations and shuffle his feet to the beat of his praise song.

Woman will still cling on to a husband who does not want her any longer; cling to his corpse if that's all she'll ever own of his; cling maybe to a faint memory of kisses and embraces and sweet pledges and vows of long ago. How some women can remember – *man alive*! They may forgive all, but they forget nothing!

Like my mother, Madikolo. My father left us when we were ten and eight, my brother and I. Just packed his suitcase and left us in a municipal house we had been occupying barely two years.

I was too small to understand the full meaning of these

events. Quarrels ... Father pounding on the door and kicking it while threatening murder and cursing with a sluggish tongue, drunk. Mother sometimes locked him out and warned us not to open the door or else she'd chop us in pieces, pieces, pieces and toss them into the jaws of any stray mongrel.

But he was never violent. Never so much as pushed my mother. And mother never permitted an angry or disrespectful word from our lips when we talked to father.

'Are we going to carry you to bed like yesterday, Pa?' I asked innocently one evening as he slumped on to the sofa. He was from his favourite spot on the next block. In no time I felt a stinging cuff on the back of my head. If the dining table was not near me, I should have fallen flat on my face. 'No more of that when you talk to your father you hear me!'

One day my brother and I asked Mother, 'Why is Pa always drunk – a teacher shouldn't do such things, Ma.'

'He's your father,' was all she said. I always remember her sitting nights at the dining table, her arms folded, staring at the candle, or digging playfully – evidently absent-minded – into the wax around the wick with a matchstick. Many a time I watched shadows come and go on that sad face as the candle fire worked its gentle wickedness on the wax, diminishing it with every tick of the clock on the sideboard. Now I think back on it, you could almost measure Mother's thoughts and feelings by the length of each candle, by the amount of wax that had collected in the candlestick.

Try as I might, I found it difficult to recapture the happier days when father used to dandle me on his knee, give me a ride on his back when he walked the narrow border between the table and the walls on all fours or out on the veranda on weekends. The grim drinking days overtook those happy carefree times and nailed our family life on the ground, so that the present seemed never to move into the future, seemed to stay with us forever. And those happy days seemed so painfully distant ...

'He'll come back, my children,' Mother said repeatedly, 'he's still your father.' As I grew up, it became clear that those words did not contain a grain of what she really thought.

She kept us in school, in food and clothing on her measly factory pay.

We overheard snatches of conversation between Mother and her friends when they were visiting. Germiston ... another woman ... a schoolmistress ... a baby boy ... conducting a school choir at the music competitions ... drinking less ... doing correspondence courses for the BA degree ... his beautiful tenor voice back in form ... singing at community concerts ... Daveyton ... back to the bottle ... stuff like that.

'I'm going to a concert to hear your father,' Mother announced one Saturday. Just as if my father had walked into the house and said, 'Aren't you folks coming to hear me sing at the concert?'

'Where, Ma?' brother asked.

'Daveyton,' she said. 'Are you coming with me?'

I shook my head. 'Yes – yes!' my brother said eagerly.

Her face was all alight the next morning. She walked with a light step. Her body stood straight up as I watched her profile against the stove.

'Father sang beautifully,' my brother told me the next day. 'Ma told me in the train he had a sweet voice. And then she told me, "You should have heard him when he was still himself. Hear me tell you, Tumi, your father used to sing as if it was the last time people were ever going to hear him – the last time, I tell you." '

And still Mother held back a lot from us, and we didn't dare ask her what had driven or dragged him out of the house. I was sure her reply would be, 'Wait until you're grown up my children, these things are too heavy for you to understand.'

Our uncles and aunts on my father's side came less and less to our home. No, Uncle Sechaba did continue to come. But very little was said between the two grown-ups. Not like old times.

'Don't waste your time eating your heart away my sister,' I heard Uncle Sechaba say. 'Our whole family have given him up. Isaka hasn't been to see our mother in years, and it seems like we have buried him already. You have been a good wife and mother, too good for the likes of him.'

'I do not know,' Mother replied. 'I do not know any longer. I still love Isaka, he is the father of my children ... I do not know, truly I do not know any longer.'

June, 1976, was upon us. I was turning eighteen then. My brother had gone to teachers' college in the north. I was doing Standard Ten. We marched. The battle cry was DOWN WITH INFERIOR EDUCATION! WE WANT MORE AND BETTER SCHOOLS! TO HELL WITH AFRIKAANS! We marched from school to school. Dogs. Tear gas. Batons. Guns. Stones. Garbage cans. Panic. Frightened teachers. Frightened students. Fire. Window busting. Looking. And as we carried the dead, we were also on the run ...

There was a continuous humming in the winter air. It lingered there, broken only by gunshots and shrieks ...

That was the day Mother was down with flu and bronchitis. When night had fallen, and I was back home, something was smouldering inside me. The city was humming, the skies were humming ... Only then did I realise I had been marching side by side with death. It frightened me. I shivered. And then I felt as if my very body were humming too. As if the killing ground I had come from had exploded and taken on the size of the planet Earth, and there was a war going on at sea, in the skies, on land ...

'How was the day, Kiso?' Mother asked in a hoarse and feeble voice when I entered her bedroom. I was lost for words. I mumbled something like, 'It was a day of blood, Ma.' Beyond that I couldn't speak. I wanted to cry, but I didn't want to look foolish and soft in my mother's presence. Nor did I think there was anything for us to be proud of. There would have been cause for pride if we had been armed with guns and all those hundreds of children had died in a pitched battle. As it was, we were mere targets for training in marksmanship. Those police and soldiers were having a gay time. Disgust, contempt was all I could feel, added to which I felt utterly weary.

Her remark irritated me a bit. It sounded so irrelevant.

I sat down on her bed. The humming had stopped now. I felt being on my mother's bed was being back in the real world. A mother, the smell of flu, her voice – the voice and inner music of a mother's love. This was a reality I needed after a day so grotesque that it did not seem to have been made of hours, minutes, seconds. Even the sun had not risen, it seemed, had not ever set.

'How are you feeling, Ma?'

'Sick all over, my very bones seem to be soaking in a pool of pain that has no outlet. I shall be all right.'

You're always all right even when everything is wrong, I thought.

'Are you hungry?'

She shook her head. 'Tea is all I need just now. Do not bother to make me food. Before I forget, I have just heard that your father is teaching in a bush school in the Western Transvaal – Ga-Seleka. He was told to leave the school in Daveyton.'

I had nothing to say, wondering at the same time if my father was ever going to leave this house, for good ...

I dozed off into a fitful sleep, if one can even call it sleep – once I had slumped on my bed ...

We lost two years, as the Government closed down some of the schools and we couldn't enter others.

During that time I worked in a tobacco warehouse. Gruelling work. It came home to me then how important schooling is; that even when one is being taught a lot of crap that has nothing to do with one's real life as a black person, it is just enough to open one's mind. One is still able to see and feel what is missing. The journey from then on is one of self-education. One has to discover for one's self the truths about our life.

I decided to go to a bush school to finish Matric. Then followed two years of teacher training.

I was home at vacation time last year when my mother came with the news that my father had left us, as she put it. 'I have asked your Aunt Dineo to keep me company on the road to Seleka.'

Aunt Dineo was Ma's older sister.

'What do you want to do that for?' Shadi, Mother's closest friend, asked when she was visiting.

'He is my children's father, have you forgotten?'

It was Shadi's turn to empty her chest of all I knew she had in store for my mother. It seemed she was never going to stop to catch her breath.

'And then?' she exclaimed, her dark eyes wide open. 'A man leaves you and his children and doesn't come back for – how many years – for eight *years* – not months – and then you want to go and see his worthless remains – jo! Mehlolo – God of my fathers! Just look at you – look at your house – no ceiling, walls not plastered and painted, your furniture a disgrace like – like the trash Goldberg buys in Westdene and comes and sells to us – just because you're dragging your soul behind you – pining over a man who doesn't care for you – that is why you can live for so many years in such a gloomy house where you expect a bat to come in and make a nest on the rafters – you should long have started to love yourself woman – you hear what I'm saying – love yourself – the next thing you will be telling us is that you want to collect his corpse and bury it – son, just talk some sense into your mother here and stop her from making a laughing stock of herself.'

I knew at that very instant that it would be fruitless. My face must have shown it, because Shadi shrugged her shoulders and nodded her head a few times.

'You can very well say that,' Mother said, in a lifeless tone, 'you long divorced your man.'

'Yes I did – and me I didn't invent divorce – me the woman

called Shadi – and again it saved me from the misery of living
with a useless dumpling perched on two legs – and again I
am not one of those women who think that by carrying a man
on their back for years is going to turn him into the perfect
husband – any man who is waiting for a woman to mother him
– to restore his manhood for him can't have been made of good
clay in the first place – let *him* deal with his own uselessness
– and you should long have divorced that man. Look at your
two sons, Madikolo – you brought them up so well and single-
handed – you should have been feeling proud and started
to love yourself sister of mine. Me I started to live when I
divorced, *you*, you stopped loving yourself when he left you.'

'I have heard you, Shadi. But I *will* go and collect Isaka's
corpse. My sons will see him and remember they had a father
and were not born like the children of a stray cat among
dustbins.'

The rest of the story came with Aunt Dineo. The two
women travelled through rough country in a jeep a former
friend of my father's had offered, the owner driving. I had
refused to go. Like Shadi, I thought my mother was debasing
herself.

They were taken by the chief to a rondavel where my father
had lived. The chief had lots of praises to sing to the dead man
for having 'picked up' his school to a level his people could be
proud of. Aunt Dineo reported the chief as having said, 'This
was a strange man, this son of Madisha. You worked hard and
made schoolchildren sing like these skies these mountains
these trees these birds these cattle these stars all together in a
chorus – and then the great enemy took possession of you, son
of Madisha – this poison the white people make and drink. My
teachers found his body right in the bush, torn by thorns and
twigs, his clothes in tatters. Something was chasing after you
Madisha, we shall never know what it was. A man just to tear
through thornbush like that – something inside him has got
to have been chasing after him – I can tell you that – and then
death pulled him out of the jaws of the enemy ... There you

are now – the journey has come to an end for your lacerated body, son of Madisha. This jacket and these trousers are all that is left of his. He just gave away his furniture and clothing piece by piece before he took to the bush.'

One of father's brothers brought a coffin the very next day. When he realised Mother was determined to have the corpse he shouted impatiently, 'Then I'll take back my coffin – take care of your man's corpse – I'll have none of it!'

And the corpse was brought home.

(1983)

Crossing Over

I have come to tell you my husband that they are taking us away, this today. I have told you many times, have I not, that they are talking about it in the villages. The cloud that has been hanging over us is at last raining whiteman's urine and excrement upon us. These are bad times for us my husband hard times. Now the chief says he cannot do anything about it did you ever hear of a thing like that! The chief not able to do anything –

Hm – mehlolo! In the old days there was nothing a king could not do – when kings were men – today all chiefs are mere maggots. They have men's pants on but let lightning strike me down if I know what they have got hanging in those pants – truly the ancestors forgive me. Now they are coming with their lorries my man let me tell you they are not playing these white people – it is not small things they are planning. What did you say husband of mine? Oh, whiteman Fatamabele? – Van der Merwe is still here. But since you left my good man no one goes to work for him any more. Only that mad Rameetse looks after his pigs. Fatamabele has sold and lost all his other animals. The field lies waste and has become a good home for rabbits and snakes. People say this. We hear tell that Fatamabele goes to Manganeng for strong magic herbs from those great mountain doctors and that Rameetse's head has been shaken up by them. You remember how he always complained that an ant once entered his nostril while he was sleeping and now it is travelling up and down and feeding on his brains and mucus. Else why should a grown man still be working for Fatamabele, why should he be taking the pigs out only to chase after them back to the sty when the boerman has gone to Mashishing, to Lydenburg. But you wait, just you watch, Fatamabele's day is coming – this land will stink from a single dead rat, you will see, let me tell you.

Where are we going? Do I know? Only they know, the men with big fat heads and hearts like rocks. We hear tell it is very far far, away from here towards the mountains of the setting sun. Have I what husband of mine? Oh no, do not worry about him, I will talk to him myself. How can I forget, eh? Forgetting him will mean forgetting the pain you carried to your grave. Sleep in peace son of the ancestors. And our two sons the other end of the burial ground – I cannot go to them because the lorries are coming soon. But tell them I am not forsaking you or else I am not the daughter of Tudumo and my totem is not kubu, the hippopotamus. Tell them I am coming to lie here with you all when the long endless night closes my eyes at last. Oh why does this man Goromente, the Government, keep us apart – does he not know that we want to be buried where the Shades will see us – who wants to die away from where they sleep!

You wait, I will come back. Let me whisper in your ear – no one else knows my secret. Just you wait my man you hear! Something tells me I shall not be long coming to you. Eh? No, I feel no pain anywhere my heart is strong and even stronger when I talk with you like this. But something tells me my days will not stretch out any more. Now I must go my man. Did I tell you also that police – many many – are waiting at Mashishing so that they drive us like cattle if we refuse to move, or did I not? Ahhhh, being here with you husband of mine is a cure for my aching bones. Like the gentle winter sun that eases the body for the blood to flow and give you new strength. Being with you also reminds me each time that I should be tying up my little bundles to come home and join you. But spare my life, badimo, spare it until I shall have done the last duty. Did you call? How can you call me when I am here at your side? Now listen husband of mine, I have hidden the firemaker in a corner that I cannot forget. He will never think there is something like it so close to the farm.

'It is me calling you, Mama, you will have to stand up; we hear the lorries are just over the hill so we must be ready. Look the sun is already bright. Everyone is ready with their things.' The voice came from a woman approaching with her son.

'Ma-Selepe turned round. 'Hao, ngwana'ka, it is you!' she said, 'and my little husband too!'

The older woman took the eleven-year-old grandson, Lefanyana, by the hand and drew him closer to the grave. 'Here is your namesake husband of mine and here also is your daughter-in-law. Pray for us to the Mighty One and ask badimo, the ancestors, to bless us and lead the way out of this home ground.'

After a few moments of silence 'Ma-Selepe, daughter-in-law Baile and her grandson began the walk into sunrise towards the village.

The trucks came.

The chief and his council were ready to take orders from the whiteman Van Rensburg, who led the convoy of authority. He was in charge of the move. The trucks set aside for personal effects, such as linen, furniture and others, lined up for the people to load. Then the vehicles set aside to carry the people of the three villages moved in – some fifty-two thousand heads all told, the officials said. A few families that had a buggy here, a trolley there and a waggon with four oxen or donkeys used their own transport. Like Motau and his wife, who lived alone. They had a trolley and four oxen. The wife sat upright with her hands crossed on her lap.

'Hei, Koffie!' Motau yelled, 'mosela'mmago! Go where the others are going, jou bliksem se donder! Wena Josefa, move, move it bliksem! It is me in charge here. Whiteman is in charge of me I am in charge of you goddammet. Hei you, Tring-Tring, sewerenoto, trek! Pull – where are you heading, if you had any balls at all you would understand what is happening to us who have come out of the black womb. Moving us, moving us – they think we are mere rocks they can roll from here to there ... My parents and their parents and those before them lie buried here at Marulaneng ... Ke maloko feela, I can tell you, just cow dung, this whole business ... I never thought I would see the day when my body would lie on the ground so far away from our people's home dear woman of mine, *never*. The ancestors are weeping for us I know ... What does the government man in Tshwane take us for – pieces of furniture?'

'They have been weeping so long, oh, so long.' It was Motau's wife saying something, and yet she spoke so calmly, with all the weight of the moment pressing on her shoulders. 'We are too old to fight, my old man, death is our only saviour now. I just know it. Every time this leburu, the Boers, they call Goromente carries our people away from their burial ground, from the soil whose dust they have tasted all their lives, the older ones simply die as soon as they set foot in the new place. You remember our friends who have been to those faraway lands have told us these things.'

Motau's wife wept silently.

To suppress his own urge to bawl out into the pastoral silence, Motau sniffed and with a rapid gesture brushed his nose with the left wrist.

The rest of the journey of some three hundred kilometres was a time of sniffles, expletives, banter, praise songs to the oxen and to the Motau ancestors. 'Ma-Motau sat bolt upright, her eyes fixed straight ahead as if her man's monologue were mere noises that did not touch her. Over fifty years she had learned to absorb grief so that it became part of her whole being instead of reacting to the minute to minute ticking of its clock, as if it were an invasion from outside. This way she was able to encompass its pain, deal with it philosophically but without any consciously devised strategy. To encompass grief was to feel its walls, its roof, its floor, its nooks and crannies, its chemistry, to comprehend it in relation to the time and place that contained it, and then to live time, live place.

Somewhere Motau said, 'Do nuttin', do nuttin', cannot do anything dammet.'

'What is it you said?' as if to grab the opportunity for a brief diversion, to shift the weight burning its way into her shoulders, ever so slightly so that it presses on another point in the body.

'The chief says he can do nuttin', just plain nuttin', niks, hm!' Motau threw in the word 'nuttin' ', 'niks' into his native speech to sum up the contempt they had for the language in which orders always came to him and his people, whether directly from the whiteman or through the chief, who was a government agent.

'Do nuttin',' Motau kept repeating, 'ka modimo – by God! He got nuttin' between his thighs – that is what the fool means … fokawl! No balls but fat hanging belly, that's all …'

'I must go, Mama, I must go.'

'You are only sixteen, what do you think you can do without a piece of paper to show you can count and read and write?'

The boy Ramushu looks away, then his eyes rove round in the truck, registering one face after another: old, wrinkled, young, smooth. The pretty face of Mantwa. About his age, he'd say. Her own eyes spell bewilderment. He wonders if his eyes are like hers, seeming to cry out for help; like the young dove she now reminds him of that struggles to disentangle itself from birdlime he has laid to catch meat for the family, and only tying itself up more and more. All a silent struggle, except for the flap-flap-flap-frrrr-frrrr of the feathers as the bird thrashes about. And then he will release it from its misery and its fear by wringing its neck with one decisive movement of the hand.

Then the boy shakes his head vigorously, as if to shake himself back to consciousness. As the truck rocks the passengers over potholes and ditches the girl's face seems to Ramushu to change moods: bewilderment, fear, expectation …

Suddenly he comes back to what he was telling his mother. 'So many of my age group have gone to the whiteman's town.'

'Stop this foolish talk,' the mother says impatiently, 'you don't know what you are saying. Your father left, your elder brother, and now *you* want to leave me. Who is going to look after me and your sisters? Besides, do you want to grow up ignorant, your brains nothing but darkness in such a cruel world. Just look at me you boy, just look at me. Your father, myself, your brothers are all ignorant. This is why white people do us such evil as eclipses the sun, we are just plain ignorant, stupid. What do we understand about this journey, just you *tell* me, tell me boy? All we know is that we are face to face with the kind of evil – that is what leburu is – we have never known before in this world. If our children and grandchildren of their own free will refuse to allow some light to enter their brains, then the ancestors help us Almighty Spirit.'

Her last words sound desperate. Like one who suspects that her son has a defective mind.

'I do not know, Mama, I do not know. But I know I want to go. There is nothing for me here. I can read and write, what more do I need?'

'You need to know more which you cannot get outside school. People are not meant to grow like trees – just because they get water and food out from the ground. People have to grow in the brain and in the heart. We had only three years of school ourselves but our people, no matter they were your parents or not – our people helped us to know how to live, how to raise you. You will have nobody out there, and a person needs people.'

Silence follows as mother and son think more about preventing excessive rocking in the truck, the wheels grinding stone and earth over a rugged patch.

'Your father will not like this Ramushu. You must wait for him to come home and talk to him. I cannot let you go unless your father tells me to.' She knows that she is clinging to a straw in the sweep of events that are overtaking the people, but she keeps pushing her argument anyhow. Also, there is that fear in her right now, the realisation that her son may not be entirely misguided.

'The only reason he is not here is that his white people refused to release him. You heard the son of Ledimo give us the message, from his own lips. You heard it with your own ears. And your brothers are too far away for me to let them know your intentions.'

Ramushu is half listening, half engrossed in his own thoughts.

Clouds of dust are swirling all over and every passenger has a hand over the mouth, which opens only to cough. Women look at one another over garments wrapped round them up to the eyes. The people on the vehicle look like cargo that has neither say nor enthusiasm over the purpose of the journey or destination. Mute Fate is in charge here, whose high priest is the Pretoria government, who in turn delegates authority to the likes of Van Rensburg. These holy messengers' response to Pretoria's deity is always swift and sure. A fierce devotion propels them across their areas of jurisdiction. They seldom if ever feel that they owe anyone any courtesy, any kindness, any understanding in return for understanding. If someone accuses them of excesses on the side of cruelty, their stock response is, 'I'm only doing my duty.' Motau's interpretation is, 'They always say that these maburu, they always come up with donkey manure when they are being mean, which is always, the man means I am only doing what I love.'

Even when the dust has settled, 'Ma-Selepe is silent throughout much of the trip. She nods or shakes her head in reply to daughter-in-law Baile's questions.

'You must not be so sad Mama. What must your grandchildren feel then? You ought to be thankful through the ancestors that you still have a good son who looks after us all, who cares.'

'Where is he now, this today? Why has he not come when these maburu have turned our lives into dead and worthless toys, carried to a place that does not even have a name? – hm – babinatau!'

'Hao Mama, the place is called Marakong, did you not hear?'

'Wherever my people do not lie buried has no name. Wherever my afterbirth does not lie buried in a homestead has no name. What name they call it by is not something I can feel.'

She begins to weep. Quietly. Like a well yielding up its water. But she says while wiping her eyes with the corner of her shawl, 'I will not cry, no I will not, Selepe, I am not crying, you hear me, just you wait, I am not weeping.' She shakes her head to emphasise her statement.

Baile lays her hand gently on the older woman's shoulder, while her fourteen-year-old daughter and eleven-year-old Lefanyana (named for Grandpa Selepe) look on. They comprehend nothing in all this, but are buoyed up by their own childlike sense of adventure.

'The children's father will come, Mama, I know, Monope will come. Perhaps his white people would not let him off today. Has he not always come, has he not always brought us money and food and sometimes sent it through some other man!' In the usual affectionate banter in which she uses mother-in-law's pet-name, Baile concludes, 'Let us not hear you complain again Ngwana'Tabane, you hear.'

'Ma-Selepe continues to sniffle. Then she mumbles some words Baile cannot make out. Lefanyana fidgets and tries to crane his neck to get the full view of the landscape that seems to glide in the opposite direction. But from where he is sitting he can only see the sky and what is defined by the rear opening of the truck. His elder sister looks steadily at her grandmother. Her face is a picture of simple, bewildered compassion.

The old woman mumbles on, 'Tell the spirits I did not want to leave you behind at Marulaneng, son of Selepe. It is the pain of the times – father leaves wife and children, brother forsakes sister, sister leaves brother, children leave parents … How are these old feet of mine going to walk on new ground … Marakong, Marakong, let it go fart in the wind – where have you ever heard such a name for a place!'

Her granddaughter's contemplative eyes stay on the old woman, as if she were observing her for the first time. Shadows play on the child's face where innocence and bewilderment alternate with something that flashes an anticipation of adult concern and insight.

'Ma-Selepe looks at the sky and says, 'I smell rain. It is

coming, I know it.' No one responds aloud, except Baile who remarks almost irrelevantly, 'We are all exhausted, the sun beating down on us like this ...'

At sunset the next day they arrived at Marakong. All covered, it seemed with three hundred kilometres plus hours of red dust.

The rain came.

It was almost as if it had been programmed to fall just when they were laying out the tents brought by Van Rensburg's people. The rain lashed about and in no time the veld was waterlogged. Wherever the veld sagged under the fury of the storm it made small dams where the rain danced mercilessly. The water seemed to dally, not knowing where to go. Dallying was short-lived. For gashes appeared that made rivulets, which in turn cut across to provide channels for the water's escape.

The confusion that reigned among the newcomers was of another order. Screams, yells, shouts, arms flailing in the night; lanterns, shadows darting back and forth to find shelter that was not taking shape fast enough. Van Rensburg himself, if he was there, was invisible. But his people were trying frantically to erect the tents, several of the male newcomers themselves hauling pole and canvas this way and that under the lashing rain.

Soon after the downpour had started, Father O'Brien's name was passed from mouth to mouth among the people. 'He has come ... he is here ... Father O'Brien has come with his people ...'

He had been following hard on the caravan's trail. With trucks carrying canned and bagged and packaged food, a van carrying medicines and first-aid kits. His people raised a huge tent to contain them and the priest.

This Catholic priest had become a notorious name among all white officials engaged in forced removals. He had been speaking out for human rights in general and the African victim's rights in particular since 1964. Now he was embroiled in this Marulaneng-Marakong resettlement process. The officials always emphasised 'resettlement', which rang kinder in the critics' ears than 'forced removals' – the blunt truth. All African political movements had been banned. The State sent Nelson Mandela and some of his associates to Robben Island for life on charges of treason. Most other leaders, big and small, fled into exile, following those before them.

Whites had barricaded themselves with iron laws in fear of a black revolution. So they told themselves and one another, the propaganda machine of their government reinforcing their tribal myths, their image of themselves as the superior people. What they didn't tell themselves was the deeper truth: fear of themselves. Conscience seemed to have gone dead. Like a torch whose battery's life has run out as a result of its own acid ooze. But in reality this death had always been the warp and weft of the white man's history in this country.

Most other clergy who knew these removals were happening chose to leave it at that. They witnessed army trucks thundering past with loads and loads of humans for dumping in some location planned for the resettlement. The authorities knew that Father O'Brien was exploiting the privilege of being born white: he was not so vulnerable to the swift reflexes of a police state. The fact that he was priest in charge in the Jesuit mission of St Augustine, some ten kilometres east of Marulaneng, was but a secondary deterrent against police action. But all this infuriated the officials endlessly. The vast area of sprawling villages that constituted Marulaneng made it one of the most spectacular in the northern region of the old Transvaal Province. Its hills and valleys, its vegetation, were the perpetual envy of the whiteman, provoking the rhetorical question, 'What was it that prevented the whites from settling here all these generations past?'

Delegation after delegation, Father O'Brien in each one of them, failed to move Pretoria to change its attitude. He travelled the length and breadth of the country recording forced resettlements wherever they occurred. In all the delegations he joined, he tried to talk reason into the authorities from Pretoria down to the local minions. He produced sheaves and sheaves of paper documenting the soul-shattering state of the areas to which people were being moved. And now Fr O'Brien found himself embroiled in the Marulaneng-Marakong process in an attempt to stall it. He had a faint hope that he might rally financial support and employ legal means to obtain a court interdict. He argued, pleaded, tried to appeal to reason, cautioned with subdued demeanour. His efforts were like trying to strike wet matchsticks on a wet box. How tone-deaf bureaucrats can be! O'Brien mused.

Government said, 'There will eventually be 700 000 residents in Marakong ... In time the water situation there will improve ... People will own plots where they can make vegetable gardens ... Eventually there will be no Bantu left in the Republic of South Africa when the homelands have been consolidated, and all will be happy in their separate homelands ...'

The law and the State's proclamations were irreversible. The juggernaut was set to go.

The delegations despaired. His Archbishop consented to join him in this crusade, but with the propriety befitting his office. They tried to bring home to the officials the brutal truth of Marakong's wretched state. The landscape bore the characteristic scars of soil erosion; a garment of sick grey covered the district, broken by a few hills, abundant thornbush, cactus. It was drought-prone: for six years running there might be no rain. A smile of half-acknowledgement on the mouth of one of the audience reminded O'Brien of so many other times when he was face to face with inscrutable bureaucracy.

On one of these occasions the Deputy Minister called the Archbishop and his priest instigators, rebels who did not have the support of their congregations. His parting shot was, 'And I don't see why you should bring God into this!'

The Pretoria masters moved the pieces on their giant draftboard at will. Every time they had to account for their policies in Parliament in response to some feeble voices in the opposition ranks, the Minister in charge of the African population or his deputy gave the same explanation in different word order over and over. And Government rode the waves of protest, the honourable members sat back and cheered and guffawed and rested their case with the usual litany of self-congratulatory utterances. The Grand Design was working, they assured their public ...

As if the Furies were providing an answer, bang! The territory was declared a 'black spot'. The authorities, using the jargon of the day, described a black spot as one that contained 'surplus people', 'redundant, non-productive people'. And the military trucks started to roll.

It had rained all that night, pelting and lashing against ill-clad bodies. Stopping for people to relieve themselves merely gave the water more time to drench them, but degrees of wetness were merely an academic matter. The next day the whole landscape was covered with clothes and blankets set out to dry on the baking surface. For the sun had come out in all its renewed fury.

'And now he's here again,' Van Rensburg was to say with a smirk, two days after the people had arrived, 'he's here again to try to prove how much cruel the white peeples is from this kuntry. Do he thinks my government cannot give this peeples food and medicines? Let him just somaar stomp my toe, poppets they will dance todays – that days. Let him keep out of my ways.'

Nothing of the sort happened, on either side. Father O'Brien stayed with the people until they were dried out, the tents had been set up. 'Temporary measures' in officialese. Government was soon going to be building three-roomed tin-and-timber structures, the publicity flyer announced.

On the third day Mulder the builder arrived with a huge squad, white technicians and foremen and African manual labourers. Materials arrived shortly afterwards. Pretoria had given him the contract to build 20 000 homes. Individual residents could obtain a permit to build their own homes, with their own materials and hands. Government inspectors would need to approve a house for occupation at the beginning of the operation, in the middle of it and at the end.

Monope, 'Ma-Selepe's son, came with a truck full of building materials. He had taken two weeks from his twenty-one days' annual leave to come and pitch up a shack for his folks. There were scores of other males who were migrant workers and came at staggered times to build for their families. One of the lasting ravages wrought by the system of migrant labour: the break-up of the family unit, the long intervals between the visits by the male head or other breadwinner. Monope helped one or two families to pitch up theirs and they in turn came to help him with his.

'Ma-Selepe is walking out of the shack in the soft red glow of sunrise. Autumn is in the air. The patches of grass are losing the only little green this part of the land can boast.

Monope and his team have long been up and hammering away to make a habitable structure. These days he does not have time to spend with his mother, as he must finish his project before the two weeks are up. His wife, Baile, is more intimately acquainted with the old woman's anxieties and fears and other moods.

'Did you sleep well, Ngwana'Tabane, you are up so early?' The voice is Baile's. She is sweeping what would have been a yard if the ground around the shack had been fenced.

The older woman does not answer. She simply sits on a nearby log of wood Monope has hewn out of a tree for her to sit on outside the dwelling in the making. Baile goes to stand by her side, broom still in her hand.

'It is going to be hard, Mother, but things will straighten out, do not cry, I do not want Monope coming here and thinking that I am not treating you well, you hear me Ngwana'Tabane?'

'Ma-Selepe chuckles. 'Cry my child? Women my age do not cry any more. We do not know the meaning of that word any more.'

'Aowa, Ngwana'Tabane, I do not believe you, there must be

things that make you want to cry, things that make you want to laugh. Is it not good life goes on? Surely life is worth the effort to live?'

'Wait till you get to my age, my child, and then you will have to ask "Is the struggle worth the life?" Take your man, Monope – what is he but a migrant worker – gone for four weeks and home for two days. Is the struggle worth the life?'

'The sun rises for all of us, Mama, it has no spite for anyone, anything.'

A low chuckle again. 'The whiteman takes it all even before it shows its head in the east – the whiteman – he is in charge of the sun and his god approves. Hear me tell you, my child, even as I say so sitting here, I know the ancestors who sleep awake in those hills we left behind and who roam about in the wind and water and move through the soil and trees – they will also be our strength. Because they have passed through other valleys as painful as ours and they know. But human beings must always have a place to go to where their forefathers lie buried, not so?

'The ground that holds them is holy and now the whiteman has dragged us out and away from them. And now in my old age I feel I have no strength to support me – like a river whose mountain source has been blasted by dynamite and now must choke on its own silt and rocks and who knows what else. I already feel like a mere echo even while I still breathe, and this should not be. It should not be like this. Because either you live in a place and you and the earth give out an echo, or you are an ancestor who is in an echo out of a certain place and a certain time. Do you hear me child?

'Do you hear me child? This is no place – where we are now – the dead hand of the whiteman has fouled it up; this is no time, the dead hand of the whiteman has poisoned it and frozen it. So I should not be sounding like an echo ... yet I do feel like it: because things are wrong, an evil thing bestrides this land and the sun will be blinded and there will be no night, no day. This is what the whiteman will never understand, never can. When you say to him this ground contains my ancestors, my husband, my children and other beloved ones and I cannot leave them I want to go to their graves so many times to talk to them, to listen to them, whiteman laughs, and then bulges with anger and impatience and he makes long tiresome speeches about somebody in Pitoria they call Goromente, and this man is the father of us all and looks after us. And you know why the whiteman will never understand – not once? Because his big stone head cannot take in anything we tell him – you cannot teach him anything, do what you like. In all my eighty years on this earth I have never known a single whiteman who learned anything or even tried to learn something from us how to live and die. And hear me tell you, child, he could not, so he decided that he did not want to learn, for the reason that he is some god, and a god must not be seen to be stupid, ignorant.'

Government brought raw goods to Marakong. Staple food such as maize-meal, sorghum meal, flour, sugar, bread, salt, dehydrated milk powder, tinned milk and so on. The people had to buy. Again Father O'Brien was there to provide money to buy food to be rationed. Government trucks brought water in huge drums.

Put a human being anywhere, under the most desolate conditions, and he will instinctively lift himself to put up a shelter, or hunt for one, gather food and clothing. Van Rensburg knew this. He was cynical enough to lecture his juniors on it – newcomers in the game of processing black people's lives and programming them. Whoever might have had doubts about the agony of removal and resettlement was bound, after the lecture, to feel that the hardships were ultimately neutralised by the human instinct to survive. In other words, you possess the instinct to survive, so what's the problem?

Once a week trucks come and carry people to the town only a hundred kilometres away to buy bigger things. They pay but it is not too heavy for them. We allow small traders to come in and sell smaller necessities. We are starting to build a school and a police station for them. What do you find so painful? Van Rensburg would ask, for he was sure he knew all about this instinctive urge. But there was a lot more he didn't know, didn't care to know, couldn't *ever* know. He was aware of this ignorance, but was not prepared to spend sleepless nights over it.

The old woman shivers slightly and adjusts her shawl tighter over the shoulders with unsteady sinewy fingers.

Standing up she says, 'Me I am going out to walk about and stretch these old knees. It is also time to find out which way the whiteman's sun is coming from and going, because I can feel that my sun rises and sets elsewhere.'

'It is all right, Ngwana'Tabane.'

She chooses a direction at random without giving it much thought. Not so long ago she would be walking along a beaten path, sure of where she was going. There would be Madinko, Tebora, Santlo, for instance. The four would sit for hours talking and taking snuff, exchanging banter and jokes and woeful stories. Now here she is among strangers from other villages. 'Ah,' 'Ma-Selepe sighs heavily.

The earth she walks on is grassy and resists her bare feet. Even the bare patches of red soil. The toes begin to tingle and curl inwards, twitching with fear of every step she is taking; twitching as if they had a life of their own, apart from the rest of the body. She turns the feet sideways to feel for softer ground. The undulations she has to negotiate are strange to her, almost hostile, and she nearly falls forward, but for the staff she immediately leans on. For a few crazy seconds she feels as if she has stopped at the lip of a bottomless hole.

When she regains her balance and rests both hands on the upright staff there is no hole, the terrain of grass and shrub lies there in front of her, unfriendly, frightfully alien, but there. The breeze comes at her from the wrong side and it chills her bones. An unholy solitude floods 'Ma-Selepe's whole being. She feels as if she can taste, smell, hear and touch something hideous inside and around her.

And as she stands there on the open barren stretch of land,

she screams at a quivering pitch, screams to her husband to come and rescue her from the coils of this unholy crushing loneliness.

It is then that she knows for certain it must be done. If she ever doubted that she still had the strength, the revelation of this morning exercise has confirmed her will to do it. The moment when she feels she can hold out her hand and actually touch the pulsating emptiness that hurts so.

In less than the two weeks before her son's departure, 'Ma-Selepe told the family that she had found a friend on the east rim of the new village. She wanted to spend the weekend with her. 'I want your father-in-law here to come with me,' she announced, referring to Lefanyana her grandson who bore the diminutive form of her late husband's name, 'Lefa'. 'Come, come with me my little husband and protect me.'

'Wooo-wooh!' Baile exclaimed. 'Just look at you Ngwana'Tabane! See there Monope! Her German print blouse and skirt will freeze lions and leopards and antelopes just where they are standing, just to admire her beauty.'

'Oh, go away,' she said good-humouredly with a gesture of self-deprecation. Baile was still laughing and full of cheer, too, as her mother-in-law and her 'little husband' were leaving.

'Wait, wait you two!' Baile called out, remembering something. She ran into the shelter and brought back an extra shirt and pants for Lefanyana.

'Ma-Selepe tugged at the fringes of her colourful shawl to adjust it with an air of finality and finesse that seemed to suggest she was ready, for now, forever. Monope waved as he said, 'Go well. Greet them all where you are going.' Calling out to his son, he said, 'I hope you have not forgotten your books I brought you, boy, remember you have some reading to do, eh!'

On the way, not far from home, 'Ma-Selepe stopped by a cluster of trees and pulled out a small bundle of clothing, two blankets, a basket containing a large bowl of porridge, a bag of cooked dehydrated spinach, a small bag of maize-meal.

Questions from the boy followed in quick succession: 'Makgolo, what is in there? Why did you hide them here Grandma? Do they not have food where we are going Makgolo? Are they stingy? Are we coming back Grandma? ...'

Grandma merely said, 'Do not be afraid ngwana'ngwanaka, do not fear child of my son.'

On the road, a donkey-drawn gig stopped abreast of the two.

The reins were in the hands of a middle-aged man who asked if he might cut short their journey? 'Ma-Selepe's nervous movements as she stepped closer to the gig indicated how much she welcomed the offer. The gigman held out his hand to help the woman up. Soon she and Lefanyana following close behind were comfortably seated behind their host.

'Where is our mother going?'

'Marulaneng,' 'Ma-Selepe replied. 'If my brother takes us as far as he is going towards Marulaneng – or is he even going that far?'

'Marulaneng?' the gigman enquired. 'Did the people not move here?'

'Yes, but does that mean there is nobody at all left in Marulaneng?' She was thinking also, *do not ask any searching questions about me, old man, let us keep things quiet, I pray ... not when I have such an awesome mission ...*

The man shrugged his shoulders, saying, 'Aretse – do I know?'

'And you, father, where are you going?'

'Nna I am going to Dilokong, still some way before you get to Marulaneng, only I have to leave this road at some point and go west.'

After a brief spell, the old woman passed her knotted unsteady fingers under the cloth belt she wore. She unmade its many folds on her lap. Then she said, 'I have fifty shillings here. It is yours, my brother if you take us as far as Marulaneng.' She held out five one-rand coins in her hand.

'I will take you to Marulaneng, my sister,' the gigman said, taking the money from her hand. 'We shall sleep the night at Mogale's village. They will give us food there to eat and to take for the road. Tomorrow we shall continue. As we say, you do not hunt for lice at night, sunrise grudges no one, it will tell us all we want to know.'

As he looked at his passenger she nodded, then brushed the heel of her hand against the tip of her nose to clear mucus. Something about 'Ma-Selepe's profile – her well-defined jaw, her largely unwrinkled face, the taut muscles of her neck – compelled him to keep throwing a glance towards her. In addition to his goodness of heart, the gigman felt a certain aura that commanded acquiescence; some mysterious force radiating from her.

As the donkey cart chewed the road, eating the kilometres, 'Ma-Selepe felt as if it were slowly chewing up the palpable emptiness that was weighing on her. Her shoulders were literally feeling light and at ease. Self-confidence had found anchor, her destination was assured.

The day was silent except for the call of some faraway bird and the jingling of the harness and unrhythmic fall of eight hooves. Here was all shrubland, where the mimosa tree dominates. Far away in the distant haze tall mountains beckoned them. Somewhere in those blue mountains lay Marulaneng. A land from which 'Ma-Selepe's people had been violently uprooted. Because it was surrounded by white people's land and was labelled 'black spot'.

She knew too that even this land she was travelling through, this vast stretch of brooding thornbush, had once been good grazing land. It fed thousands of cattle and goats and people. Scenes of her childhood and young womanhood replayed themselves before her ...

The donkey cart ground the miles, bumping over stone and gravel. It only needed her, she realised, to allow her body to hang loose, droop her shoulders, relax the thigh muscles, generally to go with the rocking instead of resisting it. The scenes of her life continued to unfold, sometimes seeming to press against her very face and her whole body by turns. Moments of fitful slumber induced by the rocking of the gig kept interfering with the sequence of the scenes.

The rattle of calabashes in earthen pots as she and her peers jogtrotted to the river to fetch water, sunup and sundown ... the echo of the noise in the valley ... the loud full-throated laughter of the girls ... The sounds came alive to her again, travelling some seventy years to remind her of the times of nature's abundance, of innocence ... She recaptured the khuui-uuui in the fields as they chased away the birds from the ripening corn and maize. The afternoon sound of steel pounding on millstones came back to her. This way the stone was made rough for more effective grinding ... The mind conjured up a picture of columns of smoke from the afternoon's wood fires, shooting up from the homesteads. Girls her age would be preparing the evening meal ...

She recalled vividly how Lefa Selepe had picked her out of a bunch of maidens who were out wood gathering. Winter time. Just came straight up to her and told her he wanted to show her something. The maiden was puzzled, a little afraid, it seemed her heart had been dislodged from its natural position. Did he beat round the bush? Oh no, not Selepe. She chuckled softly at his forthright manner. Like his name – 'axe'. He just hacked away at the bush in his way, made a clearing, told her that he wanted her to become his woman. 'I want you to be my wife, what do you say?' Her heart did a crazy dance up and down inside her and she was seized by a burning urge to run away. Just as if he had said, 'The river is in flood, get out of the way!'

She had bolted out of the clearing, back to her companions. But not before she had observed a lump dart up and down along his throat. That night, oh that night, 'What things is this man telling me!' she kept whispering to herself as she lay on her mat. And she felt an ache inside the likes of which she had never known before. Not physical, but an ache in a part of her being that was full of joy and apprehension and was afire – all at once.

'Ma-Selepe had borne him three sons. She and Lefa had known the parental bliss of raising children and seeing one of them, Monope, make his own family and home. Strange, she now thought on the journey back to Marulaneng, how it was that the simple joys of married life merged with larger life and its struggles, to be retrieved years after by the memory and so savoured and cherished even more. Joys that now took on a clearly defined face, like shining pebbles on the bed of a clear stream ...

It seemed she was never going to stop crying, when the remains of her two elder sons were brought home from the train wreckage. They had been returning home at the end of a mine-work contract that summer, intending both to marry on the same day. The stunning news of the collision: a passenger train and a freight train, one of them on the wrong track. Passengers thrown out as the train, now off its rails for the most part, rolled down the steep slope below ...

Then Selepe had joined his sons years later.

Every so often tears, which 'Ma-Selepe tried to conceal by inhaling her snuff, stood in tiny points of moisture in the inner corners of her eyes. She wiped her eyes and nose with the back of her hand. The gigman by her side looked stolidly ahead of him. He was not much of a talker, much to the relief of his passenger who had settled for an untalkative journey during which she could collect her thoughts for the ordeal ahead. The man's long silences made 'Ma-Selepe flippantly wonder if he was eavesdropping after her muted rebuke about his long tongue ... The boy sat or slept behind the couple.

And the cart chewed up the miles of kilometres ... That stifling and choking emptiness she had felt before she left was diffused, thanks to her preoccupation with the anticipated conclusion of her odyssey. A conclusion that must end all conclusions. Not long now, she would be on the turf where

IN CORNER B 225

kith and kin awaited her at the cemetery. What had to be done immediately on her arrival, in itself a task that would claim every nerve and muscle of her being, did not really possess her entire field of consciousness. For there was nothing to cause her anxiety and forebodings.

Nor did she pause to ask why it didn't. She had simply appropriated some corner of a future realm, where she was not accountable for things accomplished or undone. This intervening encounter – this task she had to perform at the end of the journey – she considered to be merely an imperative. It was too important for her to skip if she wanted to lay the matter to rest and then be ready to get on the Major Road to the happier realm. The task would also be an act of self-vindication. A reaffirmation of her state of being and its bond with the rest of nature's mysteries. From the very bowels of her soul she would cry out softly, 'Oh Supreme Guide to whom I am joined by the spirits of my ancestors!' An articulation of the very mystery of Nature's continuum. An order by and in which things simply must be done, no matter what. What is more, *we* are the inevitable agents.

'Ma-Selepe noticed that her grandson was in one of the many rounds of deep sleep, interrupted only when he asked to be let down to relieve himself, or when she wanted him to eat something. So she could say certain things with greater ease.

'Old man,' she began, 'I am going to ask you to do something for us. This child you see here with me, I took with me to protect me. He is a child but with eleven years of day and night in his blood and bones he is a brave man. Now that the ancestors brought you to our help, he can return to his parents. He is my own blood. I would ask you to come back on your return. As you tell us you often go to the villages beyond Marakong, you can carry him, he will know where his mother is. I say this because my ancestors are whispering in my ear to tell me that I may not make the journey back to Marakong right away.'

The gigman looked at her steadily, but her eyes stayed on

the course. Perhaps, aware that no amount of scanning would elicit any clue to her meaning, his eyes returned to the road ahead of him.

'Here is the last bit of money I have on me to repay your kindness, child of God, messenger of the ancestors.' As she said this she reached for her belt of cloth again to unwrap the money. Ten rands. Another reason for the benefactor to give her a look of amazement.

Lefa, old man, son of Selepe, good husband and father but stubborn, oh, so stone-headed ... Strong hands, a good farmer ... Such strength it seems no other person could possess ... I remember my good man ... Those months when government forced women to carry passes like our men ... Then the months of storms when whiteman told us to obey the chief at all times but remember always that there was the great white father in the city of Tshwane who made all the laws ... The chief was now to be that great chief's eyes and ears ... I remember all my good man ... Strange man is that one they call Goromente ... strange beyond belief ... strange man ... A long time ago he took away the chief's manhood, cut off his arms and legs and used him just like a paid policeman ... He crawled up and down the spine of the chief like a worm sucking on his marrow till the back must break like a twig in the winter time and leave the head dangling like an empty gourd you cannot even use for water to rinse your mouth with ... My good man how can I forget these things that changed the days of plenty into the desert sands of our present time ... Today you see the chief dressed in whiteman's cast-offs and canvas shoes without soles and laces, toes sticking out ... You see him sit before his court of councillors hearing cases of stock thefts and rogues who beat their wives ... No more than that ... nothing more ...

Oh, ancestors that watch over us and ask for nothing in return we have seen things that blind the sun in our time ... Mabena, Ditau, Matime, Serumula, Makuru – what did they leave behind them but these tiny men who have the time and spirit to quarrel among themselves like crows and chew each other's buttocks off while the other is not looking ... selling out and betraying each other to please the great father ... Mabena and Ditau carried away by the great chief's messengers to faraway lands for their disobedience – to Natal, to the Cape ... I remember how they were first arrested for encouraging us to rise against passes for women ... The days we were driven to jail for the first time in our lives ... I chuckle now to think that we should have felt the insult like a spear hanging from the breast ... that being arrested and pushed this way and that by special police from Tshwane young enough to be still wetting their pants ... that we should have thought the sun was going to rise in the west or a cow was going to give birth to a pig so much it seemed like woman was no longer woman, neither man, a cow no longer a cow, mountains no longer what we knew them ... Then, remember after fourteen days in jail we all said things were never going to be the same again. Funny thing, husband of mine, is it not? From day to day things change in front of our eyes and we never take notice until you are thrown into jail and insulted in a way that shakes you up and throws you bodily against the wall ...

And now they tell us those big fat red men in Tshwane that this chief is our little father ... he is filled with the spirit of the white father when he tells us they are moving us to a place of plenty and happiness ...

My old man you have seen for yourself the earlier time when the people burned down the houses of chiefs and headmen who were speaking to us with whiteman's tongue ... like Selati and Matime ... This man they call government simply sent us a useless wet-nose of a nephew of blind old Serumula to rule in his place ... a young man who has nothing but mud in his head when you put him beside his uncle ... because his uncle was on our side and said no to the wickedness of Goromente ...

The anger in the people's hearts ... think of that, old man ... because we love Serumula ... This young iguana his nephew knows no more about our life than he can see the tip of his own nose. Just went to Gauteng and dug the iguana out of the rubble and threw him on our lap ...

And 'Ma-Selepe's memory reeled off the events of her life, her husband's, her people's. The turbulent times and the quieter times; times of plenty and times of drought. The passes, land hunger, forced removals, all flashpoints of the people's anger, the consequent public stoning of Serumula's nephew to a bundle of mangled flesh and bones, reports of which were noised abroad from mouth to ear to mouth. The chase from the village to village in broad daylight when mother rat is suckling its babies, as the common saying goes … yet more stoning … and the final blow on the temple: indeed the way boys stoned an iguana because of the common knowledge that you never found it on the killing ground if you returned later … What was his name again? Do you think I still remember?

Peculiar man, is Goromente. He simply left off … did not again try to bring someone else. But how deceptive, too! Just when people are savouring victory the police come, batch after batch. Power show … They leave, almost like a dog that has urinated on a tree or vehicle in order to remember where to come next time …

Van Rensburg arrives. He is in charge of this whole removal drama. Peculiar. Lays out his net like a spider … because Van Rensburg looks all reasonable. Does not usually curse blue fire like so many other State officials. Speaks to the people as if he were actually going to advise Pretoria not to enforce the removal order. But comes the day of reckoning, he is the whiteman people in rural country are accustomed to, white to the marrow: bulging with power borrowed from Pretoria.

Certainly not the farmer type, bloated to the roots of the ginger hair on his weather-beaten arms; not stomping up and down and spewing off obscenities, generally feeling insecure. No, not that type at all. Even speaks to the chiefs with a show of respect. But when he comes back brandishing the law like a sjambok Van Rensburg will brook nothing that he does not consider to be obedience.

A number of farmers in the district were telling their labourers not to fear removal. Their place on their land was secure. But they ordered their labourers to take the news round among the villages – on weekends – that they were being moved to better land, like the Promised Land in the Bible; that they should not resist the great father's order. They should not listen to those chiefs who, the farmers alleged, were being visited in the dead of night by terrorists. These were also communists, the farmers emphasised.

Selepe was 'cheeky' enough to ask what a terrorist was, what a komunisi was, and a terorisi. For all the labourers cared, the farmer might just as well have been warning them against fireflies.

You want to know what is terorisi, komunisi? I will tell you because I can see that your understanding, your eyes, are still plastered over with black and red mud. They mean troublemakers, thieves, killers, destroyers, Satan worshippers. That is what the whiteman tells my husband Selepe. When I ask my man whether these troublemakers we never see, whether they are humans or white people, he laughs and laughs and laughs ...

'Ma-Selepe, he replies, he says, my wife, you can be so raw like the trees and the grass! They are humans like you and me and many others are white people. I ask where they come from and my man says Fatamabele told him they come riding on crocodile backs across Lepelle River. But from where? I want to know. Selepe tells me, he says, just close your mouth, God's woman, your tongue is too long.

Selepe my good man, I say to him one night before we fall asleep. It is late, and I can hear the first cocks crow for people to leave their night fireplaces. I say to him this Fatamabele worries me. Like all these farmers to tell the truth. Why are they saying we should not say No to him, I mean Goromente? What have the farmers to do with whether we go or whether we stay? What is it to Fatamabele? Why are they not sorry to lose the people who are like donkeys to them to keep in harness if we all have to move? And still they say we can stay on their land if we choose to – why? Tell me Selepe.

And Selepe makes a sound like a yawning lion and he says the white man is always full of mathaithai – just wants to trick us all the

*time. You see my good woman, he wants it to appear that the choice is
ours to stay or to go. But the truth is that they do not mind losing us
now that machines and engines do most of the work. See already how
Fatamabele is shrinking into a mere pig-keeper. Of course he is plain
lazy, drunk most of his waking life. He cannot farm crops any longer,
you wait and see. You see the trick, good woman – these farmers must
not support us and thus go against their own Goromente, and yet
they do not want to lose us all. Now, we shall go and meet – we from
Fatamabele and those from the other farms and we shall talk there and
give one another advice and hope we can agree not to tell anybody to
leave to the new place.*

'Ma-Selepe smelled treachery in Van der Merwe's exhortation
to the labourers to leave together with the villagers. *Why
should he say they may leave when he cannot do anything
without us, twenty of us?*

The land is too big for him, she mused. Especially since his
wife and three sons left home, more years ago than she can
remember – likely four.

*Have you ever seen them again? Remember how leburu went on fire
when you first asked him where his family had gone? And then what
does leburu decide? – to make you Selepe foreman. Just when tempers
were blazing in the villages.*

*Yes, Selepe affirms. Foreman on a dying farm. And just when
the new orders to move have poisoned village life and people are
sharpening knives and axes and government is loading guns. One
heart says we should leave Fatamabele, my old man says, the other
heart says let the sky rain fire or water we stay here. Then my man
breathes fast and loud and he says I am a habit of Fatamabele's, so he
cannot throw me out.*

*What are you saying, my man? I ask, fixing my eyes on his.
Sometimes my man spoke a language I believed only his own secret
heart could understand. And when I wanted to know more he simply
kept silent and then ran his hand over his face down from the forehead.
As if to say if you do not read my meaning on my face then there is*

no other way I can explain. Or perhaps, perhaps did he himself know full well what he meant deep down? I do not know.

Then there was no talk in the villages about moving any more. No more noisy talk about it. It was quiet, like when a hailstorm has been chattering on the roof with a deafening noise and suddenly the rain stops. But the sound of thunder continued to hang in the air. We all knew the storm was not gone. The all-wise Supreme Spirit alone knew when ...

Fatamabele was constantly in a drunken stupor. He grew noisier and more boorish by the day, his temper on a short fuse. Some people of his own tribe carried away his tractors and other hardware. He threw his labourers off his farm, one by one. Not in the save yourself spirit but rather in a mood that said to them, 'Get off my land, if I must drown in the raging river of brandy let it be now but not naked before staring mocking eyes of kaffers.'

Selepe was right, the farm was dying, under stinkweed and coarse grass. Only the oversize pigs rooting in front of the main house gave some indication that there was still human life there.

How could 'Ma-Selepe fail to remember the awful night? How can I ever forget it? she kept saying to herself weeks after the event. The sunset party a few metres from the house ... tall and burly men on the stoep, some standing, some sitting, all hee-hee-hawing with drunken abandon, their colour a deep brownish red, arms covered with brown and ginger hair ... Padi and another of Selepe's friends carrying her husband into their shack not far from where the red men are, indeed in full view of them. Selepe bloody all over, a tall lanky body sprawling on the earth floor, cut up as if some unknown creature of the night has mauled him ...

I can still hear my man groaning and choking on the words that were struggling to come out: they have killed me ... Fatamabele, F-ata-m-ma-b-ele and his drunken friends ... they have killed me ... hear me tell you.

We wash his face, remove his clothing and wrap him up in a blanket.

Padi my son, what happened? Padi tells me. He is not one to speak carelessly on such a serious matter. I was there, he says, I saw everything, our mother ... One of the men calls Selepe when we pass the house ... he shouts, 'Hei you, what do they call you? I mean you the tall kaffer.' It is clear he means Selepe. 'You tall kaffer,' leburu repeats ... come and fetch me water to drink ... Selepe turns round and shouts, 'You are not my baas, I do not work for you.' The man comes straight to us, takes his fist and hammers Selepe on the side of the head – ta!

Padi continues his account. Selepe holds him, shakes him and throws him hard on the ground. Another leburu and still another one, they throw themselves on top of Selepe pounding him with fists and kicking him. Fatamabele comes with his heavy kubu and gives Selepe a number of savage blows on the body and in the face – vu vu vu! Our mother! We plead to Fatamabele to let us carry Selepe away. Only then do they stop. Our mother! Where are the ancestors to give us strength against these beasts!

In the flickering light of the fire at the corner of our shack we try to stretch and rub Selepe's body. I try to speak to him but he only groans. I cry and cry and through the night from time to time we hear the hee-hee-hawing from Fatamabele, as if the night itself were laughing.

Selepe tries to raise his head and ... then he gasps ... the last thing I was ever going to hear my man say. He turns his back on us and the world forever ...

Padi and his friend report the matter to the chief and the police come from Mashishing far away ... We never hear of the matter again after this. My son comes and buries his father in the village cemetery. He brings his wife and son to Serumula's village and I go and live with them ... A woman with a beautiful heart, my daughter-in-law ...

We always hear stories about maburu beating black people to death with kubu but I never imagined something like this would visit my family, even though we knew it was always possible ...

After a good night's rest the gigman had anticipated, the cart and beasts proceeded to plough and chew up the last few kilometres with asinine endurance. Enquiries from passers-by brought out the information that Rameetse, Fatamabele's swineherd, was the only man left on the farm. Past the deserted villages the gigman, 'Ma-Selepe and grandson went straight to Rameetse's shack on the eastern fringe of the farm.

He stared incredulously at them out of his bleary eyes, as if he had the fright of his life. Must be brewing his own beer, the sot, 'Ma-Selepe deduced.

'It is me, Rameetse,' she said, 'I have not risen from the grave. I am passing on and ask for shelter for a few nights, son of the people.' Gradually things seemed to fall into place in the swineherd's mind. He smiled to show consent, although the whole situation was too complicated for him to comprehend. He seemed to be quite contented to let it be.

Next morning, after a breakfast of porridge and morogo, 'Ma-Selepe drew her grandson to her bosom and said gravely but affectionately, 'Child of my son, you are a man now. You are grown up, see how you have protected your grandmother all this way. I am so happy you will be able to look after your mother and the little ones who will come after you, not so? Yes. This father who has been so good to us will take you to his home and he will find someone to take you back to Marakong if he himself does not. Say to Mama that I borrowed you and am returning you, you hear? And greet them at home, you hear?'

'When are you coming back, makgolo?' He asked the question without showing any anxiety whatever.

'Soon, my child, soon. When I have finished my work here.'

Gigman, donkeys and grandson were released, after profuse words and gestures of gratitude and mutual regard between the grown-ups.

'Rameetse son of the people,' 'Ma-Selepe said, 'you go about your work, do not bother yourself about this old woman. I do not have many days left on this earth, and I am readier for the moment now than I shall ever be.'

He was accustomed to hear old people ramble in this manner, audience or none. A thin shaft of light managed to pierce through the thick layer of his beer-sodden brain. The light brought it home to him that it would be folly for him to stand in the way of the inevitable that he divined was already on its course. Rameetse knew that he was hearing the words of someone whose age and faith entitle him or her to catch a breeze from the ancestral valleys.

At her man's grave she merely said to him, 'I have come my good man, I have arrived. I will be talking to you as soon as I have accomplished what I have to do, which you know very well. All I pray is that you and the whole company of our ancestors with whom you live should ask the Supreme Being to give me the courage, the strength, to accomplish this. So be it husband of mine.' And she left.

Nothing happened for three consequent nights and days. On the fourth night a befuddled Van der Merwe made it known to Rameetse that he would be gone all of the next day and night and would be back the following day. He also gave the cook a day and night off.

Rameetse having gone out to seek companionship among his beasts, as the villagers used to say, 'Ma-Selepe disappeared in a nearby bush. She came out with a rusted can in her hand. Her gait indicated that the five-litre can contained something. This was the time for it. A few splashes and the house would be a sure inferno. As long as no one would die. She just had to try to make sure that neither Rameetse nor the cook would do the human but foolish thing of trying to put out the flames. She gave Rameetse a few coins to buy himself beer and to give the cook for the same purpose. She charged him with a threatening look in her eyes not to breathe a word to the cook about her presence and made him swear by his late mother. She wouldn't need to worry about the cook, Rameetse told her, because he had already gone to visit his people a long distance away.

The old woman carried the fuel can to Fatamabele's house. She placed it in a concealed place under the creeper at the back. She walked back to Rameetse's house. She needed to calculate the necessary steps and reinforce her resolve. Although she was sure Selepe and the other ancestors would give her the strength to execute this thing, she was aware of the strain of the last few days on her body and inner resources: all that intensive, almost minute-to-minute awareness of self and purpose.

'Ma-Selepe sees the sun climbing towards the meridian and goes to sit down in the shade of the shack, leaning against its wall. A picture of apparent serenity and firm purpose. Why am I not getting up to splash the petrol in every room of that beast? she dares to ask herself. Each time she wants to stand up some force seems to hold her down. She does not feel it physically, she tells herself. It is in another zone of her being. It is not even a change of purpose determined by any moral self-restraint. Because she believes she still feels the hate for Van der Merwe that has become something like a monument over the years, a bitter tribute to the man. She almost knew right after her husband's death just what she wanted to do, had to do, and how to do it. She never conceived for one moment that she needed any extra propulsion for the deed. Now, at this moment, it seems to her that she does need it. Why? Why?

Rameetse returns. He wears that perpetual smile on his face that is not connected with anything one can perceive. They exchange a few words. By all appearances he is sober. He sits in front of her, his knees raised fireside style. He fixes a steady look on the woman. She returns it. There are questions they are asking each other in this silence.

After a spell Rameetse says, 'I am not a halfwit as many people think, you know mother.'

'What gives you the idea that I am one of the many?'

'All right mother. Your secrets are safe in this heart, no living soul can unlock them. You have something terrible to do, I feel it in my bones.'

The look on his face makes 'Ma-Selepe feel there is nothing she needs to conceal from the swineherd. 'How did you know?'

My ancestors tell me things. Let me ask you: will it be with a gun, or a knife, or will you burn the house down, or will it be both death and fire?'

Silence.

'I cannot tell you that,' she replies, in spite of what her instinct tells her.

'Let me say this mother of the people, if you want to remove the man from this earth, then do it if you have the heart. Now he is away for the day, so the reason you have not done it must mean that you are hesitating, right? If you cannot do it when he is asleep or awake in his house then what is the use burning down the house? It can only mean that you are afraid, because taking a life or more is truly a terrifying thing. He will not suffer if you choose to destroy the house, because there are many homes where trash like him find refuge. And he is not going to thank you for sparing his life, and he is not going to repent. Have you ever asked yourself daughter of the people if your heart can carry the weight of such a deed? Can you carry the weight across that river we all must come to first before we proceed to the land of the ancestors? For we must all cross over, and the beauty is that we have no choices to confuse us.'

Silence.

'Think on it, good mother, think on it. I have brought some meat and will make us fire to cook porridge and pumpkin as well.' He leaves her sitting against the wall.

She unfolds her legs from under her body and stretches them, enjoying the sensuous uncoiling of the body.

Suddenly 'Ma-Selepe seems to wake up from a dream into a bright new dawn and open skies. The knot that she has felt all along inside loosens. She feels liberated by Rameetse's words. Through his voice, it seems, her own ancestors are coming to her rescue, the kind she would not have dreamed of ...

Something about the swineherd's face, in its own inarticulate way, was conveying to her some unspeakable terrible truths. She is not sure exactly what they are. She must cross over without a load on her back. Her instinct tells her: let the wind blow trash, like chaff, any way it wants. Me and my husband are together again ...

After a delicious supper, 'Ma-Selepe says slowly, 'Son of the people, night is here, and I must go and speak to my husband at the cemetery. The ancestors, like the Almighty Spirit, do not give any one by hand. They send someone, some event, some moment. So they will repay you for your kindness. Me I have only been given the tongue to thank you.'

Again Rameetse knows better than to try to stall the inevitable. He merely helps her up and gives her her staff, and says, 'May the ancestors light the way ahead for you, good mother.'

His eyes follow her until she disappears in the dark.

She walks slowly until she reaches the graves. She goes to her man's, sits down and lies on the warm earth of the mound. She is sure her people will find her in quick time – here, her last resting place ...

THE STORY OF PENGUIN CLASSICS

Before 1946 . . . "Classics" are mainly the domain of academics and students; readable editions for everyone else are almost unheard of. This all changes when a little-known classicist, E. V. Rieu, presents Penguin founder Allen Lane with the translation of Homer's *Odyssey* that he has been working on in his spare time.

1946 Penguin Classics debuts with *The Odyssey,* which promptly sells three million copies. Suddenly, classics are no longer for the privileged few.

1950s Rieu, now series editor, turns to professional writers for the best modern, readable translations, including Dorothy L. Sayers's *Inferno* and Robert Graves's unexpurgated *Twelve Caesars.*

1960s The Classics are given the distinctive black covers that have remained a constant throughout the life of the series. Rieu retires in 1964, hailing the Penguin Classics list as "the greatest educative force of the twentieth century."

1970s A new generation of translators swells the Penguin Classics ranks, introducing readers of English to classics of world literature from more than twenty languages. The list grows to encompass more history, philosophy, science, religion, and politics.

1980s The Penguin American Library launches with titles such as *Uncle Tom's Cabin* and joins forces with Penguin Classics to provide the most comprehensive library of world literature available from any paperback publisher.

1990s The launch of Penguin Audiobooks brings the classics to a listening audience for the first time, and in 1999 the worldwide launch of the Penguin Classics Web site extends their reach to the global online community.

The 21st Century Penguin Classics are completely redesigned for the first time in nearly twenty years. This world-famous series now consists of more than 1,300 titles, making the widest range of the best books ever written available to millions—and constantly redefining what makes a "classic."

The Odyssey continues . . .

The best books ever written

PENGUIN (🐧) CLASSICS

SINCE 1946

Find out more at www.penguinclassics.com

Visit www.vpbookclub.com

CLICK ON A CLASSIC
www.penguinclassics.com

The world's greatest literature at your fingertips

Constantly updated information on over 1600 titles, from Icelandic sagas to ancient Indian epics, Russian drama to Italian romance, American greats to African masterpieces

•

The latest news on recent additions to the list, updated editions and specially commissioned translations

•

Original scholarly essays by leading writers: Elaine Showalter on Zola, Laurie R King on Arthur Conan Doyle, Frank Kermode on Shakespeare, Lisa Appignanesi on Tolstoy

•

A wealth of background material, including biographies of every classic author from Aristotle to Zamyatin, plot synopses, readers' and teachers' guides, useful web links

•

Online desk and examination copy assistance for academics

•

Trivia quizzes, competitions, giveaways, news on forthcoming screen adaptations

•

eBooks available to download